Devastation

Devastation

Virtual War
The Clones

GLORIA SKURZYNSKI

Atheneum Books for Young Readers

NEW YORK   LONDON   TORONTO   SYDNEY

ATHENEUM BOOKS FOR YOUNG READERS

An imprint of Simon & Schuster Children's Publishing Division

1230 Avenue of the Americas, New York, New York 10020

This book is a work of fiction. Any references to historical events, real people,

or real locales are used fictitiously. Other names, characters, places, and incidents

are products of the author's imagination, and any resemblance to actual events

or locales or persons, living or dead, is entirely coincidental.

Virtual War copyright © 1997 by Gloria Skurzynski

The Clones copyright © 2002 by Gloria Skurzynski

ATHENEUM BOOKS FOR YOUNG READERS is a registered trademark of

Simon & Schuster, Inc.

For information about special discounts for bulk purchases, please contact

Simon & Schuster Special Sales at 1-866-506-1949 or business@simonandschuster.com.

The Simon & Schuster Speakers Bureau can bring authors to your live event.

For more information or to book an event, contact

the Simon & Schuster Speakers Bureau at 1-866-248-3049

or visit our website at www.simonspeakers.com.

Book design by Sammy Yuen Jr.

The text for this book is set in Apollo MT.

Manufactured in the United States of America

First Atheneum Books for Young Readers paperback edition August 2010

2 4 6 8 10 9 7 5 3 1

CIP data for this book is available from the Library of Congress.

ISBN 978-1-4424-1680-2 (bind-up)

These titles were previously published individually.

For Edite Kroll, friend and guide,
and
For Paul Thliveris,
who is a unique and excellent individual.

Virtual War

one

The sky was golden.

Corgan could feel sand beneath his fingers. What were those trees called, he wondered, the tall ones that curved to the sky. Ridges circled their trunks all the way up, but there were no branches or leaves except right at the top, where fingerlike green blades stuck out. . . .

What does it matter, he thought. Things don't need names. They haven't told me the names of lots of things, and I don't really care. It's nice to lie here like this under the sky and the trees and not have to practice for a while.

Someone came toward him—a girl, striding across the sand.

Her hair was more golden than the sky. As she walked,

her long hair swung from side to side, swirling around her shoulders. A Go-ball racket dangled from her right hand.

She stopped right above him and looked down at him. "Want to play?" she asked.

"Sure!"

As he leaped up, he noticed with some surprise that his LiteSuit had begun to shimmer with the color of blood. Corgan knew what blood looked like. Once, a few months ago, as he'd walked along the tunnel from his Box to his Clean Room, a tile fell from the ceiling and hit his hand. His knuckles had bled, the first and only time he'd ever seen real blood.

The way the Supreme Council had carried on, it was as if Corgan's arm had been chopped off or something. About a dozen times a day They'd examined his hand to make sure it wasn't infected, even though it was only a little cut and it healed fast and felt fine. They'd moved him to a new Box at a different location—Corgan wasn't sure where. The tunnel connecting his new Box to his new Clean Room was now made of polished steel, with no tiles that could fall off, and Corgan's new Clean Room was so sterile his nose twitched every time he used it. He was just now getting used to the antiseptic smell.

"Who are you?" Corgan asked the girl as a Go-ball court materialized around them. It was a clay court—Corgan liked that. Even though Go-ball courts were created entirely from electronic impulses, virtual clay felt different underfoot than, say, virtual concrete or virtual grass.

"Sharla," she answered. "That's my name. Do you want to lead off, or should I?"

4

"Go ahead."

She served the ball so fast Corgan was caught off balance. He recovered and shot it back, but right from the start his timing was off. Sharla was good. Really good. They had been giving him better and better opponents over the past few months, even though Corgan's specialty wasn't Go-ball so it didn't matter too much if he didn't win. Sharla was the best opponent he'd had so far.

She ran, covering the court in wide zigzag leaps. She whacked the ball harder than anyone he'd ever practiced with.

She distracted him. Not because she did anything against the rules—Corgan felt off balance because he'd never before played against a girl his own age. Boys, men, women, robots, anything They could dream up to create an image of, no matter how unreal. But this was the first time he'd played against the virtual image of a girl who looked about—

"How old are you?" he asked.

"Fourteen," she said. "Same as you."

Wondering how she knew that, he reached out to snare a wild shot and ended up smashing the ball into the net. Since the net was shaped from thin, intersecting beams of laser light, it sparked when the ball hit it. Brilliant reds and blues and greens arced and burst like tiny flowering comets that fell to the court, where they sparked again.

"Point!" she called.

Corgan stalled. "I don't know why They bother with all those flashing lights and everything when a ball hits the net," he mentioned. "It's kind of a waste of laser energy—"

5

"Do you hit the net often, Corgan?" she asked. "The idea is to knock the ball *over* the net." And she laughed.

The laugh sounded rich and impulsive and free; Corgan was so caught up in the sound of it that when Sharla served again, the ball flew past his ear.

He really was trying. But he couldn't keep his eyes on the ball. Sharla's pale green LiteSuit ended inches above her knees. All the females Corgan had ever played against before had been covered to the ankles with regulation LiteSuits. He wasn't used to seeing female legs, and Sharla's were . . . were . . . he didn't have a word for them. As she raced across the court, he noticed how her arms and chest twisted with every swing, how her face lighted with amusement when she hit the ball so hard it ricocheted off his forehead. If They had turned on the tactile simulator just then—if the ball had actually hit him on the head that hard—Corgan would have been knocked flat.

She laughed again, bending forward with her hands on her knees as if to keep herself from collapsing with mirth.

There was no sense pretending. He'd lost the game, dismally! "Sharla, are you real?" he shouted.

"Yes, I'm real. But They've made me look better in this image than I do in . . ."

Immediately she vanished.

Corgan felt a stab of disappointment, quickly replaced by guilt as Mendor's stern image materialized in front of him. This time Mendor was a man, the reproachful Father Figure.

"What happened?" Mendor asked. "That's the worst you've ever played."

Corgan shrugged.

"The War is less than eighteen days away."

"I know when the War is, Mendor. Seventeen days, twenty-one hours, thirty-nine minutes and forty-seven and twenty-three hundredths seconds from now."

"The War scene can contain any legal diversion, you know, including the image of a beautiful girl," Mendor continued. "Are you going to be so easily thrown off when you're fighting the real War?"

"No, I won't be," Corgan muttered. "But it was only Go-ball. . . ."

"This is serious, Corgan. You lost your concentration. That can't happen."

"Then bring her back and let me play her again," Corgan said. "I'll do better next time. It's just—I was lying on the sand, and the sun warmed me and the breeze felt good and those trees. . . . Mendor, what are those trees called?"

"Palm trees." Mendor's look softened. "It was a test, it's true. They were afraid you might be rattled by a pretty female. I told Them it wouldn't happen. 'Not Corgan,' I told Them. 'You can trust Corgan to keep his concentration, no matter what,' I told Them. 'Corgan always plays to win, no matter who his opponent is. You can count on Corgan,' I said—"

"Enough!" Corgan shouted. "Let me play Sharla again, Mendor. I'll *crush* her this time."

"Not now." Mendor's voice grew lighter and higher. As Mendor slowly morphed into a woman, into the Mother Figure, Corgan felt a trickle of approval brush him.

7

Then Mendor morphed completely, becoming Mother Comforter, Mother Nourisher, with gentle features and tender eyes. "You're forgiven for losing," she said. "Go into your Clean Room now. You raised some sweat in that game with Sharla, and you need sanitizing. We'll see what happens after that. Maybe in an hour or so They'll let you play a game with a different girl."

"I want to play Sharla again."

Mendor's voice deepened. "Sharla is in Reprimand."

"Because of what she said? She was telling the truth, wasn't she? Don't let Them keep her in Reprimand, Mendor! Not for telling the truth!"

Mendor's maternal voice said, "I'm sure They'll consider your request, Corgan. Now go to your Clean Room."

Disgruntled, Corgan opened the door of his Box and stepped into the tunnel. He'd lost the argument with Mendor and before that he'd lost the game with Sharla. Corgan wasn't used to losing. His straight black eyebrows pulled together in a frown.

The polished steel of the tunnel reflected his scowl as he strode to his Clean Room, only a few meters away. No curves in his path, no corners, no loose tiles. A sensor opened the Clean Room door when he came close enough to it.

Clean Rooms were always built in clusters. Corgan couldn't remember where he'd picked up that bit of information; it wasn't something he'd have learned in his regular lessons. One time, four years ago, when he was only ten, he'd let himself think about it: that on the other side of the walls of his Clean Room were other Clean Rooms with other people in them, maybe sometimes using them at the same time Corgan used his. That day he'd banged on the wall while he was being sanitized, just to hear whether someone would bang back.

Never again! He'd gotten into so much trouble— Mendor the Angry Father had used his deepest, loudest voice to chastise Corgan for a full five minutes, the longest scolding Corgan had ever known in his life. Corgan had cried for hours until Mendor finally relented and morphed into the Mother Comforter, wiping his tears away.

"Haven't They given you everything a ten-year-old boy could ever want?" Mendor the Mother Figure had asked that day. "You have toys. You have games. You have me to love you and teach you. You can create whatever playmates you want—dogs or monkeys or dolphins or other children or anything at all that your imagination can picture. All you have to do is ask and they appear in your Box, one at a time or a whole roomful of images."

All that was true. Corgan didn't know what had possessed him to bang on that wall, just to see if there'd be an answer. In the four years since then, he'd never tried it again.

Now he moved to the flush tube to pass his body fluids and solids. From there it was just one step to stand beneath the vapor nozzle. Dropping his LiteSuit to the floor, he got a quick look at his body, reflected by the stainless-steel walls. Thin. Tall. Strong legs. Shoulders needed thickening, but Mendor said Corgan couldn't expect that until a year or two more had gone by. After the War. Corgan's hands looked too big, all out of proportion to his thin arms. The fingers were long, agile, and powerful. Not much hair on his body yet, but the hair on his head stood up thick and straight and black as midnight. He flexed the muscles of his back and upper arms, pleased by the swell of his biceps. At once, the warm, cleansing vapor flowed from the nozzle above him, enveloping him. Corgan could no longer see his reflection because of steam.

He felt his head gently lifted as his hair was laser trimmed; a week had passed since the last trim. Each hair on his head had to be kept precisely five centimeters long, because that was the ideal length for cleanliness.

Hair. He thought of the girl, Sharla, and her long golden hair that swung across her shoulders as she bounded around the clay court. Was her hair really that long, or was it just the way They made her look in the virtual image? And if her hair really was that length, then why were girls allowed to wear it like that? Didn't they need to be kept clean, too? He'd have to ask Mendor.

As the vapor cleansing continued, lifting off his sweat, pulling it up into the remover pipe, Corgan pictured Sharla in his mind. The golden light had created shadows that sculpted her legs—they'd looked so lean and clean and smooth, from the calves to the thighs. . . . Was *that* part of her image real?

Suddenly the vapor that enveloped him turned icy cold.

"Hey! Stop that! I'm freezing!" Corgan yelled to his Clean Room. He was tempted to bang on the wall because the vapor cleanser had obviously malfunctioned, but he stopped himself just in time. Mendor might think Corgan was trying to communicate with someone in an adjoining Clean Room, the way he'd done four years ago. Mendor was already disgruntled because of Corgan's poor performance in the game with Sharla. Corgan didn't want to be criticized twice in one day.

His LiteSuit had dissolved and disappeared into the remover pipe. A new LiteSuit hung on a hook—shimmery blue, his favorite color. They must be trying to make amends for the icy vapor bath. Corgan frowned a little to let Them know, if They were watching, that he was still a bit unhappy with Them. After all, he was Their champion. He deserved better than a malfunctioning Clean Room and a cold vapor bath.

Back in his Box, Corgan suspended himself in the aerogel and relaxed, ready to have lunch. He turned on his favorite surround scene: ocean waves. Towering breakers rushed up to him, curled above him in crests of foam, and receded, soothing him with the throb of crashing water.

"Lunch?" he asked out loud. "Where's lunch?"

"Not yet." It was Mendor's voice, nothing more than the voice, without any face or body showing. Mendor did that sometimes. "You need reflex practice, Corgan."

Corgan sighed and turned off the ocean. Mendor was evidently in his Father Figure mode again. "Practice by myself or against a competitor?" Corgan asked.

"Competitor."

The Box crackled with laser light. "Bees," he told Mendor. "Make it bees to start out with." Corgan liked swatting at the golden bees when they darted at him, faster and faster, as they tried to sting him. They never hurt. It was just a game to check the speed of Corgan's reflexes, to challenge him at each escalating level as the program became faster and more complex. He'd never lost yet. "Bees, Mendor? Okay?"

But Mendor wasn't in an agreeable mood. "You'll practice on whatever They decide you need," he said sternly.

All right, Corgan thought. I'll show the Supreme Council. Let Them throw everything They've got at me. I'll beat Their program like I always do. I'll destruct it so bad They'll have to design it all over again.

"State your pledge," Mendor ordered.

Corgan raised his hand. "I pledge to wage the War with courage, dedication, and honor." He'd said the words so many times he no longer thought about them. "Ready!" he shouted.

"Right hand!" Mendor barked. "In place! Go!"

Lasers bombarded him, the points of light crossing his field of vision so rapidly they were almost invisible. One after another Corgan hit them with his fingertips, making them flare and die the instant he touched them.

"Left hand, middle finger!" Mendor yelled. "Faster!"

Corgan was surprised. To go straight from right hand to left hand, middle finger with no index-finger warm-up of either hand was unusual. This had been an unusual day right from the start, and it wasn't yet lunchtime. But even without a warm-up, he had no trouble making fingertip contact with the points of laser light.

"Both hands, little fingers!"

Ordinarily it wouldn't have been a difficult exercise, but suddenly they doubled the speed of the laser-light points. Corgan had to block everything else from his mind, had to focus intently on the split-second light attack. They tried to trick him by adding colors—They weren't supposed to do that. According to the rules, no more than four colors could appear on the field at a single time. Still, he never missed a point.

A terrible laugh made his arm hairs stand up. A monstrous face appeared in front of him. Steady, he told himself, it's just an illusion; They're trying to break my concentration. The maniacal laughter grew louder and swirled around his ears; They even threw in a sickly sweet smell that made him choke while the laser lights bombarded him so fast, his arms grew numb from hitting them. Now he could no longer touch the lasers with a fingertip; they were hitting him too rapidly for him to be that accurate. He had to bat at the lasers with both palms, increasing his area of contact, because, in spite of his extraordinary natural speed and precision, the laser points were coming faster than a human being could move. A small part of his mind wondered whether They would declare it illegal for him to use the palms of both hands at once, but he heard no warning buzzer. Anyway, They were the ones breaking the rules with too many colors, and that sweet stink. The lasers kept flaring, hundreds of them, faster and faster. Just when he thought his arms would drop off from fatigue, the bell sounded.

"Splendid, Corgan!" Mendor declared. Mendor had a face now, his Father Figure face, and it spread into a wide smile. "You have never played better! You didn't miss one—did you know that?"

Corgan shook his aching head. His score flashed in front of his eyes. 126,392. EXCELLENT WORK, CORGAN.

Flushed with victory, dizzy with success, he realized what that meant. No one in the Western Hemisphere Federation had ever earned a score that high. Corgan knew he could make a demand now. It was even expected of him. "I want something!" he declared.

Mendor slowly turned into Mother Figure. "Of course. Our wonderful champion deserves a reward," she said. Love, pride, approval—all of them radiated from her, washing over Corgan in a wave of maternal admiration. "What would you like?" she asked. "We're already bringing your favorite lunch—a steak."

"Real meat or synthetic?" he asked.

"A real steak from the Federation's famous cattle husbandry division. Do you know what an honor that is, Corgan? The members of the Supreme Council are really pleased with you. They're willing to forget that you lost at Go-ball this morning."

"But I want something else," he demanded, his voice catching just a little. It was always dangerous to demand, never knowing where the line might be drawn.

"What would that be?" Mendor asked, still sounding like the Mother Figure, still indulgent. "What does our hero really want?"

"I want to see Sharla."

Mendor's image smeared. Her colors changed rapidly: red, pale green, purple, black, in swirls like spilled oil. Her face hardened and became androgynous, half Mother, half Father. "Don't push too hard, Corgan," he/she said.

"Bring Sharla out of Reprimand and let me see her,"

Corgan demanded. He tried to sound forceful, but he wasn't sure this was going to work.

"Eat lunch first," Mendor said curtly.

First? First means there might be a second, Corgan thought. Are They really going to let me see her?

But the rest of the day passed, and Sharla didn't appear.

Instead, Corgan had to spend the afternoon on Precision and Sensitivity training.

TWO

The next morning, Mendor the Father Figure paced back and forth, back and forth, inside Corgan's Box. Four meters in one direction, turn around, four meters in the other direction, with his hands clasped behind him in his professor's pose. Of course it wasn't anywhere close to four meters he was pacing, because Corgan's Box was only two and a half meters wide. But the Box could create illusions of distance up to fifty meters long without any distortion. Beyond fifty meters the distortion started small but grew exponentially with each—

"Corgan, are you paying attention?" Mendor barked.

Corgan straightened himself. In the past five minutes, he hadn't heard a thing Mendor had said.

"You need a certain knowledge of history or you won't understand why this War is so important," Mendor scolded. "How much did you miss? What was the last thing you heard me say?"

No sense trying to fake it. "Uh . . . I guess . . ." Corgan searched his memory for the part he'd been paying attention to before his mind wandered. "I remember a picture of bodies all stacked together, wrapped in white cloth. . . ."

Mendor sighed. "That was Zaire—the Ebola epidemic. When they still bothered to bury the dead. Did you understand what I told you about Africa? That life could no longer exist on that continent after the year 2037? That the remaining Africans, the ones who had somehow survived the plagues, were divided among the other confederations. . . ."

Glad that he remembered *something*, so Mendor wouldn't think he'd daydreamed through the whole lesson, Corgan broke in, "Right. About a hundred thousand Africans went to live in the Eurasian Alliance, about half a million went to the Western Hemisphere Federation, and the rest to the Pan Pacific Coalition."

"Very good! Why did none go to the Middle East, Corgan?"

"Because that was where the nuclear war started."

"Correct. And how many died in the nuclear war?"

"Uh . . ." That part of the lecture must have been where Corgan's attention drifted. "Two and a half billion people?"

"Wrong! Only four hundred thousand actually died from the limited nuclear bombing. The other two billion died afterward, from radiation poisoning caused by the next two Chernobyl accidents."

"And then," Corgan began, wanting to redeem himself, "in the twenty years after that, three billion more people died from AIDS, Ebola, dengue fever, hanta virus—"

"—and Earth's surface became so contaminated that no one could survive except in domed cities," Mendor concluded. "Like the one we're living in."

Corgan intertwined his fingers and stretched, pulling his knuckles. "Mendor, there's something I want to ask you—"

"Why are you doing that to your hands?" Mendor interrupted. "Do they hurt? Does your skin itch?"

"No, I'm fine. I was just wondering—"

"Anytime you have the tiniest pain or ache, especially in your hands," Mendor ordered, "you're to report it immediately. You understand that."

"Yes, Mendor, how could I forget it? You tell me at least forty times a day."

"Don't exaggerate. What's the question?"

"Where are we?"

Mendor's image dimmed for a moment. He stopped pacing and lost his body, becoming nothing but a face that looked directly at Corgan, a face with several layers edged in different pale colors. "Where do you think? We're right here in your Box, Corgan."

"No, I mean, you said all Earth people who are still alive live in domed cities. So where is our domed city?"

Mendor's image froze. For about six and thirteen hundredths seconds it remained unmoving.

He's gone to consult with Them about how much I can know, Corgan realized. Corgan hadn't thought the question was *that* major—not so important that Mendor would need to call a conference before he could answer it.

Mendor's face came alive again. "All right. If you want to know, pay attention." The Box filled with the image of a three-dimensional sphere that rotated to show oceans and continents. "This is Earth," Mendor said. "This picture was taken from space long ago, when people called astronauts went up in spaceships that orbited Earth. The last satellites were launched around the year 2010; actually, seventy-seven of them got put into orbit. They were called the Iridium Array. After that, all space launches stopped, because no nation could afford them. Are you following this?"

Corgan nodded.

"Now, seventy years later, only five of the Iridium satellites are still operating," Mendor continued. "All the other space vehicles are gone—they wore out, fell apart, or burned up when they dropped too close to Earth. And that's why it takes so long to get data from outer space these days."

"Uh-huh." Corgan sighed. It took almost as long to get Mendor to answer a simple question. When he was in his Father Professor mode, he blathered all over the place, going off in all kinds of directions before he finally got to the point.

"Okay, I know we live on Earth," Corgan interrupted. "I know we're part of the Western Hemisphere Federation. I know we're on the North American continent—you've told me all that before. But exactly *where* on the North American continent are we?"

The image of Earth zoomed to North America and kept

zooming so fast that Corgan felt airborne. Over mountain peaks and wide valleys, across a river, a lake, waterfalls, trees, another mountain range with white snow on the peaks . . .

"Here!" Mendor announced as the image froze. "In the old days, before the Federation, this place was called Wyoming in the United States of America. This is where our Federation headquarters is located. This spot right here . . ." Again the image zoomed, but more slowly this time. " . . . is where you occupy your particular physical space, Corgan."

It was an aerial shot of a transparent dome. For a short time Corgan's viewpoint stayed motionless, as if he were suspended right over the center of the dome. He strained to see through the glass, or whatever substance the transparent sphere was made of, so he could discover what was inside, but reflections of clouds and sky blocked his view.

About two kilometers in diameter, the dome was supported by six curved beams. The whole structure rested on a circle of solid walls ten meters high. A causeway, completely enclosed, extended from the domed structure to a broad, gray, flat-roofed, windowless building.

"Where? Show me the exact spot I'm in," Corgan said.

He saw a flash of intense red light at the center of the flat-roofed gray building, which appeared to be about a hundred meters square, although it could have been larger or smaller. In virtual images, proportions were often deceiving.

"You're right here. In the spot where the light is. Now, is that sufficient?" Mendor demanded.

"No. Back off so I can see what's around us."

Again, moving slowly, the image pulled backward to reveal a paved runway on one side of the domed city. Two Harrier jet airplanes sat in front of a cylindrical hangar. As the view reverse-zoomed even farther, Corgan noticed a river curving around the expanse of land where all the buildings stood. Beyond the river grew a thick forest of cone-shaped trees that Corgan didn't know the name of.

"Why'd the Supreme Council pick here?" he asked.

"Energy. Solar power, wind power, water power, thermal power. Enough natural energy to keep this domed city running indefinitely. And the biggest reason of all—the area wasn't nearly as contaminated as most other places. That made it easier to sterilize."

The image vanished. "All right, that's enough," Mendor declared. "I think you may have even learned a little bit today. It's time for reflex practice, then lunch, and after that there's a surprise for you."

"Surprise?" Corgan rose to his feet. He'd been sitting for so long that the shape of his body had molded into the aerogel. "Good or bad surprise?"

"You'll think it's good," Mendor said. "As for me, I'm not so sure."

Corgan tried to keep from smiling. If the surprise was something Mendor the Father Figure didn't think he should have, then Corgan was sure to like it. And since it sounded like the Council was giving him something nice, he'd give Them a present in return. During reflex practice he'd pull out all the stops and play at the absolute peak he was capable of. That ought to make Them happy.

They chose to test him on button-hits-per-second. His previous high score was thirteen hits per second with the four fingers of his right hand, twelve with the four fingers of his left hand, and nine with each thumb. Because Corgan could gauge time in hundredths of a second, he calculated that by shaving just six or seven milliseconds off each hit, he could set himself a new personal record.

Concentrating hard, he pictured the neural impulses that started in his brain, then fired along his spinal cord and branched into the nerves in his upper arms, lower arms, and wrists. When the neural transmissions reached his fingertips, each tiny neuron would fire instantaneously in response to his commands. Corgan closed his eyes and visualized the sparks traveling along each nerve path. In his imagination he magnified the synapses, picturing them in full color, in full motion, in 3-D. He took a breath, recited the pledge to wage the War with honor and so on, then said, "I'm ready."

As it turned out, he didn't even need to break a sweat. His time-splitting ability kept him aware of his score even while he reacted to the voiced instructions: "Third finger left, right thumb, index finger right, fourth finger left . . ."

Mendor was ecstatic. "You've set another Federation record!" he/she crowed. "That's two new records in two consecutive days."

"Good! Let's eat."

"Corgan, dear boy—"

"Lunch, please. Now!"

The meal was nothing more than synthetic meat and tasteless hydroponic vegetables, but Corgan hardly noticed. He wolfed it down, not because he was hungry, but because he wanted it to be over quickly so he could find out what the surprise was. Mendor the Mother Figure hovered over him, pointing out each little lapse in his table manners, making him finish every tiny bit of food on his plate, stalling on purpose.

"All right!" Corgan threw down his napkin. "I'm done. What's the surprise?"

Mendor sniffed. *"They* can show you. It was *Their* idea to call it a surprise."

Corgan waited for the Supreme Council to appear on the surround-image inside his Box. Slowly, the visualization appeared before him: a long table, with six faceless humans in uniform sitting at the table, staring at Corgan with shaded eyes. In the center of the six was an empty chair.

"Corgan!" The voice came from the second faceless one on the left. "You've done extremely well. We're pleased." The other five faceless ones murmured agreement, causing light waves to shimmer where Their mouths should have been if Their mouths had been visible.

"You knew from the start," a Councillor with an echo-chamber voice said, "that you would have two partners in the War. You, Corgan, are the team leader. You are the one who will be physically involved in the War. But your team also requires a strategist and a cryptanalyst—a code breaker."

"Yes, sir . . . ma'am." Corgan couldn't tell from the voice whether the speaker was a woman or a man.

"We're ready for you to meet your cryptanalyst."

"Is that the surprise?" Corgan asked. Why would Mendor be all bent out of shape over that?

"It is. And here she is. Sharla."

The image of a girl appeared in the center chair. Sharla? This was not the beautiful Sharla who'd beat him at Go-ball. At least he didn't think so. He couldn't get a good look at her because her face was blurred. Frowning, squinting, Corgan tried to bring her image into focus, but it was as if several veils of light had been layered one over the other, slightly out of alignment.

"Hello, Corgan," she said.

Only the eyes looked like the earlier Sharla—they were blue and brimming with energy.

"Hi," he answered.

"Sharla is the most ingenious code breaker in the history of cryptology," one of Them said.

"I'm pretty good at Go-ball, too," Sharla remarked. Even though her image stayed out of focus, Corgan could tell she was smiling.

The six of Them buzzed disapprovingly. "Be serious, Sharla," one of Them said. "The War is only seventeen days away."

"Sorry!" Sharla ducked her head, but not before Corgan noticed that her eyes didn't look at all sorry. He felt a slight tug of disappointment that he couldn't see the rest of her any better, and wondered why the Supreme Council was bothering to blur her image. Just because Corgan had acted foolish over her yesterday?

"When do I meet the third member of my team?" he asked.

24

"Eventually. Soon," one of Them answered. Corgan had given up trying to figure out which one was talking. It was too hard to notice the slight wave motion where their mouths were supposed to be. "For today, we want you to become acquainted with Sharla. The two of you must learn to work together smoothly. Raise your hand, Corgan. Touch Sharla's hand."

Why bother, Corgan thought, but he did what he was told. What good was it to touch a tactile simulation of someone's hand? They could manipulate the tactile sensors to make a hand touch feel any way They wanted it to. Sharla's hand touch felt cool and rough, but it wasn't real. It was as artificial as her image. He was much more interested in how she would look in real life, but he'd probably never find out. The Supreme Council could tamper with her appearance as much as They wanted to, making her look incredibly beautiful or clouding her features in mist, like They were doing now. They controlled all the virtual images.

They controlled everything.

THREE

The next day they practiced together for the first time, Corgan and Sharla. She looked the same as she had the day before—out of focus. Corgan wondered where Sharla lived. In a Box like his? In the same domed city he lived in? In Wyoming, where the wind and sun and thermal pools made energy? She could be next door or anywhere on Earth; in the virtual world, it didn't matter.

Corgan had never before thought about where the space might be that a person actually occupied. Virtual contact was all he'd ever known—virtual images of playmates, of Mendor, of the pets he was allowed to sleep with at night when he settled down into the warm aerogel inside his Box, holding a puppy or a kitten that had molded itself, as he watched, out of the same soft aerogel he slept on. After the pet took shape, its virtual heart would beat beneath Corgan's fingertips and its virtual breath would warm his cheek as it huddled against him. But the puppy—or whatever pet he'd chosen that night—never shed hair or nipped fingers or made a mess. And it never grew or wore out, because it disappeared whenever he got tired of it.

"Recite the pledge, Corgan," Mendor instructed.

Corgan raised his hand to say, "I pledge to wage the War with courage, dedication, and honor," as he did before every practice session. Sharla seemed to be saying the pledge, too, but with her image so out of focus, it was hard to tell whether she was murmuring the same words Corgan spoke. He stared intently at her lips.

"Pay attention, Corgan," Mendor ordered. "You and Sharla will start out with a few easy exercises to warm up. We'll change trajectory codes ten times while you play the first game. Sharla will adjust the program each time the code is changed so you won't miss any hits. "You can play Golden Bees to start, since you like that game so much."

At the end of the Golden Bees session, Corgan asked, "What happened? I thought the trajectory codes were supposed to change."

Sharla laughed—at least that much of her was the same. Her laugh sounded as full of delight and amusement as when she'd hit him on the head with the Go-ball.

"The codes did get changed," Mendor said dryly. "You just didn't notice, because Sharla calibrated and adjusted each one in about a tenth of a second. She's fast."

"I really wasn't trying as hard as I should have," Sharla

said apologetically. The mischief in her eyes contradicted her modest tone.

"You must always try to do your best work," Mendor ordered.

They practiced a few more times, and then Mendor told them, "The rules governing the Virtual War were agreed upon, after five years of negotiation, by the Western Hemisphere Federation, the Eurasian Alliance, and the Pan Pacific Coalition. If either one of you breaks a rule unintentionally—even though it's just through human error—the infraction will be recorded. If you commit three such errors, we lose the War."

Corgan nodded. He'd heard it all before.

"But if you *deliberately* break a rule—just once," Mendor went on, "it's all over. We lose."

"How are the judges going to know if it's intentional or not?" Sharla asked.

Why would she ask that? Corgan wondered. Surely They'd gone over that with her. Dozens of times.

Mendor looked perplexed, but he began to answer Sharla, going off in all directions, like he always did, to talk about every other possible topic that had anything at all to do with what she'd asked. Mendor could never get right down to the core of a question.

Corgan gazed off into the distance while Mendor rambled on. Suddenly a small image of Sharla's blurry face appeared just inches in front of his eyes. "Don't say anything!" the tiny image warned him. "Just listen. Your Mendor won't catch on that I'm doing this. I fixed the codes."

Corgan was about to answer her but something slammed hard against his mouth. "Shut up!" the Sharla image hissed. "Just listen! Tonight at eleven o'clock I'll alter the codes so you can come out of your Box and They won't know. Meet me in the tunnel."

Corgan's eyes widened. It was a good thing Mendor wasn't focusing on him right then.

"Okay?" the Sharla image whispered. "If it's okay, blink real fast right now."

Corgan blinked.

"We'll meet person to person," the tiny face of Sharla told him. "Real. Not virtual." The image disappeared.

"You should be paying attention to this, too, Corgan," Mendor said irritably. "Or do you think you already know it?"

"Yes, I already know it," he answered.

"That kind of overconfidence could lead to serious mistakes," Mendor said. "Even if you think you know everything, it doesn't hurt to learn it over again."

"Sorry, Mendor," Corgan said. His voice shook a little. Mendor would think the quaver came from shame at being scolded. Let him think that. The real tremor was inside Corgan's chest, not his throat.

Did Sharla mean it? Could she do what she said—arrange it so they'd actually come face to face, and Corgan would be in the presence of *another human being* of bone and blood and muscle? He wondered if he'd have the courage to touch her, to take her hand.

What about infection? From the moment of his birth in the laboratory he'd lived inside a Box, away from any possibility of contamination. The Earth's population was so sparse now—hardly more than two million people left on the whole planet—that none of the three global confederations *ever* let people be together in the same space. Or have actual physical contact with one another. At least not as far as Corgan knew. Everything, for everyone, had to be virtual—always. Everyone lived in his or her own Box, enveloped in aerogel, nurtured by it, comforted and sustained by it.

Aerogel, the miracle substance. Discovered eons ago, back in the 1930s, but not till a hundred years ago in the 1980s had scientists figured out how to use it. Aerogel, called "frozen smoke." Light as air, a superinsulator that protected against heat or cold but couldn't be frozen itself and could tolerate temperatures as high as two thousand degrees Celsius. Made from long strands of silicon dioxide— common sand—linked together with pockets of air. Aerogel was 99.6 percent air.

In a Box lined with aerogel, a person could live his entire virtual life, because aerogel carried electronic signals. Mixed with metal ions, it became a virtual medium that delivered 3-D, wraparound images as well as sounds, smells, touch—everything but taste. That afternoon, as Corgan advanced through a dozen practice levels, his senses were reacting to signals sent through aerogel.

"Very good. That's enough drill for now," Mendor stated. "You need some physical exercise." Immediately Sharla vanished and Corgan's virtual surroundings changed into a running track—a circular dirt track with white lines marking the edges and sweet-smelling grass growing in the middle. Obediently, he started to run faster and faster around the track, and all the time he was still in his Box, running on a treadmill imbedded in the floor, not a dozen inches from where he'd spent the whole day.

Corgan's aerogel-filled Box was his whole world, safe, sanitized, and lighted by a virtual sun. It was his cocoon. The surrounding aerogel-coated walls put him, electronically, into any scene created for him. Nothing could harm him in his Box, nothing could disturb him. Except Sharla, who managed to disturb Corgan's thoughts quite a bit later that night as he squirmed inside his aerogel bed.

Usually Corgan would fall asleep right when he was supposed to. Every night at exactly ten o'clock, Mendor the Mother Figure would call out, "Sleepy time, Corgan!" in a sweet, silly, singsong voice, and Corgan would settle himself into the aerogel, which had been cooled by five degrees for nighttime comfort. Within minutes he'd sink into the light sleep that always preceded his dreams. Dreams of ocean waves, or of the huge dinosaurs and pterodactyls that he'd picked out to decorate the walls of his Box when he was little. Sometimes he'd dream of soaring over trees in a forest of tall ferns and flowering branches. But since the day he'd played Go-ball with Sharla, he'd dreamed of other kinds of trees. Palm trees.

That night, though, Corgan wouldn't let himself fall asleep. He yawned, loudly, for Mendor's benefit. "'Night, Mendor," he said. Then he waited, lying as still as possible, counting the tiny grains of time as they cascaded over the sharp edge of his wakefulness. Since his sleep was always monitored by sensors embedded in the aerogel, he was afraid to move much—if he tossed and turned, as his body urged him to do, They'd check on him to discover what was keeping him awake: did he have a fever; did his hands hurt; did his throat feel sore?

"You're such a wonderful sleeper!" Corgan had been told over and over again when he was a little boy, as though sleeping were a skill as important as his ability to tell time to the hundredth of a second, or to throw a ball through a hoop thirty meters away, which he'd mastered before he turned three.

It is now twenty-two hours and forty-seven minutes and thirteen and eight-tenths seconds past midnight, he counted in his head. At twenty-two hours, fifty-nine minutes, and forty-five seconds he would stand up and attempt to walk through the door of his Box. What would happen? Could Sharla really fix the code so no one would know, so Mendor the Mother Figure wouldn't appear the instant Corgan stood up, asking him what was wrong—did he have to go to the Clean Room, had something upset him, did he feel too warm, and on and on and on?

He stood. Nothing, no Mendor. He moved through the pliable aerogel to the door of his Box. It opened. He stepped into the tunnel.

It was dark. Sharla must not have known how to light the passageway. Or else she was afraid to because They would notice light where it wasn't supposed to be.

"Corgan?" The whisper made a chill rush over his skin.

"Where are you?" he whispered.

"In front of you. Reach out."

It was going to happen, then. For the first time in his

life, Corgan was going to touch a human being. He knew it would be dangerous, because contamination got spread by touch from person to person, which was why 93 percent of the Earth's human population had ceased to exist in the past eighty years. He'd been taught the danger ever since he could remember knowing anything, and now—he didn't care.

She touched him first. When her fingers reached his chest he trembled so violently that he almost fell against the wall—only his natural agility let him straighten himself in time.

"It's all right," she said softly. "Hasn't anyone ever touched you before?"

"No. What about you?"

Even muted, her laugh sounded joyful. "Corgan, I was bred to break codes. And on my own, I figured out how to break rules. Practically from the day I could walk They couldn't control me. I've been everywhere. I know everything. All about you, and the world, and the War we're going to win for Them, and . . ."

"All about me?"

"Sure. You and I were bred in the same laboratory. I looked up the records to find out about you."

"What about me?"

The words coming out of him sounded ordinary and rational, even though inside he felt total chaos—in his brain, in the pounding of his heart, in the way his breath kept catching in his lungs. *He was standing beside a living human being.* Except for that one fleeting brush of her fingers across his chest, they hadn't touched again. But he could feel her breath on his face when she spoke, still in whispers.

"You're one of Their greatest successes, Corgan," she said. "You were genetically engineered to have the fastest reflexes possible in a human. You and I happened to be in the same crop of genetic experiments, and the scientists almost went crazy when we were born. Because both of us turned out even better than they'd expected. We're not only superior, we're supreme. And I speak in all modesty. . . ." She laughed softly.

Her nearness made him dizzy. "What about the rest of the crop we were in?" he asked.

"Failures. The rest were all Mutants. Fourteen of them. Twelve died, and two went into the Mutant Pen. Since then, though, the geneticists have gotten better at it."

"How?" he asked, as softly as possible. If she had to lean forward to hear him, she'd be close enough that he could breathe the scent of her.

"The geneticists studied you and me to figure out what made us so good. It took a lot of years, but they've finally got a few more successes like us coming along, except those kids are all a lot younger than we are. Which is why you and I will fight the War."

The meaning of her words suddenly penetrated. Although still intensely aware of her presence, Corgan began to focus on what she was telling him. All of it was new to him. "Why didn't They teach me this?" he asked, forgetting to whisper.

"NNTK. No Need To Know. They might have told you, if you'd ever bothered to ask, but I guess you never did."

Corgan rubbed his arms. The tunnel was cold.

"I know you're a time genius, Corgan, so how long have we been out here?" Sharla asked.

"Thirteen minutes, fourteen and fifty-six hundredths seconds. That's how long it was when you asked, but whenever I count in hundredths of second, by the time I say the words—"

"Better get back in your Box soon," she interrupted. "You're lucky you have a nice warm Box to live in."

"Everyone lives in a nice Box," he said.

"No they don't," she told him, sounding impatient. "They want you to believe it's true, but it isn't. Most people live in cramped dormitories. You've been raised in a Box because you're special. I am, too, but I learned how to get out and navigate the city when I was eight years old, and They never knew. They still don't know."

Corgan wanted to reach and touch her; instead he asked questions to keep her there. "What will happen if They find out you escape all the time?"

"Nothing. I'll go into Reprimand again, but what else can They do to me? They need me. I'm the best code breaker that ever lived. I'm the best by about a factor of ten."

She was either incredibly brave or incredibly foolish. "What about contamination?" he demanded.

"Won't you get infected if you keep leaving your Box?"

"The whole city is pretty much infection free," she answered. "The Supreme Council keeps scaring you about contamination because They want to you to stay isolated."

She's got to be wrong, Corgan thought. At least about

that part of it. He wished he could challenge her on it, but they were running out of time.

"You'd better go—you don't want to get caught on your first time out," she said.

"First? Are we going to do this again?"

"Do you want to?"

"Yes!" Even though he remembered to whisper, the fervor in his voice echoed off the steel walls of the tunnel.

"Okay. Tomorrow night. Same time." Her fingertips grazed his cheek.

Not till he was back in his Box trying to settle himself in the aerogel did Corgan realize he'd never even seen her. Was she the beautiful Sharla he'd first met under the palm trees, or was she something else?

FOUR

"This is the land the War will be fought over," Mendor announced. "The Isles of Hiva."

The name meant nothing to Corgan. Tired, because he hadn't slept much the night before, he slumped into his aerogel as Mendor droned on about the Isles' location: between 7 degrees 50 minutes and 10 degrees 35 minutes south latitude, and between 138 degrees 25 minutes and 140 degrees 50 minutes west longitude. In the Central Pacific.

Slowly, the virtual re-creation of the Isles of Hiva filled the space around him, and Corgan came wide awake. Ocean waves splashed against rocky shores. The smooth circular trunks of palm trees rose high into canopies of flat, spiny fronds. Birds soared overhead and launched themselves into the water to spear fish. A warm, humid breeze skimmed Corgan's skin. The thunder of surf felt like heartbeats.

"Twenty volcanic islands forming two main groups . . ." Mendor the Father Professor's soliloquy continued, boring and lifeless. How could Mendor talk about something so beautiful and make it so dull, Corgan wondered. Was Sharla seeing and hearing this? She probably knew all about the Isles of Hiva. She'd probably broken into the code and discovered them for herself.

"A hundred years ago, seven thousand people lived on these islands," Mendor went on. "Fifty years ago, they all died in an epidemic of pakoko. That's what the natives called a particularly rapid-spreading form of tuberculosis."

"Then why are we fighting to win the islands if they're contaminated?" Corgan asked.

Mendor's color changed; it grew softer. "I'm glad you're interested enough to finally ask a question," he told Corgan. "Because amazingly enough, the islands are no longer contaminated."

"How'd that happen?" Corgan asked. He didn't really care so much about the answer; sometimes he just kept asking questions because it made Mendor happy. He felt guilty about what he'd done last night—sneaking out of his Box. If he pretended, now, to be really interested in the lecture, it might quiet his own conscience.

Mendor's image grew even brighter with pleasure. "As you know, Corgan, five satellites still orbit the Earth to send back—"

"Yes, I know."

"In 2073, scientists put together twenty years' worth of data they'd gathered about the Isles of Hiva. It was discovered that the contamination was gone. A submarine party of robots landed there to confirm the data."

Corgan lifted his hand to feel the soft virtual breeze. Mendor went on, "Why have the islands become danger free? No one is certain. Perhaps because for a dozen years in a row, they received excessive rainfall—a hundred inches each year. That might have washed them clean and swept all the pakoko bacteria into the cold ocean current that flows north from the Antarctic, past the islands. Then the cold current might have killed the bacteria. Whatever the reason, the islands are safe for people to live on again."

Now Corgan really was interested. "You said the scientists figured this out in 2073. This is 2080. Why'd They wait so long to have a War over these islands?"

Mendor became a pulsing fount of radiant androgynous light. "Because of *you*, Corgan! For all these years the Supreme Council has used every excuse They could think of to delay this War. They stalled Their negotiations with the other confederations. They wrangled over rules and details. They demanded additional meetings and procrastinated at those meetings until it became embarrassing. All because of *you*. They were waiting for you to grow up, Corgan. Waiting for your skills to peak. And it's happened! Your abilities go far beyond anything ever measured before." Mendor's light dimmed a bit. "Sharla's, too, of course."

* * *

There were so many things he wanted to ask her. Things he could never ask Mendor. What was the Mutant Pen she'd mentioned? He'd never heard of it. What was it like in Reprimand? Why did she take so many chances?

But when they met in the tunnel that night he forgot all his questions. Sharla had brought a light.

"It's not very bright—it's just a piezoelectric stone. You squeeze this clamp on it and the stone glows for a second. I wanted to get a look at you," she said.

The stone measured only three centimeters wide on each side. "Let me," he said, taking it from her. "My fingers are strong."

The more pressure he exerted on the clamp holding the stone, the brighter the glow. Still, the piece was too small to cast much light. He was able to see Sharla more clearly than her blurred image at the War games practices, but not as well, in the dimness, as he would have liked. He saw that her hair was shorter than on the Go-ball court, yet it looked more golden. And her mouth! For a long moment he let the light shine on it. No virtual image could ever do justice to those full, moist lips.

"Better let the stone go out before They come snooping," she told him.

They stood together in the dark, with Corgan resisting the urge to reach out to her, feeling awkward because he ought to be saying something and he didn't know what to say. When two people were connected in the virtual world, conversation was easy. But here, with Sharla only inches from him, Corgan became tongue-tied.

"Uh . . ." All he could think of were the fractions of

seconds being wasted while he stood there, as dumb as the stone in his hand. "Uh . . . what about me? Do I look the same as in my virtual image?"

"Exactly the same. No surprises."

Corgan's ears started ringing from the flood of sensations coursing through him, from the novelty of not only standing beside another human being, but this time, being able to actually see her. *Talk!* he commanded himself. A hundred phrases darted into his brain but shriveled there. *What should he say?*

Sharla took over. "Do you know that tomorrow we're scheduled to meet our Strategist?" she asked him. "Virtually. Right before lunch. And tomorrow night, I'm going to bring him here with me. If you want to meet me here again."

"Tomorrow?" A few seconds passed before Corgan nodded, hurt because she intended to let a stranger come with her the next time. Just when he was trying so hard to know her, to know how to act around her. He realized she couldn't see him nod in the dark, so he mumbled, "Yeah, I guess it's all right." Then he thought, Wait! Is she going to think I'm not anxious to meet *her*? "I mean, it's more than all right with me for us to meet again," he stammered. "I mean, you and me. And I guess it's all right if you bring him along. The Strategist. Do you have to?"

"Look, he's just a little kid," Sharla said. "Only ten years old."

"Then what's he doing on our team? Why would They put a ten-year-old with us to fight the War? That's crazy!"

She rested her hand on his arm. "This kid's a real prodigy. His name's Brig. I've seen him in real life. When They show him to you virtually, he'll look like an ordinary boy. But wait till you meet him tomorrow night."

It was a strange feeling—trying to push down his resentment over some ten-year-old intruder at the same time his blood raced because her hand was on his arm. The brand-new sensation of human touch: he wanted it never to end. Who cared what this Brig looked like? As long as Corgan and Sharla could stand together in the tunnel, Brig could look like one of those bodies consumed by flesh-eating bacteria, for all Corgan cared. Mendor had shown him images of those bodies, once, to convince him how important the coming War would be. "Safe, uncontaminated land is the most precious commodity on Earth," Mendor had said. "Do you understand? Contamination has almost killed off the human race."

"What if the kid's infectious?" Corgan asked now.

Her laughter escaped before she could cover her mouth with her hands to stifle it. "Corgan, you really are funny," she whispered. "Brig won't be any more infectious than I am."

Stumbling over the words, he asked, "Could you put your hand back on my arm? I like it when you do that."

"Even if my hand has germs? Tell you what—how 'bout if I really contaminate you." She reached up in the dark and brushed his lips with hers. "That's called a kiss, in case you don't know. Remember it, because I won't do it again. From tomorrow on, we won't be alone anymore. Brig will be with us."

Corgan had never met Brig but he already hated him. "Then do it once more. Right now," he demanded.

"*Shhhh.* They'll hear you, and we'll both be in trouble."

"Would you like to hear how loud I can *really* yell?" he asked her. Then he said, "I'm sorry. I—I don't know why I said that. It's just that I've never been out of my Box before these last two nights with you, and I don't want it to stop, and this stupid clock keeps ticking in my head, eating up the time. . . ."

He felt her lips touch his face again, but this time, they lingered against his own lips a little longer—four and thirty-seven hundredths of a second.

"Good night," she whispered. "Till tomorrow."

"Did you brush your teeth?" Mendor the Mother Figure asked.

"Yes, I brushed my teeth," Corgan shouted. "I always brush my teeth. I always do what I'm supposed to, don't I?"

"What's the matter with you today, Corgan?" Mendor wondered. "Why are you so grouchy?"

"Because it was a stupid question you asked me. You had to know I brushed my teeth because you know everything I do—I'm monitored every second of my life. Even in the Clean Room."

That was not something Sharla had told him last night in the dark. It was something he'd figured out for himself as he lay awake, tossing and turning, remembering that kiss, not caring if his restlessness made all the sensors go off to alert Mendor.

Now Mendor's image changed through several shades of green.

"I'm sorry," Corgan told her. "I guess I'm starting to worry about the War. I think I need more practice sessions with Sharla." He was twisting the truth, and he felt a moment of guilt. But the Supreme Council lied to *him* all the time, didn't They? Making him think everyone lived in a Box, like he did.

"If that's all that's bothering you, we'll increase your practice time," Mendor said. "It's good for you to be conscientious, Corgan, but you don't need to worry. Judging from what our surveillance teams have learned about your competition, your skills are infinitely superior to theirs. There, I probably shouldn't have told you that because They don't want you to become overconfident. But you shouldn't become *under*confident either. Now, why don't you relax a little before the first practice session? Do you want me to turn on Ocean Waves?"

"No. Not now." Corgan realized he still sounded like a cranky child. He softened his voice and asked, "Could I please have the Isles of Hiva, Mendor? All of it—image, sound, smell, touch . . ."

Mendor turned pink with pleasure. "Splendid!" she said. "The more you learn about the Isles, the more you'll understand our need to win them in a bloodless War. Naturally, the other confederations want the Isles, too. . . ."

Corgan breathed deeply. The smell of salt water reached him, carried on the island breeze. "Mendor, when you say 'bloodless War,' does that mean there once was a war with blood?" he asked. "I mean, people actually bleeding?"

Mendor hovered halfway between Mother Figure and Father Professor: If Corgan started to ask hard questions, Father would probably take over. "Even as little as a century ago, people killed each other in wars," he/she said.

"Yes, I know about nuclear bombs. But they didn't make people bleed, did they? They just gave people radiation sickness, and that's how they died." Corgan's attention was caught by a funny little creature with a shell and spindly legs. In the simulation, it skittered sideways across the beach. Corgan reached out a finger, but the creature dug into the sand and disappeared.

Mendor the Mother Figure was still talking. "Corgan, I realize that you're growing up and you want to know more about Earth's past, but we should wait until after the War," she said soothingly. "Don't clutter your mind now with unnecessary details. After you win the War for us, I'll answer anything you want to ask me. I promise!" When Corgan slumped in mild disappointment, Mendor added, "Just be glad you live in a time when wars are fought virtually."

The morning dragged as Corgan practiced alone. For two hours Mendor made him do P and S drills. In Precision and Sensitivity training, Corgan had to bring his hand as close as possible to a square of laser light without actually touching it. He couldn't determine his closeness visually; he had to use the nerve endings in his palms and fingers to feel the strength of an electromagnetic field between his hand and the image.

From ten millimeters away, he couldn't feel anything. Within one millimeter of the laser square, he would barely begin to sense energy. At five hundred microns from the image, the surface of his skin could perceive a tiny magnetic sensation. At two hundred and seventy microns, a slight tingle.

P and S workouts were the most difficult part of Corgan's training, and the most important part, Mendor said, although Corgan didn't know why. He'd practiced for two full years before he could turn the energy of electromagnetism into movement. It required all his concentration to bring his hands to within two hundred microns of a laser image—a distance the width of a delicate strand of a spider's web—and still not touch it. But when he learned to do that, he could make the laser image move. By itself.

Only half a dozen people in the whole world—at least as far as the Council knew—had control as precise as Corgan's. Because of it, he was favored, indulged, and given privileges that no one else got. On the down side, he was watched over and guarded every second of his life, day and night.

"Can I quit now, Mendor?" he asked after exactly two hours.

"Yes. Sharla's here, ready to practice with you."

It was the virtual Sharla, still unfocused. Doesn't matter at all, Corgan thought, because I know how she really looks. They can make her as blurry as They want, but I've seen the real Sharla.

"Recite the pledge," Mendor instructed them. Since Corgan had to repeat the pledge before every single practice session—sometimes as often as five times a day—he said the words automatically and never thought about what they meant. Now he stared at Sharla's out-of-focus mouth, trying to decipher whether she was saying the same pledge or something different. He couldn't tell.

"Ready?" Mendor asked. "Begin!"

They started with Triple Multiplex, a three-dimensional, three-layered maze that pitted artificial intelligence against Corgan's decision-making speed. He performed so well that Mendor heaped lavish praise on him, and Sharla smiled.

They had three more practices. Sharla needed to adjust the program to handle twenty-five switched codes, involving Corgan so intensely that he couldn't think of much else. He was sweating.

He asked Mendor, "Did you know we ran thirty-seven hundredths of a second over the time limit on that last game? If we do that in the War, we'll be penalized."

"Very good, Corgan. You caught that."

"Did you think I wouldn't notice?"

"Your proficiency was a bit off in the first game," Mendor said. "Not by much—just about three hundredths of a percent. Letting this last game run overtime by a fraction of a second was a little test They devised to make sure you were back on track. I told Them you'd be fine, and you were. Go to your Clean Room now and sanitize yourself. When you come back, you'll meet someone new."

Yeah, I know all about it, Corgan thought as moisture swirled around his naked body, as his hair got cleansed and his LiteSuit melted in the vapor before disappearing. He began to wonder—did everyone wear LiteSuits?

For the sake of sanitation, these seamless suits of PVA—polyvinyl alcohol—were formulated to dissolve in water so they couldn't be worn more than once. But they were expensive; especially the kind Corgan wore, which reflected subtle highlights of color to match the wearer's mood. Sometimes he pretended to feel angry, then happy, then sad in rapid succession just to see how fast his LiteSuit could ripple with pale traces of gray or yellow or brown.

He'd have to ask Sharla if those people she talked about who lived in unsanitary dormitories got to wear LiteSuits. He'd ask her tonight. Except tonight, Brig would be with her. Ten years old! What kind of kid could be smart enough at the age of ten to plot strategy? And what was it about the way he looked? Sharla had hinted, but she hadn't really told Corgan anything except that Brig's virtual image would look a lot different from the way he was in real life.

When Corgan reentered his Box sixteen seconds late, the same faceless members of the Supreme Council were already there in virtual form, seated in the same straight line as before.

"Where's Sharla?" Corgan asked.

"She'll arrive later. After you meet your Strategist."

Brig's chair was in the middle of the row. Why did he need a chair anyway? Even real bodies didn't need chairs—aerogel let them sit suspended in comfort. And virtual bodies didn't need anything at all to hold them up because they were nothing but electronically transmitted impulses.

Except for his flaming red hair, Brig looked pretty ordinary. Corgan would never have guessed he was only ten. It was hard to tell what age he was supposed to be in the virtual image—not as old as Corgan and Sharla, but not especially young either.

"Corgan," one of the Councillors said. Corgan didn't bother to notice who was talking. "This young man will be your Strategist in the War. His name is Brig."

"Hi," Brig said. Corgan raised his hand in a small wave.

"You may be wondering, Corgan," another one of Them said, "why we've waited so long to introduce you to your two team members. Have you wondered?"

"Not really," Corgan answered.

Mendor suddenly appeared at the right shoulder of the Councillor who'd spoken last. "Corgan is an exceptional boy," Mendor said softly. "He rarely questions anything. He always does what's expected of him, no questions asked."

Corgan saw a tiny, scornful flicker cross Brig's eyes, and wanted to punch him in the mouth.

Another Councillor spoke. "Wise elders on the Council decided it would be best to bring the three of you to your highest skill level as individuals, before letting you practice together. Do you think that was a good idea, Corgan?"

He shrugged. "I guess."

Brig butted in. "Several conclusions could be drawn. Why waste valuable practice time when our abilities weren't yet at the peak of perfection? Now that they are—at least mine are—each practice will have greater value. Still, drawing on my instincts as a Strategist, I suspect the real reason hasn't yet been mentioned. My guess is that the

War rules prohibited us from meeting before now."

Corgan's jaw dropped. The Council members laughed and congratulated Brig on his clever answer; some of Them even applauded.

Ten years old! The little toad talked like an old man of forty! Corgan said sarcastically, "Brilliant deduction, Brag. I mean Brig."

Mendor's image flared into all the colors of the rainbow. Corgan had embarrassed him.

In a chilly voice the Councillor said, "Corgan, the three of you are required to interact in cooperation and good-will. No rudeness will be tolerated."

Corgan nodded, his cheeks flaming. He'd never before been rebuked in front of the whole Council.

Sharla appeared then, and Mendor the Father Figure announced, "You three will begin practice with an easy exercise and build to increasing levels of proficiency. Corgan, Brig, and Sharla. *As a team! Starting now.*"

Sharla, Corgan, and Brig the Mouth. Together for a whole afternoon. What fun.

FIVE

Eleven o'clock. Without even wondering whether Sharla had set the code, Corgan stepped out of his Box. Far down the tunnel, well past the door of his Clean Room, he saw a dim light flash on, then off. Sharla was signaling him to their meeting place, much farther along the tunnel than where they'd met before.

Moving silently, he reached her, took the piezoelectric stone from her hand and held it up to illuminate her face. "You came by yourself," he said. "I'm glad."

"I'm not alone," she answered. "Brig's here. Look down."

Startled, Corgan saw him. He was only half as tall as a ten-year-old should be and his head was twice as big. His arms and legs looked spindly. Even through the cloth of his LiteSuit, his torso appeared twisted.

Astonished, Corgan exclaimed, "You're a dwarf."

"No I'm not! I'm a Mutant." Brig's real voice was high and childish, much different than it had sounded that afternoon, when it must have been electronically altered to make him seem older.

"A Mutant!" Corgan had never seen one; he barely knew that such creatures existed.

Wobbling unsteadily on his twisted legs, Brig stared up at Corgan. In the dim light his features looked grotesque—bulging blue eyes, ridged forehead, ears that stuck straight out from his head through a great mop of flaming red hair. His nose was too big and his mouth too small, but as Corgan slowly took in Brig's appearance, he realized that shadows from the piezo light were exaggerating the boy's weirdness. "I thought all Mutants were . . . um . . . kind of retarded," Corgan said.

"Well, I'm a Mutant and I'm not the least bit retarded," Brig huffed. "You're right, though. Some of them are. Most of them are. Most of them die before they're seven. But here I am and I'm ten and I'm brilliant. A lot more brilliant than you are, Corgan-the-good-boy-who-never-questions-anything!"

"Don't be so prickly, Brig," Sharla chided him.

"Well, it's true. Corgan was bred for swift reflexes and incredibly precise control. But his brain barely hovers around genius level. Mine's *double* genius."

"And mine's *triple* genius, so back off, Brig," Sharla told him. "If you want to have a brain contest, you lose."

"Corgan loses worse," Brig muttered.

Sharla shook her head. "You can tell he's just ten," she said. "Still a big baby."

"The only thing big about him is his mouth," Corgan answered.

"Don't be nasty! You're worse than he is—you're older, so you ought to know better. Both of you better stop it right now or I'm leaving."

"No!" Corgan's hand shot out to stop her. "You promised me fifteen minutes, and there's still twelve left." If he had to put up with Brig to keep Sharla there in the tunnel, it was worth it. Fighting down his irritation, he said, "Sorry, Brig."

Brig muttered, "Apology accepted." He reached up to put his hand into Corgan's. "Shake!"

The hand was so small! And warm. It filled only half of Corgan's palm, and felt as delicate and fragile as a hummingbird he'd once held, created for him to play with in the tactile simulator. Brig's fingertips twitched against Corgan's palm as if he knew Corgan could very easily crush him—fracture those frail, vulnerable, metacarpal bones—just by squeezing them in his own powerful fist. And Corgan could have. But Brig let his hand stay where it was until Corgan gave it an abrupt shake.

Sharla said, "I'm going to lift up Brig so we can all see each other's faces. You hold the stone, Corgan, to make enough light."

Brig's face did look less grotesque with the light shining directly on it, but Corgan wasn't looking at Brig. In the glow from the piezoelectric stone, Sharla reminded him of an electronic painting he'd once seen of a mother holding a child. A madonna. He sucked in his breath.

"What is it, Corgan? What's wrong?" Sharla asked.

"Just . . . the way you look. With him. I never got held that way when I was little. Not by a real person."

"Neither did I," she answered. "Only by robots." She paused, then said, "At least you had your Mendor, Corgan. Brig and I were raised by nonthinking robot caretakers."

"But not always. Not at first." Brig leaned his forehead against Sharla's cheek. "That's one advantage I had in being a Mutant. They put all the surviving Mutants together in a pen, like a litter of puppies. We could touch one another and crawl over each other, and some of the babies even sucked each other's thumbs. Robots took care of us, but we had the . . . the comfort, I guess you'd call it, of human touch. Even if some of the Mutants didn't look too human."

Brig twirled Sharla's hair with his spidery hand and said, "I spent six years in the Mutant Pen before They discovered how smart I was and took me out. So I got plenty of touching, like this. . . . Not to mention I got drooled on and slobbered over, too, 'cause that happened all the time in the Pen."

"Why are you so—I mean, you're right, it's easy to see you're intelligent, but—what made you look the way you look?" Corgan asked.

"I'm a case of genetic engineering gone wrong. Usually all the FLKs—"

"FLKs?" Sharla asked.

"Funny-Looking Kids. Actually, we were more than funny looking, we were flat-out weird. Usually kids like that are retarded, so that's why I was put into the Mutant

Pen in the first place. But I'm different from the rest. I may be small and . . . and . . . deformed—" The last word was mumbled softly. Then Brig puffed out his scrawny chest to declare, "But I'm a *mental* giant!"

"Absolutely," Sharla agreed. "Corgan, how much time do we have left?"

"Two minutes and seven-some seconds. Listen, do we always have to stay out here in the tunnel? Could we go someplace else?"

"Where do you want to go?" she asked.

"To see some things. I've never seen anything in the real world. For a start, I'd like to see the Mutant Pen."

Angrily, Brig arched himself backward in Sharla's arms. "They're not a bunch of freaks for you to laugh at," he lashed out. "Mutants are people. It's hard enough for them without idiots like you coming to point at them and ridicule them."

"I would never do that!"

Sharla patted Brig's shoulder. "He really wouldn't," she told Brig. "But if we do what you want, Corgan, I'll have to program your Box so you can be out of it for a whole hour. What if you get caught?"

"I'll take a chance."

"The practices went *reasonably* well today," Brig said the next night, "only we have to do better. The problem is obvious. Corgan, you just don't trust me."

Corgan didn't answer, because he couldn't deny it. The games were set up so that Sharla directly handled each code adjustment—it all took place between Sharla and the program, so Corgan rarely knew what she was doing.

Brig's role was different. Brig had to feed strategic decisions very fast into Corgan's mind through an auditory connector, with no time to explain why he'd made a certain choice. Corgan was supposed to act on Brig's input without hesitating. But each time, Corgan hesitated. And each fraction of a second counted against their score.

Maybe the Supreme Council members knew what They were doing when They made Brig's virtual image appear normal, made him look older than ten, and altered his voice so it didn't sound squeaky. Because Brig was right—Corgan really didn't trust him. That stunted, twisted, big-headed Funny-Looking Kid—how could anyone so weird be able to make good judgment calls?

Corgan didn't want to think about that now, not tonight. He was scheduled to have a whole hour with Sharla, and that was all that mattered. Even if Brig had to tag along.

"He can't walk like we do," Sharla said when they started out. "His legs are weak."

"I'll carry him," Corgan offered, although it was the last thing he wanted to do.

"No, Sharla will carry me," Brig said.

"How far is it?" Corgan asked.

She answered, "The Mutant Pen is too far for us to walk to, but there's something closer I think you'll be really interested in, so we'll stop there first."

"So pick me up, Sharla."

"I said *I'll* carry you." You little slug, Corgan added silently.

"No, no, no, no, no! I know who I want, and it's not you," Brig whined. "Sharla, carry me, pleeeease!"

"I can't believe you!" Corgan cried, barely able to keep his voice down. "Half the time you talk like some grown-up professor and the rest of the time you're a big crybaby!"

"Yeah, well, I'd rather be a paradox than an ape-armed troglodyte like you."

Frustrated, Corgan clamped his jaw shut so tightly his molars hurt. He was sure he'd been insulted, but how could he fight back when he didn't understand the words Brig used? Paradox? Troglodyte? He'd never heard them before.

"Are you two finished? Can we get on with it?" Sharla asked, picking up Brig. "Make sure you stay right behind me, Corgan. I know my way through these tunnels. Brig, you hum or something—but keep it low—so Corgan can follow the sound of your voice."

Oh great, Corgan thought. Now I have to listen to the little toad croaking in the dark. He decided to ignore Brig; there was no rule that he had to talk to him. "When you said it's too far to walk, Sharla—how else are we going to get there?" he asked, trying to stay right behind her without stepping on her heels.

She whispered, "Better not tell you now. These walls echo. Anyway, you'll find out soon."

The tunnel widened, and a small amount of light glowed in a thin strip set flat into the middle of the floor. "Okay, we're here at the first stop," Sharla murmured.

Corgan asked, "Where's here?"

"We're about a quarter way through the causeway that

connects our building to the domed city. Brig, brace your legs. I'm going to set you down."

Corgan could barely make out Sharla in the darkness. She seemed to be holding something in one hand and tapping it with the index finger of her other hand. "What's that?" he asked.

"My code alteration device. There's a shielded window here, with a room behind it. I'm trying to realign the numbers and make the window transparent so we can see through it."

"Me too," Brig said. "I want to see. Pick me up again so I can see."

Gradually, like a steamy wall in Corgan's Clean Room when dry air hit it, a clear spot expanded in the seemingly solid panel in front of them. "Look in there," Sharla said. She picked up Brig. "See them?"

"People," Corgan answered. There were six of them, four men and two women. None of them was young; none of them looked especially out of the ordinary. One had lost most of his hair; one slumped in a chair as though he didn't have the energy to sit up straight; one of the women rubbed her temples as if her head hurt, and as she rubbed, her fingers pulled her eyes into ugly slits. The six of them talked listlessly. They seemed to interrupt each other a lot.

"Who are they?" Corgan asked.

"The Supreme Council."

"*What! No!*" Corgan remembered the way They'd looked in the virtual world—large, faceless, eyes hidden in shadow, erect bodies dressed in flawless uniforms with fluorescent medals.

"It's true," Sharla said. "There They are. Take a good look."

Corgan stared for a full minute. Then he asked, "In our meetings, why do They make Themselves look so—"

"Commanding? Mysterious?" Sharla finished. "Mind control. They don't want you to know They're just ordinary people who could maybe make mistakes."

"Why not?" Corgan asked.

"Because They don't trust people to handle truth. They have to make everything seem mystical so They can dictate to people. So people will do exactly what They tell them to. That's why They love you so much, Corgan, because you never question anything." She shifted Brig in her arms. "Seen enough?"

"Too much!" Corgan cried.

"Not so loud! If They hear a sound, They might look over this way and I'm not sure how opaque the wall is from inside." She set Brig on the floor. "Anyway, They're not such terrible people," she told Corgan. "They really want to do what's right for the Western Hemisphere Federation. The bad part is that They think They're the only ones who know what's right, for the Federation and everyone in it. And They're the ones that get to make the rules."

Corgan stared at the plain, unimpressive people beyond the wall. One of Them kept pinching his nostrils together and sniffing as if to stop a sneeze. A woman scratched the top of her head, then examined her fingernails.

"What are They doing there?" Corgan asked.

"Having a secret meeting. They come here when They want to talk privately. They'd have fits if They knew I knew about this place."

The Supreme Council! Average-looking people who couldn't even keep Their hideaway secret from a fourteen-year-old girl. Disillusioned, Corgan turned away, and Sharla closed up the transparent circle. "On to the next stop," she said.

"The Mutant Pen?" Brig asked.

"That's the last stop. We're going to pass the hydroponic gardens on the way—I thought Corgan would like to know where his meals come from."

"Make sure you leave enough time for the Mutant Pen," Brig pleaded. "I want to see it again—it's been a long time."

They'd walked rapidly for six minutes forty-three and seventeen hundredths seconds when Sharla said, "Wait here. We have to take a hover car."

Corgan was about to ask what a hover car was, and how they could take one without anyone finding out what they were doing, but Sharla disappeared. After fourteen seconds she came into sight again, under a ceiling light. She was talking to a man who wore a dark one-piece outfit of heavy cloth, definitely not a LiteSuit. Five more seconds and she gestured for Corgan and Brig to join her.

"This is Jobe," she said, introducing the gray-suited man. "Jobe, I'm not going to tell you the names of these two guys. Just being safe, you know."

Jobe held out his hand for Corgan to shake, but Corgan couldn't make himself touch it. He'd barely overcome his fear of contamination enough to touch hands with Sharla and Brig. And Jobe's hand looked disgusting. Little cracks in the skin were ingrained with dirt, and the fingernails were rimmed with black grease. That thick, rough, filthy hand had to be crawling with bacteria.

"Well," Jobe said, grinning as he dropped his hand after a moment, "here's a hover car comin' along right now. It's not supposed to stop here, but I can maybe slow it down a little. You three will have to jump inside real fast. I'll flip up the dome when it gets close enough, and you can run alongside the car and hop over the side. Once you're in, I'll close the dome again. If you miss this one, you're out of luck. Okay?"

"Okay. Thanks, Jobe," Sharla said.

"So run!"

Corgan scooped up Brig into his arms as the hover car, moving silently only three centimeters above the floor, drew close to them. It followed the path of the dimly glowing magnetic strip in the floor. The car moved forward quickly, but neither Sharla nor Corgan had trouble keeping up with it. Sharla leaped over the side and reached for Brig.

By then the car had traveled into total darkness. Corgan kept his hand on the edge of the dome so he could feel where it was going.

"Hurry up!" Jobe cried, panting as he lumbered along beside them. "Jump in now. Fast!"

Corgan managed to clamber inside just before the dome slammed shut, grazing his knuckles.

"I hope I'm not bleeding," he said.

"Afraid of a little blood?" Brig mocked.

"No. Mendor will pester me about how I got my knuckles skinned, that's all." He slid back onto something hard.

"These are real seats, aren't they?" he asked. "They're not aerogel."

"They're aerogel," Sharla answered. "Only they're rigid-molded, not flexible. They last longer that way."

He felt along the back of the seat until he touched Sharla's shoulder. She reached up to squeeze his hand. "Enjoying the ride?" she asked.

"How'd you arrange this?" he wondered.

"I know all the hover-car maintenance people. I don't need a whole lot of sleep, Corgan, so I prowl at night. And this whole city is too big to travel around on foot—we haven't even reached the domed part yet. But we're getting close. Right now we're still in the connecting causeway."

Brig burrowed backward, wedging himself between them as though he didn't want to be left out. "You are one very impressive contriver, Sharla," he told her. "How do you get the staff people to let you ride these hover cars?"

"Bribes," she answered.

Corgan said, "I don't know that word."

"It means I give them something, and they let me sneak on the cars."

"What do you give them?" he asked.

"Tips on the lottery. You know what a lottery is, don't you, Corgan?"

"Uh-huh. Sure." He really didn't, but he was tired of sounding ignorant.

"Since I was genetically engineered to be a code breaker," Sharla explained, "I'm also great at figuring the probability of numbers hitting in the lottery. I'm not right all the time, but enough that my tips give the guys a winning edge. I just told Jobe to play 716."

Corgan didn't have any idea what she was talking about.

"Is that legal?" Brig asked. "To give them tips?"

"Do you care?"

"No, but Corgan the Obedient probably cares." Brig's sharp little elbow dug into Corgan's ribs.

"It's the way I operate," Sharla said. "I was genetically engineered to calculate numbers. And somehow, I got this strong urge to take risks. Plus, I like to find out things. So I use my numbers genius to pay for the risks when I snoop around. It works great. Usually."

The hover car had come alongside a lighted area: a huge room filled with tables that held growing plants. Dozens of people, dressed in dark suits of heavy cloth like Jobe wore, walked between the tables. They talked to each other, and they stopped every few meters to examine leaves and spray mist on the plants. Farther along, others cut plants and dropped them into square aerogel boxes. Sometimes their hands touched. Apparently all of them breathed the same air. Didn't anyone in there worry about contamination?

"This is where your food comes from, guys," Sharla said.

Corgan asked, "What are they growing in there?"

"Soybeans, mostly. Just about everything we get fed, from turkey to toast, is really soybeans in disguise," she answered.

"I get real steak sometimes," Corgan told them, and instantly wished he hadn't said that.

Brig sneered, "Of course Corgan would get steak.

Corgan, the darling of the Supreme Council. Corgan, the fabulous physical animal that gets favored and fussed over and fed real steak while Mutants like me get recycled garbage."

"Quit complaining," Sharla told him. "It's probably better for you anyway."

Corgan stretched to see better. "There's the dome!" he exclaimed. "The dome that covers the whole city! I've only seen it virtually before. And—*I can see through the dome! I can see real stars!*"

"Let me see, too!" Brig scrambled onto Corgan's lap. "Where? Show me! Lift me up! I haven't seen true stars since I was six, when they took me into the other building."

The hover car kept moving but the stars stayed still: tiny chips of cold light in the darkness outside. As they traveled the corridor that bisected the hydroponic gardens, both boys sat in silence, fascinated by the night sky. "Those stars look so much nicer than virtual ones," Brig murmured. "See there? That's Orion. I remember Orion. Doesn't he look great?"

Corgan nodded. "Really great." Without realizing it, he tightened his arm around Brig.

SIX

Corgan was so enthralled by the night sky that he hadn't even glanced at Sharla for seven full minutes and thirty-two and a fraction seconds—not since the hover car had entered the domed, lighted area. He regretted it the instant he turned toward her.

Illumination from the hydroponic gardens gave him his first-ever look at her in a decent light. For once she was fully visible from head to toe, from her boots to her shining blond hair.

She turned and caught him staring at her. Embarrassed, Corgan stammered, "Uh . . . I was just wondering. About your hair—isn't it too long? I mean, it's really nice, but the rules say hair can't be longer than five centimeters. So why is yours—?"

"I told Them it's my hair and if I want to wear it long I will," she answered matter-of-factly.

She amazed him. Sharla seemed to break rules and suffer no consequences. How did she get away with it?

"I could look at these stars forever," Brig said, "but when do we get to the Mutant Pen?"

"Soon," Sharla answered.

Corgan kept watching her in the pale light. Suddenly it occurred to him that the same light must be making him visible, too, and not just to Brig and Sharla. "All those people working there in the gardens," he said, "can't they see us? I mean, the light from there is shining in here. On us."

"Don't worry. The car's bubble dome has a reflective coating on the outside. If the people in there bother to look up from their work, all they'll see is glare." She peered ahead. "Something's wrong, though, on the track about twenty meters in front of us."

"Get off my lap, Brig," Corgan said. "I need to look out."

He leaned forward, pressing his face close to the transparent bubble dome. "We're coming up on it pretty fast, whatever it is."

"It's another hover car," Brig announced. "Looks like it's stalled. See, it's not moving. It's just sitting there on the floor."

"Move, move, move, MOVE!" Sharla cried, clenching her fist.

"Who, me?" Brig asked.

"No, that car up ahead. Get out of our way!" she ordered, as if saying it would make it happen.

Brig braced himself. "Are we going to crash?"

"No, we can't crash. This car stops automatically if it comes within three meters of any obstruction. But I can't tell if there's another car in front of that one," Sharla said. "If there's a real jam-up and we get stuck here, we're in major trouble. Corgan, how much of our hour is left?"

"Twenty-three minutes, forty-seven seconds and . . ."

Their car came to a sudden halt, rocking them forward. "We've got to get out of here!" Sharla cried. "There's at least six stalled cars up ahead."

"Can't we just reverse this one?" Corgan asked.

"Hover cars only go in one direction. They loop," she told him. "Corgan, if we run from here back to our Boxes, how long will it take?"

"I don't know! I don't know how fast you can run, and Brig . . ."

"You'll have to carry him. Right now we need to get this bubble dome open so we can get out. See that handle on your side? Push it hard."

He pushed, but nothing happened.

"Harder!" she commanded.

Corgan pushed with both hands. Nothing.

"Okay!" She took out the small flat control box she'd used to make the wall turn transparent at the Supreme Council's meeting room. "I've got to figure the code that secures the latch. Lean back, guys. The beam has to focus straight on the door."

Her long thin fingers flew over the numbers on the control box. "I don't know what's wrong," she said through clenched teeth. "Either something's jamming the door or the whole hover-car system's down."

Corgan stayed quiet. This was outside his area of expertise. Sharla would have to handle it.

Desperately, she kept punching numbers. "I can't make it work!" she cried.

Corgan asked, "Do you want me to break out the bubble dome?"

"Yeah, right!" Brig scoffed. "You break it, and every security guard in the gardens and every mechanic in the whole transport system will be here in about ten seconds."

"Yeah, well, there's about nineteen minutes left right now before we're locked outside of our Boxes for the rest of the night," Corgan lashed back at him. "So come up with some other strategy, Double Genius Mouth-Off."

"Break the bubble dome, Corgan." Sharla sounded grim. "We're out of options. Just do it."

Corgan had no experience with molded aerogel. Regular aerogel, the kind that lined his Box, was too flexible to break, although with enough pressure it could be torn. All he could try to do now was smash the molded bubble dome with both arms and hope it would break outward, hope it wouldn't explode into fragments that could fly into their eyes and cut them.

"Here goes!" he said. He raised his arms chest high, with his fists together. In a burst of force he flung both fists outward against the dome. His first blow shattered it.

All the pieces flew away from them in a spray of chips that caught the light like tiny stars.

"Get out!" Sharla picked up Brig, ready to hand him to Corgan as soon as Corgan climbed over the side.

"They'll see us!" Brig wailed. "It's light out there!"

Sharla hesitated. "You're right." Once more her fingers flew across the controller box. Suddenly everything went dark.

"Here, Corgan, take Brig," she said. "I'll lift him out to you."

Corgan heard a tearing sound and whispered, "What happened? Did someone get cut on the shards?"

"Just my LiteSuit. It's ripped," Brig answered. "Don't drop me, Corgan!"

"Go!" Sharla cried. "Corgan, follow that magnetic strip— it gives off a glow. Run back the way we came. Fast!"

"I'm gone." Even carrying Brig, Corgan could move faster than Sharla. She stayed behind him, close enough that he could hear her breath coming hard as her feet pounded the floor.

"How much time?" she panted.

"Eight minutes seven seconds."

"Go without me," she said. "You have to get Brig back to his Box first. Brig, can you tell Corgan how to get there?"

"I'm scared!" Brig whimpered.

"Can you tell Corgan how to get to your Box!"

"I guess so."

"That's not good enough!" Corgan hissed in his ear.

"YES! I'll tell you! But you probably won't listen to me anyhow," Brig whined. "You don't trust me."

"You crybaby! Do you want to get us all into trouble?" Corgan shook Brig in exasperation, but stopped shaking him because it broke the rhythm of his running stride, and anyway Brig really was starting to cry. "We're a team!" Corgan barked. "Act like a team!"

"Go on, pull ahead of me," Sharla said. "I know I'm holding you back. How many minutes left now?"

"Six minutes and twenty-eight and nineteen hundredths seconds."

"Dammit, Corgan, do you always have to be so exact? 'Six and a half minutes' would have been fine."

That was the last he heard from her. Sharla dropped back at the same time Corgan increased his speed. He felt exhilarated. He'd never before run in an open area. Always before he'd run on a treadmill on the floor of his Box, although it never looked like a treadmill: The virtual images that surrounded him made it appear he was on a sandy beach, or running along a forest path, or a mountain trail, or a racing track. Now his legs stretched almost straight out as they pumped faster and faster in a sprint. His balance adjusted easily to the slight weight of Brig in his arms.

"Turn! Turn!" Brig yelled. "Over that way!"

"Are you sure?"

"Do you think I don't know where my own Box is?"

"You didn't seem to know back there."

Corgan spun into the turn without losing momentum. He felt great! He'd never tried anything like this before: running at top speed on a real floor, carrying an awkward, lumpy weight, and yet being able to talk in whole sentences without even panting. He was stronger than he'd thought. Brig's skinny arms clamped Corgan's neck like a vise, but even with that little leech hanging on to him, Corgan ran like a champion. I'm the best! he thought.

"Here! Stop! This is it." Brig tried to leap from Corgan's arms and almost tumbled to the floor. Without as much as a thank-you he scurried into his Box, scrabbling like a scared rat.

"And good night to you, too, Big Brain," Corgan said. Then he turned and raced back along the passageway. He reached the fork where he should have angled toward his own Box, but he was enjoying himself so much he spun around and retraced his path, sprinting back in the direction of the abandoned hover car, just for the freedom of it. And to see if Sharla might still be in the corridor. But she was gone. The clock ticking in his head told Corgan he had enough time to make it back to his Box and slide through the door with at least a tenth of a second left before Sharla's programming clicked the door shut. He laughed out loud.

seven

"Where did you get that cut on your hand?" Mendor demanded.

Corgan had forgotten about his scrape from the hover car. He hadn't even noticed it during the morning sanitizing in his Clean Room. "It's nothing," he said.

"Let me see!" The tactile simulator turned on and Mendor the Mother Figure reached out to grasp Corgan's hand. "How did this happen?"

"I don't know. Leave me alone!"

"Any little break in the skin can be dangerous," she said patiently. "Be a good boy, and—"

"Stop it!"

"My, we're a bit testy today, aren't we?" she crooned

as tiny flashes of light went off over his scraped knuckles. He was being cauterized with laser beams. "Your hands are extremely important, Corgan. They must always be protected."

With a strong pull he yanked his hand free.

"Corgan!" It was Mendor the Stern Father now, glowering at him. "Since you seem to have no concern for your own safety, let me remind you what can happen. A microscopic bacteria called streptococcus pyogenes can invade your body through any chance opening in the skin. It can cause an infection known as necrotizing fasciitis, also called 'flesh-eating disease.'"

Mendor's image enlarged until his purple-gray face filled the Box. "If you get this disease and you're lucky enough to survive, Corgan, you may lose quantities of skin and fascia—the fibrous tissue surrounding your muscles. Then your gangrenous fingers and toes will be amputated. Would you like to see some of the victims?" Instantly, pictures of grotesque, dripping bodies filled the surround-scene, their lesions so repulsive Corgan threw his hands over his eyes.

"Turn it off!"

The images slowly faded as Mendor said, "Tell me, Corgan, you're a boy who was born with the fastest reflexes and the most unerring precision ever known to humankind. Just how would you play games if you had no fingers?"

Corgan shook his head.

"Now, Corgan, how did you get that broken skin on your hand?"

"Dammit, Mendor, I told you I don't know." Mendor's gasp was like a gale blowing through the Box.

"Where did you learn that word, Corgan?"

"What word?" But he knew exactly the word Mendor meant.

"That swearword. Never in your entire life has that word been spoken in your presence. Where did you hear it?"

"From you. You said it—you just don't remember. Your internal programming must have some kind of a memory glitch. . . ." Corgan felt the sweat break out in his hands as the lies came out of his mouth.

"My programming is never faulty," Mendor hissed. "This time you really have gone too far, Corgan. You're lying! I have no choice but to send you to Reprimand."

Reprimand! Corgan's LiteSuit turned dark from apprehension. He had never been put into Reprimand—he'd never before had to be punished for wrongdoing. He couldn't even imagine what Reprimand would be like, except that it had to be something awful.

His ears filled with a staticky whirring that swelled and ebbed from loud to soft and back so rapidly that his head started to spin. Then he felt his whole body rotate, spiraling, whirling, pivoting, head up, head down, sideways. . . .

And there he was. In Reprimand. But it wasn't a place; it was simply total emptiness and almost total darkness and gloom. A feeling of despair swept through him, filling his heart, his whole body, and even his skin, down to each separate pore. He wanted to run, but couldn't move. He hung suspended, motionless, not sure whether he'd landed vertically, horizontally, or at any other angle up or down.

"Corgan! Corgan!" It might have been Mendor's voice he heard or the voices of the Supreme Council; it seemed he recognized all of them in the words. "We have given you everything. Isn't that true?"

He nodded, glad he was able to move his head, at least.

"From the time you were a tiny boy, we've done all we could think of to make you happy. Haven't we, Corgan?"

"Yes," he whispered.

"We gave you toys. Dinosaurs decorating your walls. And do you remember the koala bear, Corgan? You wanted a koala with blue eyes and soft fur, one that would chase a ball like a puppy. You named it—what did you name it, Corgan?"

"Named the bear Roland," he answered, the words like ribbons unwinding from his throat.

"Ah yes," the voices continued. "We had to create a special program to make Roland do all the things you wanted him to. We set our cleverest engineers to work on the project, and we told them, 'Don't worry about how much time it will take you to perfect it. Don't worry about expense. This toy is for Corgan.' They worked night and day to build Roland for you."

"I loved Roland." Tears stung Corgan's eyes as he remembered.

"For a little while," the voices murmured. "For only a little while you loved him. Then you stopped playing with him."

Now a whole additional chorus joined in to sigh, "We asked why you no longer played with Roland. And you said . . . you said . . . that Roland had bitten you. Do you remember that, Corgan? You told a lie."

Lie! Lie! Lie! The word echoed as if from a deep cavern.

Incredible, Corgan thought. They had to go all the way back to when I was six to find the last lie that I told.

"We didn't mind that you'd stopped playing with Roland," the voices lamented. "Even though we had put so much time and effort and scarce resources into that special koala that you wanted, and you only played with it for a few days—we were glad it made you happy. Even if just for a little while. We've always tried to make you happy, Corgan."

"Yes," he gasped. His throat felt like it was closing from the inside.

"But when you lied, Corgan . . ." Now the face of Mendor the Mother Figure wrapped around him, gray and furrowed, the surface sliding downward in despair. "You broke Mother's heart."

"And you wounded Father's pride." Slowly Mendor the Father Figure appeared, somber and dark.

"I've been bad," Corgan whimpered, sounding like a six-year-old. He hadn't meant to say that—where had it come from? He cleared his throat, wondering why his voice had suddenly turned thin and high-pitched. Then he saw himself in the wraparound image: He *was* a six-year-old, with straight black hair falling in bangs over his forehead, with his mouth drawn down and his soft lips trembling.

"No . . . you're not a bad boy, Corgan," Mendor the Mother Figure said once again, as she'd said so many years before. "You're a very good boy. But you mustn't tell lies."

"I'm sorry! I won't tell lies ever again."

"We've always done everything we could to make you happy. We gave you everything you asked for. We gave you our trust. You must always tell us the truth, Corgan."

He said, "Yes," through trembling lips, not sure whether he was Corgan the six-year-old or Corgan the long-legged, strong-armed virtual champion. Discovering he could move his arms, he reached up to knead his throat, trying to get his real voice back.

"We trust you to do what is right."

There was nothing Corgan could safely reply. A faint chord of music, deep and dolorous, rumbled across the dark emptiness.

"Your happiness matters to us, Corgan, more than anything." The words matched the tempo of the barely heard music, which built slow, heavy, minor chords into a song of infinite sadness. "Your happiness will always matter. Our love for you will never diminish. Even when you betray us." Betray! Betray! Betray! It hung in the air, vibrating.

"Honor, Corgan. Truth. These matter most. The trust between parents and son."

He didn't answer. Couldn't answer, because it was guilt, now, that rose into his throat. They were right. He'd told a lie. Lying was wrong.

"After all we've done for you, Corgan, can you give us just one thing in return?" The music throbbed softly, like a slow heartbeat.

"What's that?" he whispered. "What can I give you?" He knew what They were going to ask for.

"The truth, Corgan. All we want is that you tell us the truth."

"What truth?"

"A very small matter. So small! Just tell us—where did you hear that word you used this morning?"

"I can't remember."

The music grew louder, anguished. The space around Corgan seemed crowded with creatures, all of them weeping, pressing against him, smothering him, drowning him in their tears.

"Please, Corgan, try to remember. We don't blame you. You're the innocent one. Others have led you into error. We want desperately to believe in you again. We love you. Tell the truth, and all will be forgiven. All will be forgotten. Nothing will be held against you."

Shadows filled the darkness, moving shapes bent over in sorrow. The shapes hovered around him. Phantom hands reached up to touch him in supplication.

"Where did we fail, Corgan? What more can we give you? We gave you so much, but it wasn't enough!" The music grew louder; the weeping rose to a new level of anguish.

Corgan's tears rolled slowly down his cheeks. It was true; They'd always been good to him, and now he'd caused Them pain. Would it really matter if he admitted everything? He'd insist on taking full responsibility. They said he'd be forgiven.

"Once more, Corgan. Who spoke that word to you?"

"Sharla," he whispered.

"When?"

"Last night. I don't know!"

"Where?"

"In the corridor. Don't punish her!"

Light blinded him. He was back in his Box, with Mendor beside him.

"We will not speak of this again," Mendor the Father Figure thundered. "Ever! How many days remain before the War, Corgan?"

"Twelve."

"A full morning of practice has been lost because of this lie you told."

"It's only been a few minutes!"

"The matter must be pursued further. Be cautious from now on, Corgan. That is all I have to say to you."

Corgan sat up, wet from sweat and tears. His gut felt raw, and his ears rang. His Box filled with images of the Isles of Hiva—palm trees with their broad leaves waving in the wind, the surf rushing up on sand and then rolling back. So it was all supposed to be over, and They were trying to soothe him with Hiva while They—did what? Went after Sharla! And Brig, too, probably!

Corgan paced his Box. He'd been forgiven quickly enough, or at least he was out of Reprimand. So Sharla and Brig ought to be forgiven, too. After all, the three of them were in it together. The other two would probably be questioned in Reprimand just as he'd been. It hadn't been so bad, really. Yet, remembering it, his skin turned clammy. If nothing really terrible had been done to him, why did he feel so rotten?

He knew why. He'd betrayed the people he cared about. Not Mendor, not the Council. He'd betrayed Sharla and Brig.

* * *

A whole hour late, practice was about to begin.

"Where's Sharla?" Corgan asked.

She appeared, even more out of focus than before. What a joke, Corgan thought, the way They make her look. Are you all right, he tried to ask her with his mind, but her eyes didn't respond. "What about Brig? Where's Brig?" Corgan demanded.

"Brig is—not here. He won't practice with you today." Mendor spoke in a flat, unrevealing tone.

"Why?"

Mendor didn't answer.

The tiny image of Sharla's face appeared close to Corgan's eyes, as it had that one time before. "Keep quiet, don't say anything," the image told him. "Brig is still in Reprimand. They want him to tell why his LiteSuit got ripped, but he won't talk. He's really scared! They put me in Reprimand, too, but I'm used to it and I didn't admit anything."

Brig, that little crybaby, was holding out against Them? And Sharla hadn't admitted anything. Only Corgan had! He stood up halfway as the Sharla face vanished.

So! The Supreme Council wanted honor? Mendor wanted truth? Fine! He'd give Them truth.

He shouted, "Sharla, listen to me! I told Them wha—"
Inhumanly high-pitched shrieking hit his eardrums with such force he felt as if he'd been thrown against a wall. The piercing sound paralyzed him while every visual image in his Box got snuffed out. Each pixel of color sputtered into darkness.

Corgan threw his arms over his ears to try to block the

excruciating pain, but the sound kept blasting. "No!" he wailed, curling up in a ball. "Stop!" Nothing helped. The screeching shrilled louder and louder, stabbing his brain. His body shook in spasms. Then he thrashed with convulsions, his arms and legs lurching out at angles unnatural to human anatomy.

Suddenly it was over.

He lay helpless, unable to move, tears streaming from his eyes, blood from his nose, and moans from his lips.

"Get up. You're not hurt," Mendor the Father told him. "I never thought it would be necessary to use that kind of punishment on you, Corgan. But you were out of control."

He must have lost track of time. Had he lost consciousness? Because now it was Mendor the Mother leaning over him, and Mendor had never been able to morph that quickly from Father to Mother. "Wipe your nose, dear boy. The bleeding's already stopped. Here, take a sip of water," she was telling him, but even before he could swallow, Mendor the Father loomed over him again.

Corgan squeezed his eyes tightly and then opened them, bewildered. "These are the rules!" Mendor the Father was saying harshly. "You will be given an hour to pull yourself together, to prepare for today's practice. From now on, at practice, you will not speak without permission, unless you need to communicate with the other two members of your team about the practice session. Nothing else! You will focus all your attention on one objective: winning the War. Is that clear?"

Corgan nodded. Just that small movement made his

head pound. Instantly Mendor the Mother was there, rubbing his forehead.

"From this moment forward," Mendor the Father thundered, "you will obey all orders. You will always tell the truth. When the time comes, you will wage the War with honor. You must promise this."

"I promise," he whispered.

"You give your word? Good. I trust you."

"We'll warm up slowly." Mendor was doing the instructing, but Corgan sensed that members of the Supreme Council had been summoned and hovered close by, watching Corgan. Sharla and Brig had not yet appeared.

Though he was still hoarse, Corgan had recovered from the high-decibel shock waves. He no longer felt frightened because he knew exactly what he was supposed to do: follow orders, tell the truth, and win the War honorably.

"Recite the pledge," Mendor ordered.

Corgan raised his hand, which still trembled very slightly. "I promise to wage the War with courage, dedication, and honor."

This time he took definite notice of the word "honor"— it slammed his brain with such an impact, he winced.

"Begin."

The figures of a common board game appeared, three-dimensionally, in front of him.

Chess! Corgan almost smiled. They'd given him *chess*, an easy game like that. To make amends for his punishment? But when he began to play, the chess pieces turned monstrous. The most horrible images They could throw at him materialized on the chess board, and grew enormous until they towered over him: An octopus slithered over the board and reached for Corgan's hands with slimy, sucking tentacles; huge, mossy-scaled, misshapen fish gaped toward him with undulating mouths. . . .

"Confront your fears, Corgan," Mendor urged him.

"What, these? I'm not afraid of these." Allotting no more than seven-tenths of a second to each chess piece, Corgan demolished them, one by one.

"Play again!" he ordered. "Where's Brig? I'd like some strategy input from Brig, please. He needs the practice."

"I'm here, Corgan." Brig's image appeared, as ordinary as always, but his eyes looked haunted. "I'll try to provide useful input," he said softly.

"See that you do." Corgan couldn't stand to look at Brig when he said that. Couldn't think about Brig's eyes or about Brig in Reprimand or anything except the practice game. Had to focus all attention on one objective. Play to win.

Swiftly, the two of them dispatched the chessmen to monster hell. Then Sharla appeared, and the team moved on to harder games, playing for an hour without a break. The three of them performed well, their skills blending seamlessly.

"Splendid!" Mendor the Mother said. "Go to your Clean Rooms now. You'll meet again later for further practice."

The images of Sharla and Brig vanished instantly, and Mendor said, "Why are you waiting, Corgan? Off to the Clean Room with you, like a good boy, and when you come back, you can choose a nice scene of galaxies to go with your dinner. Stars and planets and comets—"

"No, thank you." He'd already seen real stars. Virtual galaxies could mean nothing to him from now on. "I'd like the Isles of Hiva again, please," he said. First, though, he had to deal with a nagging puzzle. "Mendor, I timed you once. It takes you fourteen and thirty-three hundredths seconds to morph from Mother to Father. Or from Father to Mother. Has that changed? Has it speeded up?"

"'What a strange question, Corgan. No, it hasn't. Why did you ask that?"

"Never mind." Biting his lip, Corgan moved into the tunnel.

When he returned from the Clean Room, his steak was waiting. Not soybeans in disguise—this was real beef, hot and perfect. So he'd been forgiven completely, and his trespasses were to be forgotten. Be a good boy, do what you're ordered, always tell the truth, and you'll get steak. Were Sharla and Brig getting real meat, too?

A faint drumbeat throbbed as the Isles of Hiva surrounded him, the ocean waves rushing toward him, flecked with foam, while sea birds cruised on air currents above his head. But he couldn't really enjoy it. He was too puzzled about why Mendor had seemed to morph so fast.

He considered the possibilities. Maybe he'd been partly unconscious. He knew that a condition known as unconsciousness existed, where a person's brain shut down for a certain period of time, although he'd never personally experienced such a thing.

The other possibility was more ominous. What if the sound-shock punishment had damaged his time-splitting ability? But why would Mendor or the Council take a chance of hurting him when the War was so close?

"Mendor," he asked the Mother Figure, "has anyone else with my kind of time skill ever been sound-shocked before?"

"Why talk about unpleasant things?" Mendor replied. "The incident is over. Finished. It's best forgotten now."

"Please, I need you to answer that."

"All right. If you promise to eat while I talk," Mendor fussed. "Sound-shock is used as punishment because it's effective and causes no permanent damage. Admittedly it's unpleasant while it lasts—"

"It's a lot more than unpleasant!"

"—but it has been fully documented in hundreds of cases and it's totally harmless. Eat, now. Your steak must be getting cold."

The steak tasted flat but he chewed and swallowed to satisfy Mendor. "You didn't tell me what I asked you, though. Has anyone with my time-splitting power been sound-shocked before?"

"Corgan . . ." Mendor the Mother's warm image wrapped around him. "Don't you understand? There *is* no one else who can calculate time like you do. There never has been. You're unique. You're a mutation, with a skill never before known to humankind."

"I'm a *Mutant*?"

"No, a mutation, in the best possible sense of the word. That's how the human race evolved, you know. How *everything* evolved. The superior mutations, the exceptional ones, have always thrived and flourished; the weak ones die out. Now finish that last bite, and then, would you like to take a nice little stroll across the beach before it's time to practice again? You'll have an extra practice session this evening to make up for the time lost this morning."

"No. No walk." It was too much for him to handle. He felt overwhelmed by all that had happened that day, by all that had been done to him, and now, by what Mendor had just told him. Shoving it out of his mind, he said, "I think we should get back to practice right away."

Mendor beamed. "What a dedicated, industrious boy!"

He was neither of those things. He had an urgent need to check his timing, to make sure it was functioning right, and to see Sharla, to try to contact her with his eyes. Had she understood what he tried to tell her before the blast of sound knocked him senseless?

But for the first hour, he practiced alone: Precision and Sensitivity training again. Lately They'd been doubling—even tripling—his P and S sessions. Using electromagnetic energy to move a twelve-centimeter-square patch of laser light seemed an odd exercise to concentrate on, but Corgan asked no questions.

Later, when the team assembled for practice again, Sharla, Brig, and Corgan glanced furtively at one another. After that Sharla avoided Corgan's eyes. When they recited the pledge this time, she seemed to be saying the same words he did.

They played hard, doing Triple Multiplex, and Corgan was relieved to realize that his timing ability worked fine. But as he checked the score, he saw that it was a little lower than usual. "Mendor, is that score right? Oh, sorry, Mendor, I should have asked permission before I spoke."

"Forgiven. I will double-check the score, but you must rest now. Tomorrow will be another day for practice."

As Corgan settled into the aerogel, time ticked away in discrete hundredth-second intervals inside his head. Perfectly. Yet, during that incident earlier in the day—whether it had been brief or otherwise, he didn't know—he hadn't been able to calibrate time. And his score tonight had been a little off. *If* it was true that he was having a bit of trouble with his timing, why should it affect his playing ability? Calculating time was one kind of skill and playing games with his hands was another entirely different skill, and the first shouldn't have an impact on the second.

At eleven o'clock he stood up and moved toward the door, knowing it was futile to bother, but doing it just the same.

He couldn't find the opening. In the dark, he felt all over for a way out, but the exit was gone. He was locked in.

What had he expected? That They'd let those secret meetings in the tunnel keep happening, now that They knew?

He'd ruined everything when he confessed. Now he'd never see the real Sharla again. Never be able to touch her. That, on top of everything else that had come crashing down on him today, crushed him with despair.

He slammed his fists into the soft aerogel.

EIGHT

The next day Sharla wouldn't meet his eyes, and Brig wouldn't *stop* looking at him. Spooky little Brig, pleading without words. Because no matter how hard Corgan tried, he couldn't match his usual high score in the War-game practice.

He was only a little off, and no one said anything, but everyone noticed.

That night the door was locked again. In his sleep, Corgan ground his teeth and pounded his aerogel pillow.

The following morning he got up and ran a thousand meters on the virtual racing track in his Box, then lifted weights until his biceps burned. When he took his place at practice, Mendor stated, "Ten days remain until the War.

According to the rules agreed upon by the three confederations, this is the day your team will be introduced to the actual format the War will take."

Corgan tensed as the Box filled with surround-images of hills and dusty ground, pockmarked by shallow depressions. A shell exploded right next to him, sending up a plume of orange flame and smoke and a shower of dirt that fell back on his head. He grabbed his ears—since his high-decibel punishment, he shuddered at every loud noise.

"That's the way wars were fought seventy years ago," Mendor explained. "Fortunately for you, the War you're going to fight won't be quite as brutal, but it will have all the noise of the old-fashioned wars."

Corgan frowned. That didn't sound good.

"You will not see the other two teams," Mendor went on. "We know nothing about them except that each team consists of three players. Age, gender, area of expertise—none of that is known." Mendor's harsh voice softened a little. "Conversely, they know nothing about the three of you, either.

"Now, here are the rules: The images you play with will be of actual soldiers in battle dress. All the moves were programmed to re-create real warfare as it was fought at the beginning of the twenty-first century. Tanks, fighter aircraft, aerial bombardment, and artillery—they'll all be directed against you. Not to mention poison gas attacks, toxic agents, chemical and bacterial contaminants. *Your only defense will be to evade these assaults. You will never go on the offensive. All you are allowed to do is protect your troops by moving them to safe ground.*"

Corgan asked, "May I speak, Mendor? If we can't attack, if all we can do is stay out of the way, how do we win the War?"

"Patience!" Mendor the Stern Father demanded. "I'll explain the rest of the rules later. For now I want you, Corgan, to move the soldiers around to get used to the feel of them. Brig will observe."

It was as though they were real people, perfectly three-dimensional, with distinct facial features and skin colors, but each one was no bigger than Corgan's hand. They milled around aimlessly over the pockmarked ground.

"Pull them together, Corgan. Line them up in platoons," Brig instructed over the audible connector.

Corgan reached out too quickly and obliterated a dozen troops. Brig gasped. Stricken, Corgan looked up at Mendor.

As though trying not to reproach Corgan in front of everyone, Mendor spoke quietly. "Isn't it obvious, Corgan, that all your Precision and Sensitivity training has been for this one purpose? You must move your soldiers the way you moved the laser square: by compressing electromagnetic force. Never touch them directly! They have been designed so that your hand will set them in motion when you come to within five hundred microns of each image."

Sharla spoke then. "I could change the codes to increase the magnetic force field a little," she suggested. "That way Corgan could move the images from farther away—like, seven hundred microns?"

"No!" Mendor was adamant. "The War rules won't allow that. Corgan can do this. It's what he's been trained for. Try again, Corgan."

Concentrating so hard that sweat broke out on his forehead, Corgan moved his hands toward the images. Although the soldiers looked real and solid, they were only millions of holographic projections of colored lasers, as delicate as moonbeams. If he pushed just a fraction too hard, his hand went through them and they died.

Now he understood why Mendor and the Council had always fussed so much about his hands. Why he'd had to practice countless hours reaching to within a hair's breadth of the laser square. Strength, stamina, speed—all of them mattered, but not as much as P and S. In this War, Precision and Sensitivity would be the winning factor.

By the middle of the morning, Corgan had gotten the hang of it, sort of. "Now," Mendor said, "the object of all this is to move your soldiers onto designated territory: the top of that hill, where the flag is. Of course the other two teams will be trying to do the same: to get their soldiers onto the same hill. The team to reach the hill with the largest number of surviving troops will be declared the winner. It's as simple as that."

"That's it?" Corgan asked.

"That's it. Your job is to move the soldiers without touching them, using electromagnetic force. Sharla's job is to change the trajectory codes of artillery launched against our troops. At the same time she must jam the codes the other teams use as they try to block barrages aimed at their own troops. It won't be easy—destruction will rain so thick and fast on all three teams that most of it will be impossible to stop."

"I'll do my best," Sharla said.

"All the bombardment, against all three teams, will originate at the same source," Mendor continued, "the Coordinated Confederations Command Control Center."

"Wait a minute! I mean, do I have your permission to speak, Mendor? Are you saying that the three confederations are banding together to blast their own armies?" Corgan asked. "That's a weird way to fight a war."

"It will be perfectly fair. Each explosion, each assault, each demolition will be counted out equally. Each team gets the same amount of bombardment, down to the last bullet. War-game designers from all three confederations have worked for years to make this War scrupulously equitable."

Corgan didn't know what "scrupulously equitable" meant, but he figured it must be the same as "fair."

"It will be a war of defense," Mendor told them. "Strictly defense. The team with the largest number of surviving troops on the hill at exactly five P.M.—wins!"

"What about Brig?" Corgan asked. "What's his job?"

"Brig will be the only member of your team who witnesses the entire, overall War scene. At every moment, he will know how many soldiers remain in each of the three armies. He will see where they all are in relation to the hill. He will communicate this information to both you, Corgan, and to Sharla, and he will tell you where and when to move your soldiers. And while your team is busy communicating and changing codes and dispatching troops . . ." Mendor paused for a long moment. ". . . Bombs, mines, and heat-seeking missiles will be exploding; machine guns will fire on your soldiers; poison gas, chemical weapons, and all the other destruction that we talked about will be deployed against you."

Corgan leaned back and let the breath he'd been holding rush out between his lips.

It had been a hard day. Corgan felt drained. Learning to manipulate the virtual soldiers, to protect them from twenty deadly explosions all hitting them at the same time—in spite of Sharla's skill at deflecting shells and air missiles, there were land mines and ground fire—it was tough work! The only thing that gave him hope was that it must have been just as hard for the other two teams that would play in the War. It was the first day of real practice for them, too.

Still! Corgan hadn't played well. The harder he tried, the more mistakes he made. He'd concentrated as hard as he could, and tried to focus himself completely on the job he had to do, but it wasn't turning out right. He kept snuffing out his own troops.

"There are so many of them!" he'd protested to Mendor. "In P and S training I only had to move one laser square at a time."

"In P and S training your hand needed to come within two hundred microns of the laser square. Here, the distance is greater—five hundred microns. That makes it easier. You should have little trouble maneuvering more figures at once. Concentrate!"

He'd concentrated until his brain went numb. The day dragged out so long he couldn't wait for practice to end.

That night, wearily, he got up at eleven o'clock and

moved to check the door, not expecting it to be open. But it was. He went through it, to find Sharla and Brig waiting for him in the tunnel. Without a word, he threw his arms around both of them. They sank together onto the cold floor, arms entwined, and just kept hugging each other.

"They locked me in," Corgan whispered. "Were you locked in, too? Last night and the night before?"

"Yes. They changed the codes."

"Couldn't you break them?"

"I didn't try too hard," Sharla answered, "because there was a lot to think about."

"So why did They let us out now?"

Neither Sharla nor Brig answered right away, and Corgan's mind jumped to something more important. "Sharla, could you understand what I was trying to tell you the other day, before They hit me with the sound shock?"

"I got it. When They had you in Reprimand, you told Them about our meetings," Sharla answered.

"I—I'm sorry." Corgan dropped his head into his hands. "I feel so bad!"

Brig chimed in, "So Corgan the Bold and Magnificent cracked under pressure, while Brig the Weak and Ugly held out. Maybe big and strong isn't the same as brave."

"Stop it, Brig," Sharla told him. "It didn't really make any difference. They would have known, anyway, as soon as They read the morning reports. Or maybe They already knew, before They even put Corgan into Reprimand."

"What?" Corgan raised his head. "What morning reports?"

"Our chemical analysis reports. They must have been all out of balance. . . ."

"He doesn't know what you're talking about," Brig said, tapping Corgan on the head. "Corgan the Squealer is also Corgan the Clueless."

Corgan knocked Brig's arm away. "You'd better explain things," he said to Sharla. "What chemical analysis?"

She moved a little apart from him. "Don't you ever wonder about it," she began, "that everything from your body is collected? Your sweat gets sucked up in the vapor tube when you're sanitized. Your body fluids and solids go into the flush tube. Even the breath you exhale gets collected in the aerogel. Didn't you ever try to guess why?"

Corgan shook his head, then remembered they couldn't see him in the dark. "No."

"Everything your body puts out gets analyzed, Corgan. Every day. They want to make sure all your physical systems are working right. You've missed a lot of sleep lately—that shows up in the reports. And your midnight run the other night: Think what that did to your endorphin count."

"And me," Brig said. "I was so scared that night my adrenaline went off the charts. Sharla told me. She broke those codes and read our charts."

"The Council's not stupid," Sharla went on, "and we left enough clues for Them to figure it out. Brig's torn suit, the smashed dome on the hover car . . ."

After the first astonishment, rage began to seep in. "So They knew all along! And They took me on that guilt trip into Reprimand all for nothing. They must have been laughing Their stupid heads off back there behind Their invisible barriers."

"I don't think so." Sharla gripped Corgan's shoulder to calm him. "Really, all They want is for us to win this War."

Shaking off her hand, Corgan exploded with fury. "They talk about truth and honor, and then They do that to me! Play me like a puppet! Blast my brain with sound shocks! All for their dumb bloody War. That's all They care about. Not us! They only care about Their War. So we win the War for Them, and what do we get out of it?"

"Real steak?" Brig suggested.

"I can't believe what you just told me about Them ana-lyzing my sweat and my . . . it's *my* body, isn't it? They don't own it."

"They created it, Corgan," Sharla said quietly. "Yours and mine and Brig's and quite a few hundred others that didn't turn out so well. They manufactured us, so I guess They think we belong to Them."

"Damn Them!" Corgan cried, using the only strong word he knew. "So I'm supposed to give Them everything They ask for. And what do They give me?"

"They're giving you us," Sharla answered. "Brig and me."

"Think about it," Brig said. "They know all about what's been going on between us, and still They let us out of our Boxes tonight. To be together. Aren't you wonder-ing why?"

If he'd wondered about it a little earlier, it had been driven out of his mind by bitterness over what he'd just learned. "So you must know the answer to that question, Big-Brain Strategist, or you wouldn't be asking me," Corgan said. "Are you going to impress me, or do I guess?"

"Just think about it," Brig said again.

With great effort, Corgan pushed back his anger so he could speculate. Why was he let out tonight, after being locked in his Box the previous two nights? What was different about tonight? What was different about today? Yesterday? Then it came clear.

"My scores," he said. "They were lower. Did the Council think I was holding back?"

"Possibly," Brig answered.

"No, I don't think so," Sharla told them. "It was pretty clear you were doing the best you could. But your edge was gone. I think They decided to give you what you wanted—meaning meeting us in the tunnel—to see if your playing will improve."

Fear knotted Corgan's stomach. "What if it doesn't? I really was trying. Honest!"

"I believe you," Sharla said.

Brig declared, "They keep trying to manipulate us like we do the virtual soldiers. What we need is a plan of our own. And I happen to have one. I'm a Strategist, remember? And it's a great plan." He wiggled himself comfortably between the two of them, picked up their arms and wrapped them around him as if he were a doll.

"So what's the plan?" Corgan demanded. "Not that I'm going to need it or anything. I just had a minor performance lapse. It happens to lots of people. By tomorrow I'll be playing better than ever."

"Well, just in case you mess up again, we need a fall-back plan," Brig said, "and I really look forward to sharing my brilliance with you both. But not till you pay me what you owe me."

"What are you talking about?" Corgan tried to push him away, but Brig clung tightly to Corgan's arm.

"Remember where we were supposed to go the other night?" Brig asked.

"The Mutant Pen."

"Well, we never got there, did we? And I want to go. So after the two of you take me there tomorrow night, I'll tell you my plan." He giggled. "And I guarantee it'll knock you over with its sagacity."

Sagacity! What a toad! This time Corgan managed to shove Brig away, using more force than necessary. "We won't need any brilliant plan," he growled. "I'll be great tomorrow. Anyway, what makes you think They'll let us meet again tomorrow night?"

"Just wait and see," Brig said.

nine

The next morning at practice, Sharla held up both hands and wiggled her fingers and thumbs. "Exercising," she announced for the benefit of Them, wherever They were. Corgan knew what she really meant. Ten o'clock. The three of them could meet in the tunnel at ten that night rather than at eleven. Now that everyone knew what was going on and the policy was to keep silent about it, why wait that extra hour?

At ten he didn't even grope for the door of his Box; he walked right through it. Was it his imagination or did the tunnel seem slightly brighter? Sharla and Brig were waiting even farther along the corridor than before, because, Sharla explained when he reached them, she wanted to save Brig from walking more than he had to.

"So just carry me, then," Brig said to Sharla, lifting his arms.

Corgan didn't understand why Sharla found this so amusing. "Forget it. Let me carry the little monkey," he said, and swung Brig up onto his shoulders.

Pummeling Corgan with his small, crooked feet, Brig squealed, "I want Sharla! Give me to Sharla!"

Corgan grabbed the flailing little feet and held them so tightly that Brig couldn't move. "Keep quiet, or I'll bounce you on the floor," he threatened. "Or maybe I'll just bounce you." Corgan broke into a trot, loosening his grip on Brig so the stunted boy whipped around on Corgan's back, his big head wobbling from side to side on his spindly neck.

"Stop it, Corgan. You'll hurt him," Sharla pleaded, but Brig only whacked Corgan on the side of the head.

"Me hurt *him*! He's the one pounding my ears!" Corgan grabbed Brig by one ankle, held him upside down at arm's length, and started shaking him up and down.

"Corgan, *stop it*! Look at him—he's almost convulsing!"

He was. With laughter. Giggling so hard he could barely talk, Brig gasped, "Ole Ape Arms thinks I'm a co-co-co-co-co-nut. He's sh-sh-shaking me out of a tree."

"You two are disgusting," Sharla scoffed. "I hope They're watching you. It's scary that the fate of the Western Hemisphere depends on you two idiots."

"*I'm* not an idiot," Brig yelled. "*Corgan's* the idiot. He didn't play any better at practice today, just like I said he wouldn't!"

Corgan fought the urge to drop Brig on his head. Instead he set him down feet first, so hard that Brig's legs buckled.

In a beat, the little Mutant jumped back up and cried, "But the Federation doesn't need to worry about Corgan being such a pathetic flop—"

"Flop! You little—," Corgan sputtered.

"—'cause *you'll* save us, Sharla. You'll carry us to victory. And you can start by carrying *me*! Right *now*!"

"—you little slug! I'm gonna drag you back to your Box right now and you can forget all about going to the Mutant Pen—"

In the almost dark corridor, Sharla grabbed Corgan's arm. "Get control! Don't let him make you so mad. Just because he's acting like a baby—"

"Yeah. A baby monster. A baby fascist dictator. A baby leech, a baby pervert—"

"Oh, Corgan! Show a little sensitivity! Don't you ever think about what it would be like to be *him*?" She broke away, went back to Brig, and picked him up. "We're not too far from the hover cars, Brig," she said as he put a strangle hold around her neck. Corgan couldn't see too well in the dark, but he imagined Brig smirking at him.

He wanted to punch the walls in anger but he couldn't take a chance on hurting his hands. Flop! That was what Brig had called him. He searched his vocabulary for all the nasty names he could think of to spit back at Brig, but Corgan's list of expletives was pretty limited. Instead, he fired off a couple of swift kicks at the empty air, and by the time they reached the hover-car track, he had himself under control. Why let Brig spoil his time with Sharla? Ignore the brat, he told himself. Hard as it is, ignore him.

At that minute Jobe materialized out of the shadows. "Hi, Sharla," he said, waving a wrench in greeting. "Looking for a ride?"

"Yeah, Jobe. You looking for a tip?"

"Not tonight," Jobe answered. "Don't need nothin' tonight. You and your buddies just go right ahead and get in the hover car. I stopped it for you so you can climb in easy. It's been polished and disinfected nice and clean."

Inside, after Jobe closed the dome, Sharla said, "No running beside the track and trying to dive into a moving car this time."

"I want to go straight to the Mutant Pen," Brig announced. "I hope the cars don't jam up again."

"I have a feeling everything's going to go as smooth as soy sauce tonight," Sharla told him.

Corgan leaned back into the molded seat, getting pleasure from looking at Sharla in the light. "Your cheeks are flushed," he said. "They're like—like the sun when it first comes up and it brushes the bottom of the clouds over the ocean." Corgan wasn't good at pretty speeches; he must sound like a dolt.

Sharla seemed to like it, though. She smiled and said, "I wish I knew how clouds look when a real sun rises over a real ocean."

Brig bounced in the seat between them and grinned, showing his small, crooked teeth.

"What's into you, Strategist?" Corgan asked him.

"Nothing." Tilting back his big head on his thin neck, Brig looked through narrowed eyelids first at Corgan, and then at Sharla, all the while grinning at them like a clown.

"Who knows what he's up to," Sharla said, shrugging. "But here we are. At the Mutant Pen."

It was as if everything had been prepared for them. The hover car stopped and the bubble dome opened at a touch. When they got out, they found themselves next to a wall that was already transparent; Sharla didn't need to work her code box. A little stool, just the right size for Brig to climb on, stood near the clear section of the wall.

Silent, the three of them stared through the opening.

Inside were babies, mostly—or at least undersized, stunted, helpless little creatures that looked more or less like human babies, lying in cribs. The ones who had arms waved them; some had grasping, prehensile, clawlike fingers that could hold little rattles and dolls. Only a few of the thirty or more Mutants in the Pen looked older than two. Only a few had the right number of eyes, ears, fingers, arms, and legs.

Her voice shaking, Sharla said, "I didn't think there were still so many genetic failures."

Brig had his face pressed against the wall. "I know him," he said, pointing to a big Mutant who sat in a corner, rocking on the floor, his arms crossed over his bloated chest. "That's Rojean. He was there when I was there."

Rojean had no legs. He swayed back and forth, eyes dull, face expressionless.

"Rojean's not dumb," Brig said. "When I was in the Pen, he could talk. Why's he just sitting there like that?"

Some of the older children rolled or crawled on the floor, if they had enough limbs to propel themselves. Corgan wanted to close his eyes to blot it all out, but at the same time he felt compelled to watch. The scene horrified him, yet overwhelmed him with pity. Brig had said that most of them died young. Maybe that was for the best, and yet Brig—what if Brig hadn't lived? Brig was brilliant. He was irritating to the infinite power, but he was smart enough to have been pulled out of that awful Pen, and to take part in a War for the most valuable commodity on Earth: uncontaminated land. In spite of his deformities, Brig was a useful human being. What did it matter if he looked like—those things in there?

The Mutants. Brig was a Mutant. And Corgan was a mutation, Mendor had said. It seemed the only difference between a mutation and a Mutant was that one turned out right and one turned out wrong. I could have been one of them, Corgan thought, staring into the Pen.

I could have been Brig.

Imagine what it would be like to be him, Sharla had said. Corgan tried to imagine. *Undersized. Weak. Ugly. And knowing every minute that people found him repulsive.*

Tentatively, he put his hand on top of Brig's head and ruffled the flame-colored hair. Brig turned his huge, sorrowful eyes to Corgan. "When I was in Reprimand," he said as tears streamed down his cheeks, "They told me how kind They'd been to take me out of the Pen. They said how lucky I was to be alive, because from now on, Mutants like me won't be allowed to live."

"What!" Corgan couldn't believe he'd heard it right.

"They said resources are too limited now and Mutants take up too much time and effort and they don't pay anything back. From now on, when they're gestating in the laboratory and tests show that they won't be normal, they'll be destroyed. And maybe even these ones in here . . ." He pointed through the window. "The Supreme Council's trying to decide whether to let them keep on living."

"Keep on? . . . That can't be true," Corgan muttered.

"It's true, all right. And They kept saying how kind They were to me because not only was I allowed to live, but They've given me an important job and They've cared for me and . . ." Brig leaned his big head on Corgan's chest and sobbed.

"Come on, don't do that," Corgan said, lifting him up. "Let's get out of here, Sharla. This was a bad idea."

The hover car stood waiting, its dome still open. "It'll be a long ride back," Sharla said when they were inside. "The track loops through this whole city. It'll be nice, though; we can lean back and look up at the stars."

Brig lay between them with his head still on Corgan's chest, his small hands crossed underneath his chin. The anger Corgan had felt earlier was now gone. Trying to choose his words carefully so he wouldn't hurt Brig any further, Corgan said, "Genetic engineering might not be such a great idea—for any of us. I mean, why does it have such a high failure rate?"

"Do you know how many genes are in a human being's DNA?" Sharla asked him. "Two hundred thousand. Each human cell has about forty meters' worth of DNA that's only a couple of angstroms wide. And the scientists have to locate the one little part of that DNA that holds the trait they want, and chop it out, and splice it into another section of DNA. And they don't even have any decent equipment here. All the good stuff, like automated DNA sequencers, is still out there in the contaminated world where we can't get it. No wonder we have failures."

Sharla looked down; Brig had fallen asleep on Corgan's lap. "Poor little guy. He's not very strong," she whispered, stroking his damp red hair. "It's kind of a miracle that he's made it this far. Most times, after the gene splicing, the altered cells die, or just don't grow, or else they're so obviously weird that they get destroyed right in the beginning."

"How do you know so much about it?" Corgan asked.

"Because," she said, "that's what I want to do with my life. I want to be a genetic engineer. I was bred to work with codes. Cryptanalysis or DNA analysis—it's all coding."

He wasn't especially surprised. Mostly he felt curious about just how she'd been bred, and what had made her the way she was. But he didn't want to pry. Anyway, he was even more curious about himself.

"Where did I come from?" he asked. "I mean, how did they make me? Do you know?"

"Sure. I looked you up. You got your fast reflexes and precise hand control from your mother and father."

"You mean Mendor?"

"Corgan, Mendor is a *program*. You're a human being. I mean your biological parents. The sperm and the egg that were taken out of the frozen-tissue bank and combined in a test tube to make you. That, plus some traits spliced in from donor tissue."

"Does that mean? . . ." He was trying hard to understand it. "That I have two parents, or more than that? And anyway, who are they? Or who were they?"

Sharla answered, "It says in your records that half of your original genetic material came from—get ready for this—a champion tennis player who died in 2057."

"Mother or father?" He could say those words without any emotional tug, because there were no human memories attached to them.

"Mother, if you want to use the old-fashioned term. The other half, the father half I guess you'd call it, was a surgeon famous for reattaching severed nerves. Little tiny nerve endings." She smiled at him. "Then you got bits of DNA from other people added to you for time measurement, stamina, and hand strength."

Corgan raised his agile right hand and flexed it. He flexed his biceps, stretched his arm across the back of the seat, and reached to pull Sharla against him so their cheeks rested together. When she turned to face him, he kissed her. He put both arms around her and kissed her again.

"Stop," she whispered.

"Why? Because of Brig? He's asleep."

"No. Because I asked you to stop."

Corgan leaned back, confused. "That time before," he said, "you let me then. In fact, you were the one who kissed me first."

"It's different now," she said.

"How is it different?"

She turned away from him and looked out the dome of the hover car, although there was nothing much to see in the dark corridor. "Because I hardly knew you then, and now I really like you."

"*What?*" It made no sense to him.

"Before, I was just sort of—I'm sorry—playing with you, Corgan. It wasn't fair. You're so innocent."

Hurt, he pulled his arm away. "You make it sound like a disease—being innocent," he told her, sulking.

"It's not your fault," she said. "They've kept you away from everyone else. They've filled you full of Their thoughts and Their words and you only think what They want you to think and say what They tell you to say—"

Is that so wrong? he wondered. Every time he tried to do or say something outside the rules he got yelled at or punished. He couldn't be like Sharla, who did and said anything she pleased and always came out of it just fine.

"Sharla," he asked, "when we recite the pledge, are you saying something different?"

She smiled. "So you noticed. I just make up some nonsense words that sound pretty much the same."

"Like what?"

"You say it first, Corgan. Repeat the pledge."

He almost raised his hand but caught himself in time; if he had, she'd probably have laughed and counted it as one more sign of his innocence. "I pledge to wage the War with courage, dedication, and honor," he said slowly, seriously considering the meaning for the first time in a long while.

"Okay, here's a couple of my variations." Sharla did raise her hand and, in a mocking, singsong voice, recited, "I wedged the cage's door with birds and red carnations,

Your Honor. Or, *I educated Lori, urging meditation upon her.* Or, *I fled the raging boar with furry dead—*"

"You're making fun of the pledge," he accused her.

"Why not? The Council forces me to say it. They can't make me believe in it. To me, the War's just a silly game."

Frowning, perplexed, he studied her in the soft light. She was so clever and so pretty that she filled him with all kinds of longings, but she made him feel off balance. "Don't you believe in anything?" he asked her.

"Sure. I believe in myself."

TEN

"Brig, wake up. The ride's over. Time to go home." When Corgan lifted Brig, he felt dampness on his sleeve where Brig's sweaty head had lain against it for so long.

"Do you want to tell us your plan now before we get out of the hover car?" Sharla asked.

"No. Too tired. Tomorrow night." Brig wound his arms around Corgan's neck and went back to sleep.

"I'll carry him back to his Box," Corgan said. "Maybe we ought to meet earlier tomorrow night so he won't get so tired out."

"Okay. Nine o'clock tomorrow. 'Night, Corgan." She brushed his cheek with her lips, which was better than nothing, but not nearly as much as he would have liked.

After depositing Brig in his Box, Corgan walked slowly to his own. No sprinting tonight. It was past midnight. He was tired, too, and he needed to wake himself early in the morning to allow time for an intense physical workout. He flexed his hands, wondering what was wrong with him. In the last warm-up practice game of Triple Multiplex, his score had been off by a half percent. By itself that wasn't too significant, but added to his disappointing performance on the two previous days, he was down by a total of a percent and a half. That was significant, considering that his performance score should have been going *up* by that much margin each day, rather than down.

At six the next morning he rolled out of his aerogel bed, pulled on his running shorts, and did forty laps around the virtual track. After that he practiced with weights and after that he did fifteen minutes of finger-flexing exercises. Mendor the Mother watched all this but said nothing, except, "You'll have to sanitize yourself now to have time for breakfast. Your food intake is important, too, you know."

Later, when the team assembled in the War-games room, Mendor the Stern Father announced, "We'll start without a warm-up practice this morning."

Corgan felt both relief and anxiety. Unless he practiced on games where his earlier scores were already recorded, he had nothing to measure his performance against. He wouldn't be able to tell whether he'd broken out of his slump and was starting to play better. On the other hand, at least he'd be spared from knowing it if he was playing worse. "May I speak, Mendor? Why is that?" he asked.

"Because in the actual Virtual War, which is *eight days*

from now, there will be no warm-up. All three teams will begin the War at precisely nine A.M. and will play straight through till precisely five P.M. No breaks for meals, for Clean Rooms, not even to wipe the sweat from your brows. *Eight straight hours of war!"*

Corgan looked at Sharla, or at least at her virtual image, which was all he ever saw of her during these practices. First at Sharla, then at Brig. Both of them returned his stare with eyes that showed the same alarm he was feeling. No breaks at all during the War?

"Will we have a chance to practice nonstop like that before the War?" Corgan asked Mendor.

"No. That would be too much of a strain on your health. You must conserve your strength now to maintain your physical peak for the actual War. Which means all extracurricular activity should be limited from now on!" Mendor's eyes changed into narrowly focused red beams that bored into Corgan.

"Limited," Mendor had just said. Not "stopped." "Extracurricular activity" meant their meetings in the tunnel at night. They'd been given a little freedom, but since nothing was ever discussed in actual words, Corgan had to keep feeling his way through each situation and then trying to guess Mendor's meaning. He didn't like this; he was too tired to play doublespeak games. It made him feel like he was slogging through glue. Why couldn't the Council and Mendor just say what They meant? He stretched his arms and yawned.

"Begin!" Mendor bellowed. Corgan scrambled into position, two seconds late.

If each coming day of practice was going to bring a new element to the War, Corgan hoped They'd added the worst one first. Because it was pretty bad. Blood! They'd thrown in very realistic-looking blood.

Before, when artillery had hit his soldiers, they'd fallen down in a clean simulated death. Today, heads got blown off, arms got severed, and blood spurted so far that Corgan involuntarily jerked back his hands to keep them from getting bathed in gore. And when he did that, he missed the chance to move his soldiers, so more of them got killed. He wanted to scream for Time-out, but for the past two days Time-out hadn't been allowed. He wanted to close his eyes; instead he forced himself to keep his attention on the game.

Brig seemed calm about the bloodshed. "Over there!" he'd shout into the audio connector. "Watch your flank, Corgan. *Move that platoon!* Pull them behind that wall."

Corgan felt his stomach heave as the simulated battle-ground grew sticky with blood. He swallowed hard and focused on his soldiers, forgetting that they were only virtual images no bigger than the height of his hand. He smelled ozone and smoke and chemicals—

"Gas attack!" Brig screamed. "Get them *out* of there, Corgan!"

It seemed to go on endlessly. When Mendor finally stopped the game, he glowered at Corgan. "That lasted a full minute longer than the prescribed two-hour interval for today," Mendor rebuked him. "Why didn't you call time? If this had been the real Virtual War, Corgan, you'd have forfeited the battle."

Mortified, Corgan dropped his head onto his folded arms. It had happened again! He'd lost track of time!

It wasn't that he'd been *unable* to count time; he'd just become so intent on what he was doing he'd *forgotten* to count time. At least, that's what he told himself.

"Go to your Clean Rooms," Mendor ordered. "Then eat. If this were the real War, you'd still be fighting. No breaks. Remember that."

The afternoon practice was as brutal as the morning had been. When it was over, and after another bath, Corgan fell asleep over his dinner. He woke up, startled, with Mendor the Mother smoothing his hair and telling him to brush his teeth before bedtime.

He met Sharla and Brig in the tunnel that night at nine.

"Pick me up, Corgan," Brig whimpered. "I'm too tired to stand. I didn't think it would be this hard."

Corgan lifted Brig and held him head-high to both himself and Sharla. "I wonder why They let us stay out so late last night," he said. "They knew what today would be like."

"I think They wanted to make a point," Sharla answered. "So we'd find out for ourselves that we can't keep losing sleep. From now on, we'll have to cut back to fifteen minutes again if we want to stay competitive. Because if you think today was bad, tomorrow will probably be worse."

The tunnel felt cold and was completely dark; Sharla had forgotten to bring the piezoelectric stone. The three of them huddled together for warmth. "You'd better tell us your plan quick, Brig," Corgan said. "They're trying to freeze us."

"Yeah, just to make sure we know They're still in charge," Brig agreed. "That's Their strategy. My plan, okay . . . but I feel kind of bad, because I wanted to see your faces when I sprang it on you, and now I can't."

"Never mind," Sharla soothed him. "After we hear it, we'll tell you how we feel about it."

Brig shivered and his voice shook. "To begin with, They've conceded a few things to us, letting us make some choices, like how long we'll stay out here tonight. That shows how much They're depending on us. There are no back-up replacements for us, which means They need us *really* bad. So . . . if we demand a reward, They'll have to consider it."

"What reward? Come on, spit it out, Brig," Corgan urged.

"We win the War for Them, and They . . . for our reward . . ." He paused. Whether it was for dramatic effect or because Brig didn't feel too confident about what he was going to suggest, Corgan couldn't be sure.

"We make Them promise to let us live on the Isles of Hiva."

Corgan sucked in his breath. Sharla's arms tightened around both of them.

"Do you think They'd go for it?" Corgan asked.

"If you guys let me do the negotiating," Brig answered.

"You?" Corgan sputtered. Weird little Brig, to be trusted with something that enormous, that would change their lives?

Brig's voice still shook from the cold. "Sharla told me who my biological parents were," he said. "The male reproductive cell had been frozen for seventy-four years, which maybe is why I became a Mutant, 'cause that's probably way too long. Anyway, my natural father was the head coach for a basketball team called the Boston Celtics."

"What's basketball?" Corgan asked.

"It's a sport people played back in the old days. It was fast paced and complicated and my biological father told all the players what to do. Perfect genetics to breed a Strategist. Plus, my mother was the head of a big law firm. She never lost a case in court." Brig giggled. "What a combination I am! I wish I could have met them."

"Then he got some extra DNA from a top-ranking diplomat," Sharla said. "I think Brig can negotiate."

"If you agree, I'm going to present our demand right before War games tomorrow morning," Brig said. "They probably won't give us an answer right away. But who knows? Maybe They will."

Corgan asked, "Do we have a chance?"

"Why not?" Sharla demanded. "We were bred for something like this, we've been trained for this particular job, and when it's over, They won't need us anymore. Will They even care where we go? I think it might work, Brig."

"Yeah, so do I," Brig agreed.

"That means," Corgan said, "from now on we have to play perfectly—no mistakes—to show we can win for Them."

Silence. Neither Brig nor Sharla said anything, and Corgan squirmed. Both of *them* had been playing just fine all along.

"Look, I know my proficiency's been off," he said. "But I'm working on it. It's under control now."

After another pause, Brig mentioned, "You went a minute overtime today."

"I said I'm working on it!"

In the dark, he couldn't read their faces. "Hey, if They promise us the Isles of Hiva, I'll get my winning edge back for sure. I'll play my brains out."

"That's what we were hoping," Brig said. "I mean—"

"Anyway, we don't need to worry," Corgan said with bravado. "We're unbeatable. Even if we don't play as well as we used to, we're still way better than the other two teams. Mendor told me that."

"When?"

"What does it matter when? We were genetically engineered, remember? To be the best in the world. Right? Right, Sharla?"

Quietly she answered, "So were the players on the other two teams."

"What!" both Corgan and Brig exclaimed in disbelief.

"All three teams will consist of genetically engineered players."

"How'd you find out?" Brig asked grimly.

"How do I find out *anything*?" she answered. "Trust me. It's true."

The coldness of the tunnel seemed to seep into Corgan's lungs, chilling his heart. Brig whimpered.

"Maybe I shouldn't have told you," Sharla said. "Anyway, like we talked about, we need to get more sleep. Let's not meet tomorrow night."

"Not meet? How are we going to communicate if there's something we need to say to each other?" Corgan asked, subdued.

"That's easy. I'm in touch with both of you over the audio connector," Brig answered. "I mean, Sharla tells me the code changes, and I tell Corgan the strategy changes. If Sharla wants to throw in a personal message, and if she keeps it real short, I can pass it on to you, Corgan."

"What about the other direction?" Corgan asked. "Can I send a message through you to Sharla?"

"Sorry. One-way is the best I can do. Sharla to Brig to Corgan."

"Okay. We're in this together. If we win the War, we go to the Isles of Hiva," Sharla said, taking both their hands. "It's a pact, right?"

In the dark, they squeezed each other's hands.

His voice choking up, Corgan said, "We have to win. Because more than anything else, I want to get out of this place. I want to feel real ocean waves and run on sand. And I want to be where things can be out in the open. No more sneaking around and being spied on every time we breathe. No more Them knowing everything and pretending not to. No more Them keeping back information like . . . like—"

"The truth about our competitors," Sharla finished.

ELEVEN

The next morning, before Brig had a chance to speak, Corgan announced, "Mendor, I request permission to discuss something."

He could see the alarm in Brig's eyes, that Corgan might say something to spoil his plan. Corgan shook his head to reassure him.

"Permission is granted," Mendor said. "Go ahead, Corgan."

"My team," Corgan began, "Sharla, Brig, and myself, need to see each other the way we really are. There's no reason any longer to show false images of Brig and Sharla. I know what they look like in real life."

He could almost hear Mendor's various programs

whirring as he/she searched for instructions to handle this. Corgan was unmasking something that had been deliberately concealed.

Forty-six and thirty-one hundredths of a second passed while Mendor's image stayed dimmed. During that time Brig's and Sharla's virtual images were stopped in freeze-frame. Then, gradually, they faded in, changing right before Corgan's eyes. Into themselves.

"Thank you, Mendor," Corgan said.

Brig rose to his feet. Now he was only half as tall as he'd looked earlier. "I have a request, too," he said.

"You, too?" Mendor cried. "We're wasting time, but go ahead."

"I'll try to keep it brief," Brig answered, his voice frail, "but could you please ask the Council to come? They're the ones who will have to decide on my request. . . ."

This time only twenty seconds elapsed before Mendor said, "Go ahead. The Council is waiting."

"If . . . if you don't mind, I'd like to see Them, please," Brig said.

Immediately Their images became visible. They were seated in Their usual row of six, Their faces featureless as always. The Councillor with the echo-chamber voice said, "State your reason for this delay in the War-games practice."

"Yes, sirs. And . . . madames." Short, twisted, and homely, the true-to-life virtual image of Brig stood up to approach Them. He gave a funny little bow, bobbing his big head, and said, "The three of us on the War team respectfully wish to submit a proposal to your honors, the Supreme Council."

Six faceless, motionless images waited, saying nothing.

"We . . . uh . . . we want to discuss a reward," Brig said. "We want to negotiate."

"What reward do you want?" The words seemed to blare equally loudly from all six mouthless, faceless heads.

Brig's voice faltered a little. "We've practiced diligently. We will fight the War with total dedication and undivided loyalty."

Oh, Brig, get to the point, Corgan thought. Don't let Them spook you.

Brig stiffened, trying to make himself taller. "But after the War is over, whether we win or lose, You will have no further use for us. Is that correct?"

Silence. Then, "Losing is not acceptable."

Brig stammered, "You're absolutely right. We're not going to lose." He took a deep breath. "This is what we'd like to negotiate for. We want to go to the Isles of Hiva after the War. Corgan and Sharla and me. To live there."

Nothing moved. It was like an image-generator malfunction when the motion shut down. The seconds ticked off inside Corgan's brain—seventeen seconds and a fraction.

"We will take it under advisement," a frosty collective voice declared from the Council. "That's all. Now begin your practice."

Brig scurried back to his War-game position. So the big scene was over. Had it done any good at all? Corgan doubted it. Brig seemed to shrink into himself, looking even more deformed.

* * *

The next day was War Day Minus Six. It began with an explosion that shook Corgan to his toes, and Sharla was right. That day was worse than the day before, which had been worse than the day before that.

Added to the blood and gore were the soldiers' screams. Now when they died horribly with their eyes wide open in shock and terror, their cries twisted Corgan's insides.

"Focus! Focus!" Brig shouted. "Block out everything extraneous."

Corgan tried to ignore the screams and mutilation, tried to remind himself that these were only virtual images, not living people, but it was hard.

Yet, miraculously, when they broke for lunch, Mendor told Corgan that the Council had agreed to their request. If the team won the War, they'd be allowed to live on the Isles of Hiva. *If.* Corgan wanted to feel glad, to feel excited. A day earlier he would have. Now, knowing the kind of competition he was going to face in the War, he just felt scared.

When they met for the afternoon session, nothing more was said about the Isles of Hiva. No announcements—not a word, before or after they recited the pledge. Corgan wondered whether Sharla and Brig had been told, but he couldn't make eye contact with them. The game started then and it escalated in savagery until he felt physically sick.

He slept badly that night, his dreams filled with horror. When he woke up whimpering, Mendor the Mother Figure was there to soothe him, stroking his forehead, speaking softly, humming the little lullabies she'd sung to him when he was young. "Think of Hiva," she crooned. "Win the War and the Isles are yours."

War Day Minus Five brought more land mines. He could hear Brig shouting, "Sharla, find the right code! Disable the mines. Corgan, move your troops to the rear. No, Corgan! You pushed too hard—you destroyed nine of them."

He kept having to choose: Move his troops to the left or to the right or straight ahead. There were never any clues which way they should go. If Corgan chose straight ahead the platoon might enter a minefield, where a dozen of them would get blown to pieces before he could move them out. Or the minefield might be to the left or to the right; planted at random, land mines were undetectable. Even worse than getting his troops blown up was penetrating them with his hands because he wasn't careful enough. That killed them just as dead as the land mines did.

He had the fastest reflexes ever recorded, but in this War, speed wasn't much help. It was precision that mattered. He could move his hands quickly to the images, but if he didn't stop in time to keep from touching them, he destroyed them. And when they died at Corgan's hands, they screamed horribly.

By midmorning, he found that he was hardening himself against the screams. That let him calculate better the microscopic distance between his hands and the troops, and not kill so many through his own clumsiness. All that fierce, unending slaughter was starting to lose its impact. Blood, torn limbs, disembowelment—it was all part of the game. Concentrate. Focus. Compress the force field. Feel it, he told himself. Don't notice the horror. When he stopped for lunch he could eat the food put in front of him, and not turn away, nauseated, as he'd done the day before.

"I think I might be toughening up," he mentioned to Mendor.

"Good for you," she answered.

His toughness lasted most of the afternoon, until a message came through Brig: "Sharla says no meeting tonight. Wait till tomorrow." That left a hollowness in him that he couldn't deal with then, couldn't even wonder about, because he had to fight. Had to concentrate. Had to move those troops without perforating them.

Even that night he couldn't mull over why she decided against meeting him, because he was so tired, the minute he fell into bed he fell asleep.

Then came War Day Minus Four, when They threw in the civilians. Women holding babies, old people who could barely walk, staggering along with their belongings, children fumbling onto the battlefield where land mines blew them apart. And beautiful girls, with haunting eyes, who held out their arms, beseeching him. He wanted to move the civilians to safety, but Mendor the Stern Father bellowed at him, "Forget those people! They are not your job. You are responsible only for your troops. Civilians mean nothing! Do you want to lose the War?"

And so he had to block out the images of the terrified girls. "They're not real, they're not real," he kept muttering to himself until his brain believed it even if his heart didn't.

"Message from Sharla," Brig managed to say. "Not tonight, either. Tomorrow, she promises."

Corgan cried in his sleep all night. "You must eat," Mendor the Mother coaxed him in the morning. "Look at this nice hot oatmeal."

"Made from soybeans," Corgan muttered.

"With brown sugar and milk . . ."

"Made from soybeans."

Mendor lost patience. "Corgan, you have to keep up your strength. You're not eating and you're not sleeping." She surrounded him so closely he felt as if she were smothering him. "Be a good boy now and eat your breakfast, or you won't be able to win the War. And if you don't win it, you'll lose the Isles of Hiva."

"Mendor, tell me the truth," he said. "Am I playing any better at all?"

Mendor dimmed. Then she said, "Be a good boy and eat your breakfast."

Hollow-eyed, he took his place on the morning of War Day Minus Three, steeling himself against compassion for the civilians, and against his need to see Sharla. He had one job to do: Move his troops to the designated area. Keep them alive as long as possible, because the rules of War stated that whichever side reached the goal first would win, but the number of troops left alive would also be factored in. If he got there first with hardly any soldiers left, he could still lose to the army that reached the goal a bit later, but with twice as many living soldiers.

That was the day the vicious air attacks began. Helicopters flew straight into his face. His instincts made him flinch, while Brig shouted in his loudest voice, "Ignore the air attack, Corgan. You lost three soldiers because your hand brushed them when you jerked away from that chopper." Very quietly, Brig added, "Sharla says tonight at nine."

When they met that night the tunnel was lighted, although only dimly. At least he could see her. "Where's Brig?" he asked.

"He didn't come. He needs all the sleep he can get. This is harder on him than it is on us." She put her arms around Corgan and they stood together, leaning against each other for comfort.

"Sharla, you're the only one I can ask. Tell me the truth. Am I playing any better?"

"No," she answered.

He slumped down onto the floor of the cold tunnel, arms crossed on his knees, head bent to lean on his arms. Sharla knelt beside him and, after a minute, said, "That doesn't mean we're going to lose the War; it only means you're not playing as well as you used to."

"So we're going to lose," he said. "No Isles of Hiva." His eyes stung with tears, and he turned away.

"Not necessarily." Lifting his face so he had to look at her, Sharla said, "I'm still tapping into the Council's daily records. What They're saying is that you're improving every day, but not fast enough. By now you should be able to move the troops without damaging any of them at all. But who knows? You still might be just as good as the other team leaders."

"I need to be better than they are, or we'll lose. What happened to me? I'm trying as hard as I can, but it won't come out right."

She didn't answer at first. Settling beside him, so that both of them were leaning against the cold steel wall, she reached for his hand. "Maybe I can help," she said.

"How? There's nothing wrong with the way you've been playing. You and Brig are great. It's me who's bombing out." He laughed bitterly. "Yeah, that's the right word for it. I bomb out every time I hear a bomb go off. The noise is making me crazy. And not just the explosions—the screams, and the—"

"Corgan, stop! Listen to me! I said I can help."

He turned to gaze at her, studying her face. If only he could win the War and spend the rest of his life on the sandy beaches of Hiva. If only he could forget the War and spend the rest of his life with Sharla.

"Don't say anything until you hear this, Corgan. The reason I waited till tonight to meet you was to see if—well, if when you got Hiva as an incentive—your playing would improve enough."

"And it didn't."

"I know. But remember the War rules They pounded into us over and over? 'If our team breaks a rule, even unintentionally, three times? . . .'"

"Right. We lose. And if we break a rule on purpose even once, we lose," Corgan said. "So what about it?"

"Remember me asking Mendor how the judges would know whether it was on purpose or not? It turns out the guidelines are pretty vague about how They figure out whether an infraction was really meant, or if it just happened by accident. So here's what I think."

She leaned close to him and spoke so softly in his ear

that he could feel her breath on his cheek. "Right now, your hands have to come within five hundred microns of the soldiers to make them move. That's half a millimeter. But remember when I told Mendor I could enlarge the width of the force field to seven hundred microns?"

"And Mendor said it was against the rules."

"Right. But what if I mixed up one of my codes— accidentally, of course—and no one noticed for a while. It would be hard to prove it wasn't just a mistake. At seven hundred microns, you wouldn't have to be quite as careful. You could move your troops quicker without crushing as many."

His eyes widening, he drew back to stare at her. "What are you saying?"

"That you'd have easier control if the force field got compressed enough at seven hundred microns, instead of five hundred."

"You're talking about *cheating*!"

"I know it's risky, but it might give us enough of an edge to—"

"*Sharla! No!*" Corgan jumped to his feet.

"Don't say no so fast. The stakes are awfully high here—" Still on her knees, she held on to his hand, but he pulled it away. "Corgan, please, just think about it," she said, scrambling up to face him.

"I gave my word that I'd fight the War honorably," he told her.

"Yeah, well, you gave your word to obey, and to tell the truth, too, and here you are out in the tunnel with me, which we have been lots of times lately and Mendor and the Council are still pretending it isn't happening. So this whole phony Supreme Council moralistic garbage is just one big lie anyway."

Backing away from her, he flattened himself against the cold wall. "That's Their problem. I can't control what They do, or how They run things. Only what I do."

"It's just—you don't know, I want so much to win—"

Corgan stared at her. "Once you told me the War was just a silly game. Now you're desperate to win it. What changed?"

"Nothing," she said. "I don't want to talk about it."

"Talk about what?"

"I said it's nothing. Just forget we had this whole conversation, okay?" She turned and would have walked away, but he grabbed her by the shoulders and swung her around.

"Sharla, I don't want you to cheat. I know you can probably pull off that code change and I wouldn't be able to stop you, but promise me you won't do it."

"Why should I? I *need* to win. And I don't care one bit about honor. Look around you, Corgan. Everyone cheats, everyone lies."

"I don't," he said. "Yeah, I've gone along with the pretending, but since that day after Reprimand, I've never spoken any lies and I've never disobeyed an order. I told Them I'd fight honorably. I'm going to."

She slammed her fists against his chest. "Why . . . *why* . . . is honor so important? It's just a word."

"No it isn't. It's a promise I make every day. Over and over. When I say the pledge."

"Can't you just leave it to me?" she begged. "You don't even have to know it's happening. You *won't* know. Those codes are easy! I can change them and *no one* will know!"

"That's not good enough," he said. "I need to trust you."

Suddenly she collapsed against him and began to cry. "All right! You're so damn noble! I'll give you what you want. I don't believe in the system or the Council or the Federation or anyone in the whole world. Except you, Corgan. Too bad for me. I believe in you."

Somehow—and Corgan couldn't tell how it was done—on War Day Minus Two the soldiers seemed more real, like living, breathing, bleeding human beings. To his relief, he began to maneuver them with much less damage. No matter what horrible carnage got hurled at them, or how many devastating weapons exploded in his ears, he moved his troops steadily toward the designated target area with only half as many losses from his own mishandling.

"Splendid, splendid, splendid! You're doing better!" Mendor crooned at the end of the day. "Now eat everything on your plate and get ready for a good night's sleep."

But Corgan couldn't sleep. The terrible war scenes he'd suppressed all day came flooding at him in the night to haunt him. Children with limbs torn off, lying facedown in bloody mud. Soldiers' bodies, male and female, stacked naked and decaying like fallen leaves.

When he did sleep, bits of lectures he'd heard from Mendor long ago flared into his dreams, in Mendor's stern Father Professor voice. "War is obsolete. We must stop aggressors from taking lives, but we must engage the enemy without killing them."

"So much blood," Corgan wept in his sleep.

"In the old vicious wars, there were no noncombatants: women, children, the innocent, the helpless—all died."

"No. No dying," Corgan tried to cry out, but sleep smothered his cries.

"What was the point of bloody, bloody wars when they were so destructive that nobody won?" Mendor's voice rang through the nightmares. "Even the winners lost."

"No blood!" Corgan moaned, and woke himself from his restless sleep.

"There, there," Mendor the Mother quieted him. "You cried 'no blood.' Of course there will be no blood, Corgan—only in the virtual images. You know that's just pretend."

"But they used to fight like that, didn't they, Mendor? All the killing . . . people really killed each other in the old days, didn't they?"

"Yes. For thousands of years."

"Why did they?"

"Human nature, Corgan. People's instincts can be selfish and ruthless."

"But why do we have to show slaughter in the Virtual War games? Can't we just play a bloodless Virtual War?"

Mendor answered, "There are reasons. You're all sweaty. Let me wipe your face with a cool cloth. Sleep, now. Sleep. It's the middle of the night."

"Two A.M.," Corgan said, "and seven minutes forty-six and nineteen hundredths seconds. But I didn't know the time the other day, Mendor. What if I can't count time again when the War is happening?"

"You'll be fine," she soothed him. "You must trust me, Corgan. This past week, you worked yourself into a state of anxiety over nothing. Didn't you notice how much better you played today? Anyway, tomorrow won't be a hard day. It's the day before the War, and They want you to save your strength. It will be easier tomorrow. Rest now, Corgan. Dream of the Isles of Hiva."

TWELVE

"It's time," Mendor whispered, gently shaking Corgan. "This is the day."

He groaned, and fought against waking.

"It's seven in the morning, Corgan."

"I know what time it is, Mendor. I'm the world's most accurate human clock, remember?"

Without touching him, Mendor the Mother Figure wrapped him in a cocoon of love. "Corgan, dear boy, this is the day that may change your life."

"The Isles of Hiva," Corgan murmured. "What will you do if I go there, Mendor?"

Hesitant, she answered, "You won't need me anymore then, so I'll cease to exist."

"I can't imagine you not existing."

Her face hovered over him. She was pale pink, with cheeks so moist and fresh he wanted to touch them, with eyes that radiated love. She said, "If you don't get up now, Corgan, you'll be late for the War, and if you lose the War—no Isles of Hiva. Then the matter of my existence will become irrelevant."

"Right." Wearily, he rolled out of bed and went to sanitize himself in his Clean Room.

Breakfast was tasteless brain-potency-mineral cereal plus some chemical-laden juice that made him gag. "This drink is awful!" he exclaimed.

"It will help your muscles avoid a buildup of lactic acid," Mendor told him. "Save some of it so you can swallow these pills. They're to enhance your synaptic nerve pathways."

"I don't even know what that means," he said, but he took the pills. "I'm ready now," he said.

When he faced Sharla and Brig in the Virtual War Room, their images looked to be so nearby that they could have been within touching distance. But he was inside the confinement of his Box, and they were in their own Boxes, and the Virtual War Room didn't exist except in electronic impulses carried by metal ions embedded in aerogel. No matter how broad the battlefield appeared, no matter how real the soldiers and shells and bombardment and dirt and blood seemed—they were only combinations of light and sound created by clever virtualizers: artists, historians, programmers, and engineers from all three confederations. Those electronic geniuses could pack an entire vast War inside the walls of Corgan's small Box. And inside Sharla's, and Brig's. And the three team members would almost forget they were in separate cubicles; would almost believe they were together. Fighting the War.

"I sense that everyone is prepared," Mendor the Father Figure said. "The Western Hemisphere Federation is counting on the three of you. I know you will fulfill your destiny. Come forward now to stand before the Supreme Council."

Corgan stood up and watched his virtual image join Sharla's and Brig's in front of the Council table. Subtly at first, then more quickly, the Council members morphed from faceless, identical images into true-to-life representations of Themselves, the way They'd looked when Corgan saw Them, that time, through the transparent wall.

"Since you prefer the look of reality, Corgan . . ." the tall, stooped one said, but he didn't finish the sentence. He just gestured to indicate the others.

Six distinctive, individual right hands raised in a blessing. "Our trust is in you," stated the dissimilar mouths in six unalike though ordinary human faces. "Please recite the pledge."

"I promise," Corgan began, "to wage the War with courage, dedication, and honor." He twisted to get a look at Sharla's lips. Was she saying the real pledge, or was she faking it?

"Take your places now. The countdown begins."

Corgan sat flexing his hands, wondering what exactly had been in the pills Mendor gave him at breakfast. He could feel every nerve ending, each tiny neuron in his arms and fingertips. His hands generated power as he contracted them into fists. Yet each centimeter of his skin had become so sensitive he could feel dust motes that he couldn't even see.

"Eighteen, seventeen, sixteen . . ." Even as the seconds were audibly counted off, Corgan's mind divided them into fragments of hundredths. His internal clock seemed to be working perfectly.

"Begin." The word was spoken so quietly that Corgan might have missed it if his sense of time hadn't been flawless. He waited for the explosion that always signaled the beginning of the practice sessions, but the battlefield stayed so silent he thought the sound effects must have malfunctioned.

Fog rolled in, making it impossible for him to see anything at first. He strained his eyes until he was able to pick out his one hundred soldiers, huddled together in small groups behind camouflage netting.

Then, "On your left!" Brig screamed.

Corgan threw his whole body across the scene and managed to sweep all his troops to safety before the bomb exploded. The blast was so ferocious it shook him physically. It left his ears ringing with such terrible echoes he couldn't hear Brig, who was shouting something and waving his arms, his eyes wide with fear.

Corgan looked up. A heat-seeking missile shrieked toward his troops at such tremendous speed he couldn't hope to save them. Then, too high to cause real damage, it exploded. Sharla! Decoding the trajectory, she'd managed to defuse the warhead. Just in time.

So much heavy artillery flew at Corgan's troops that all he could do was move them out of the way, time after time. Not only was he unable to advance, but his troops kept getting shoved backward, kept losing ground.

"Land mines!" Brig yelled. "Retreat."

"No. I won't." If they did nothing but retreat, there'd be too much ground to make up later. Cupping his hands to intensify the electromagnetic force, he moved his soldiers forward a few at a time, weaving them cautiously across the dangerous minefield for seven minutes forty-two seconds until two mines detonated and three of his troops got blown to bits.

"Do what I say!" Brig screeched. "I'm the Strategist—do you want to lose?"

"Can't help it if there are casualties," Corgan panted, struggling to keep down his breakfast. His stomach heaved at the sight of his soldiers—two men and a young woman with long golden hair—lying entangled in a bloody mess, with the life ripped out of them and seeping into the ground.

"Back! Back!" Brig had to yell to be heard over the rattle of attack rifles. "Now! Around the side, behind that barn!"

"What's the score?" Corgan wanted to know.

"You've lost three. Pacific's lost eight. Eurasia's lost five."

They were ahead! Exultation filled Corgan—he was playing well! At that exact second an armored tank rumbled through the barn, crushing four of his troops. Even as he watched in horror, the tank burst into flame and disintegrated. Sharla again!

Corgan maneuvered his troops into a stand of trees where the fog lay thickest. Again the battlefield fell silent except for muffled explosions in the distance, where Pacific and Eurasia troops were defending themselves. He used the pause to take stock. He'd lost seven soldiers, 7 percent of his total force, and he hadn't gained a single meter of ground. He decided to pull his troops into squads of eight: better to realign them, and advance some of the squads toward the target area. Just as he thought of it, Brig said the same thing over the audio connector.

As the hours wore on Corgan wished he could be Brig, who looked down through smoke and flames and fog on the whole picture: at the patterns made when the troops regrouped—his own troops and the ones from the other two confederations. They came together, moved out, died, formed new units, retreated, skirted around buildings and avoided—sometimes—the minefields. Or didn't avoid the minefields and got blown apart.

Corgan's viewpoint was right in the thick of it, at ground level. His hands moved soldiers and when he didn't do it right he watched them die screaming, falling, rising above the earth as their bodies separated into bleeding limbs, torn heads, and eviscerated torsoes.

Brig had stopped shrieking out orders; his commands were now terse and low. At five hours fourteen minutes thirty-seven seconds they had fifty-two troops left, and they were halfway to the target area. Corgan regrouped his squads again—eight soldiers to a squad with four left over for reconnaissance.

It was then he noticed his blistered hands. Five hours of

compressing electromagnetic energy, nonstop, to move his virtual troops, no matter how gently, had burned the skin on his fingers. He put them into his mouth to suck the blisters, and at that second a bomb killed four more of his troops, four that he could have moved to safety if his hand had been where it was supposed to be instead of in his mouth.

"Damn!" he screamed, and swept his remaining troops inside a barricade, bursting a blister on one of his fingers. There was no stopping to have it cauterized; as Mendor had made abundantly clear, there would be no stopping for anything until exactly five P.M., when the War would end. No food, no water, no wiping away of sweat, and no damage control for raw-skinned team members. And no Mendor, Corgan realized thankfully. No Mendor to chastise him for whatever stupid mistakes he was making during the course of the War. The team was on its own.

"What score, Brig!" he demanded.

"We have forty-eight troops. Pacific fifty-seven. Eurasia fifty-one."

Corgan groaned aloud. They were down!

"But we're nineteen meters closer to the target area than the other two armies," Brig announced.

So it wasn't totally bad news. Then sweat fell into Corgan's eyes and while he tried to blink away the stinging, a helicopter dropped a fire bomb behind the barricade where three of his squads were waiting.

Forgetting his blistered fingers, forgetting his sweat-stung eyes, Corgan lunged forward to move out what remained of his troops and assess his losses. Two more dead, but that wasn't so bad considering the suddenness of the fire bombing. He advanced them once again to behind the camouflage nets.

Each time a bomb burst, the heat was so searing it made his skin ache. Flares from the explosions blinded him so that he could hardly tell the true colors of anything: All he saw were reverse-color afterimages. The continuous roar deafened him so much he had to try to read Brig's lips, because half the time he couldn't hear the audio connector over the ringing in his ears. Hour after grueling hour the battle raged. Once Corgan used a brief moment's lull to wonder how frail little Brig was managing to hold up. Brig's voice was now a gravelly rasp.

"Sharla says," Brig reported hoarsely at half past three, "we're doing okay."

Corgan wasn't too sure. His fingers had grown numb, and his hands functioned only about half as well as they had when the War started. But by now he had only half as many troops to maneuver.

"Position to target?" he yelled to Brig.

"A hundred and two meters."

So far to go! Corgan wanted nothing more than to lay his head on his arms and blot out the whole bloody battle, but he wiped his eyes with the sleeve of his now-black LiteSuit, and struggled on.

"Brig, report our position to me every five minutes," he ordered. He counted the number of troops remaining to him. Only thirty-seven.

"Wow!" Brig cried hoarsely. "Sharla just threw a code that disabled a huge missile before it even got close to us."

Corgan had no time to worry about Sharla, because

he had to maneuver his troops into a ditch. He did it just before another missile streamed over their heads and exploded harmlessly in midair.

"Wow!" Brig cried again. "That was Sharla's doing, too. Wait a minute—she's telling me something. She says—she's broken all the artillery codes. She'll call it out each time they lob something at us so we can cover our troops."

"I've got a better idea. I'll move them between bursts." Again he regrouped his soldiers, this time into parties of three each.

"Now!" Brig called.

Corgan kept his troops down until the artillery passed, then moved a group quickly up the hill.

"Now!" He moved another group.

Each time Brig called out that a shell was coming, Corgan moved his soldiers to cover. Then, in the seconds between shellings, he moved them out, one small party after another.

"How much time left?" Brig asked.

"Fourteen minutes seven and . . . bomb!"

Surprised, Corgan realized he'd already moved all his soldiers from the ditch, and he hadn't lost any for the past twelve minutes. "Score, Brig!" he demanded.

"Us thirty-two; Eurasia thirty-seven; Pacific eighteen."

"Distance to target?"

"We're strung out between twelve and twenty-nine meters to target. Consolidate them, Corgan. Uh-oh, Sharla says they figured out she hacked their artillery codes. They've changed crypto keys now. Look out!"

The next bomb found its mark. Corgan lost five soldiers. In another minute one more soldier stepped on a land mine. He was down to twenty-six.

"Sharla's coding to lay down a smoke screen," Brig reported. "Move! Move! Move!"

Under cover of smoke Corgan pulled his twenty-six remaining soldiers into four tight groups, inching them closer to the target area at the top of the hill. He could feel the seconds ticking away; his body vibrated with each fraction of time. Another bomb exploded—two more troops dead. A heat-seeking missile blew up out of range; Sharla had evidently altered its trajectory.

One more minute.

"You're close to target," Brig rasped. "The periphery will be heavily mined. Send the troops in one at a time until you find a safe passage. As soon as one of them gets inside safely, let the others follow the exact same path."

"Okay." He moved one soldier forward. A mine blew her into shreds.

"Use that path!" Brig screamed. "Move your troops one at a time over her body. The mine is already detonated, so that path is safe."

It worked. As the seconds counted down, Corgan propelled his troops one at a time onto the hilltop. At exactly five P.M. he screamed, "Time!"

It was over. Twenty-three Western Hemisphere Federation soldiers were inside the designated area. Twenty-three Eurasian soldiers were also in the area, along with thirteen Pacific troops.

Mendor appeared, to announce, "It's a tie," just as Corgan screamed, "Default!"

The silence was sudden and astonishing, even though Corgan's ears still rang from the explosions.

"No tie!" he cried. "No tie." He could barely speak the words. His lips were cracked dry, his throat swollen almost shut, his tongue raw from grinding his teeth. "Eurasia ran seven hundredths of a second overtime getting their twenty-third soldier across the line. They lose! We win!"

Again silence, but only for eight seconds. Then the War Room erupted in brilliant colors; Corgan could feel the exhilaration. Feel the cheers of triumph. He dragged himself to his feet, grabbed his head with his blistered hands to clear his thoughts, and forced himself back to reality. He was still inside his Box. Everything that had happened had taken place in a world of virtual images while he sat imprisoned in his Box. "Sharla!" he cried.

"Corgan, get back here!" Mendor the jubilant Mother/Father cried. "You're the hero. This is your moment."

He lurched to the wall. "Open the door, Mendor," he rasped, "or I'll shred it into splinters. *I want out!*"

There was no resistance. He fell into the passageway, reeling, staggering from one side to the other of the stainless-steel tunnel until he saw her. She had Brig by the hand. Both of them looked terrible—drained, pale, sweat-stained, tear-stained. With tormented cries the three warriors fell into one another's arms and sobbed.

No one came after them. No one bothered them as they hugged each other and wept, both from the horror of what they'd been through and the joy that they'd won the War.

Sharla rubbed tears from Corgan's face and kissed him on the mouth. "Me too," Brig whimpered. "Me too, Sharla."

She picked him up and kissed his gaunt cheek. The weary Mutant smiled and patted her. Through cracked and swollen lips, he said, "Watch me now! See if I turn into a prince."

THIRTEEN

The walls of the stainless-steel tunnel pulsed with color as the three of them walked side by side. Color and light.

They'd been given three days to recover from the devastating effects of the War, but Corgan knew he'd never really recover. Every night he woke shaking from terrible dreams—of blood and viscera and shrieks of fear and torn men and women with wide, shocked eyes. His hands still trembled when he ate his excellent meals; they were giving him real eggs now, and as much steak as he could hold. For the first time he'd tasted actual bananas, and if he'd had the stomach for anything, he probably would have liked them. But even the real food soured his mouth.

Nothing much mattered, not even this day, when they

were to be honored at some kind or other of award presentation. He hoped the Supreme Council would announce when he and Sharla and Brig could leave for the Isles of Hiva.

They'd been perfectly groomed for the occasion. Their hair had been trimmed, and not just for reasons of sanitation, but to make them look good. All three of them wore matching LiteSuits in shimmering rainbow hues. If Corgan hadn't still been emotionally wasted, he might have felt somewhat happy.

"Could you slow down a little?" Brig asked hoarsely. Brig's skin had a gray pallor, his eyelids were swollen, and his big head shook with a slight tremor. Right after he said that, he stumbled and would have fallen if Corgan hadn't caught him.

"Look, I'm going to carry you till we get to the door, and then you can walk through it when we make our so-called triumphant entrance," Corgan told him.

"Hail! The conquering heroes staggereth in," Brig said. "I just hope it doesn't last too long. I'd like to sleep for about a month."

The wall parted into two doors that rolled back soundlessly. "Enter, please," they heard, and when they moved inside, they saw that they were walking on a red carpet. It extended all the way to the far wall of the room, where the Council members sat on an elevated dais, waiting.

The Council Room was much bigger than it had looked from the outside that night Sharla made the wall transparent. There were no walls or flat ceiling, just a dome covered with a seamless virtual image of wildly cheering people, tens of thousands of them.

"Are they real?" Corgan asked.

Mendor appeared, both male and female. In the tight, confined space of Corgan's Box, Mendor had always loomed large, wrapping around Corgan until he sometimes felt smothered. Here, in this much bigger room, Mendor seemed less real, just one more image among thousands projected on the wall.

"Your fans," he/she said, gesturing around the dome. "Yes, they're real people. Their images are being transmitted here from all the domed cities in the Western Hemisphere Federation. You're their champions."

The Supreme Council members were also real, and not at all electronic: They were bone-and-flesh, living, breathing bodies, warts and whiskers and thinning hair and bad posture and all. Corgan suspected, though, that to the masses of people cheering out there under their domes in their own enclosed cities, wherever they were, the Council members showed only Their usual faceless masks.

"Come forward," They said. One of the Councilwomen stepped out to meet them. In a surprisingly pleasant voice, she said, "Corgan, Sharla, and Brig. You won the War, which means the Western Hemisphere Federation will now take possession of the Isles of Hiva."

At the mention of the Isles, Corgan's fingers twitched.

"But there's more to it than that," the woman continued. "You no doubt wondered why the War was fought so realistically. After all, we could have achieved the same results with a mathematical contest, or a simple athletic event, since the battlefield troops were only virtual images, after all."

Corgan nodded. Sharla didn't.

"The three of you were unaware of it, but every human being in the entire world watched the War being enacted. In all three confederations, every citizen was allowed a work-free day to follow, visually, the progress of the War."

That was a surprise to Corgan.

"It was a reminder," the Council member said, "of what happened when wars used to be fought the old way. It was meant to show why humans can no longer solve disputes by killing one another." Her voice increased in volume, amplified by whatever electronic equipment was broadcasting it. "You three sacrificed yourselves"—she paused dramatically—"so that thousands of others will be spared. With the world so sparsely populated now, peace is the only way to achieve survival."

The nearly bald man stood up and began to speak. "Not only are the citizens of the Western Hemisphere grateful to you, but everyone, everywhere in the three confederations is grateful. You young people"—he swept his arms in a wide gesture that included the three of them—"may have lost your innocence, but humanity has once again been convinced of the futility of war."

Do I believe that? Corgan wondered. Or are they just empty words to impress those crowds on the wall?

Now the man with the bad slouch took over. "You, Corgan, the team leader, have won your reward," he said. "You will live on the Isles of Hiva for as long as you want."

"Me?" Corgan asked. "All of us! You mean all of us."

Sharla took his hand. "Let Them finish!"

"But he said—"

"We'll talk later!"

"Talk? About what!"

"Please, Corgan," she whispered. "Shut up till it's over."

Corgan didn't care about the gold medal. He didn't pay attention to the speeches, or to the gift of a sixty-year-old pair of blue jeans that one of the Council members told him was what people wore on the Isles of Hiva before they became uninhabitable. When the Council member held them up, the *oohs* and *ahhs* from the electronic spectators nearly stopped the ceremony. He didn't know why everyone made such a fuss—as if the jeans were some premium bonus or something. To him, they looked pretty faded.

Sharla got a dress of a fabric They called cotton. She seemed pleased, but it probably wouldn't last a tenth as long as a LiteSuit, Corgan thought.

Brig, tired little Brig, got candy. They told him it was real candy made from real sugar—worth as much as the gold medal They'd hung around his neck. Since Brig was so short, the medal hung down a lot lower on him than Corgan's or Sharla's did on them.

Brig held the candy—a sticky red-and-white-striped rod thirty centimeters high—then licked his fingers. *"Mmmmm,"* he said, his eyes brightening. He broke off a piece of it for Sharla, but Corgan refused any.

Let's get this over with, Corgan said inside his mind. Inside his chest, a heavy weight kept growing as each minute passed. He needed to find out what that Councilman had meant when he mentioned Hiva.

One at a time, the Supreme Council came up to shake the

team's hands; Brig was standing on a chair between Sharla and Corgan. The Council members kept saying congratulatory things, and Brig and Sharla answered nicely with all the right phrases, but Corgan just mumbled, "Thank you," over and over.

After the Council retreated to hide once again behind their electronic disguises, ordinary people from the city were allowed into the room. They streamed past Sharla and Brig and Corgan, gushing about how the three of them were heroes and were a real inspiration to young children and grown-ups, too. Why was the Council letting those people into the chambers? Didn't anyone worry about contamination anymore? It seemed to go on and on, people Corgan had never seen before filing past to look at him like he was some kind of curiosity. Some even reached out to touch him—his LiteSuit, his arm—all the while they were mouthing words of praise Corgan didn't listen to. Why wouldn't they just go away?

Then he recognized Jobe.

"Hey, you guys," Jobe cried. "You did really great!"

"Thanks, Jobe," Sharla answered.

"I just got a copy of the game stats," Jobe said, waving a sheaf of papers. "You know, you didn't make a single error. Not one infraction of the rules, not even by accident."

Corgan whipped around to glance at Sharla. That was the first confirmation he'd heard that she hadn't cheated. She raised her eyebrows and smiled wryly, as if to tell him: So it's official. To Jobe she said, "What can we say? We're just good, that's all."

"Well, hey, I want to thank you all," Jobe went on. "I

picked up a bundle on that game. My buddies here—see these guys behind me? I told them I'd bring them here to meet you." Two burly men shuffled and grinned, peering around Jobe to get a good look at the team.

Jobe's words pierced through Corgan's indifference, although he wasn't sure what they meant.

"Anyway," Jobe went on, "before you guys played the War, these here guys said, 'No team can play eight whole hours without any errors,' and I told them, 'Hey, I know Sharla and Corgan and Brig. I've met them personally. I know they can do it.' So I told my buddies, 'If you don't think so, put your money where your mouth is.' And they did, and I won big!"

"Wait a minute." Now Corgan was staring intently at him. "You mean you bet on the War?"

"Sure. Everybody did—well, maybe not everybody—"

"You bet on the War!" Never in his life had Corgan felt such a surge of rage. It swept up from his chest to throb in his ears. He could taste it in his mouth. *"You bet on the War?"*

"Yeah, well—it was a game, wasn't it?"

Corgan stormed, "All those people *died* so you could *bet*?"

"People! They were nothing but—"

Corgan's fists slashed out before Jobe could say any more.

"Corgan!" Sharla screamed.

He punched Jobe's face till blood spurted from the man's lips, then pounded his soft gut until Jobe's buddies grabbed Corgan and pinned his arms behind him.

Brig shouted, "Take your friends and get out of here, Jobe. And lock the doors behind you!"

"What's the disturbance?" Mendor the Father Figure demanded, his image looming large on the wall behind them. Several members of the Council crowded forward, asking, "What is it? Is something wrong?"

"It's nothing. Would you kindly have the room cleared now?" Brig asked Them. "We'd appreciate it."

As soon as Corgan stopped struggling, the two men let him loose—releasing his arms slowly, but standing poised to grab him if he started swinging again. Corgan stayed passive, head lowered, fists clenched.

Backing up awkwardly, the men led away the bleeding Jobe, who held a cloth against his lips. One of his friends muttered, "You know these athletes. They get real stressed out after a big game. It's normal."

"But he *won*!" Jobe protested. "So why'd he go all freaky? It was only a game—not like a real war or anything. . . ."

Hesitantly, the Councilwoman with the pleasant voice said, "Are you all right now, Corgan? Would you like to stay here with your teammates for a while? You three may stay as long as you wish."

"Alone?" Sharla asked.

"Certainly. If you wish."

Morphed once again between male and female, Mendor asked, "Do you want me to leave, too, Corgan?"

"Yes I do."

Reluctantly, Mendor disappeared, and then they *were* alone. Corgan rubbed his shoulder, which throbbed with pain from being twisted by Jobe's buddies.

"Does it hurt?" Sharla asked. "Jobe and his friends—they just don't understand, Corgan. How the War was the most important part of our whole lives for so long—"

"Forget that!" he barked. "There's something a lot more important going on. I want to know what."

"You mean about the betting?" Brig asked.

"Dammit, you know what I mean! About the Isles of Hiva."

Sharla and Brig glanced at each other, questioning which of them would answer first. "I'm sorry it turned out like this," Sharla said. "We should have talked yesterday, or the day before, but Brig was exhausted—"

"So talk now!"

Brig began. "It was strategy. Your game was off. The Council called Sharla and me to a meeting. They asked if we could suggest some reward for you that might make you play better."

Taking over, Sharla said, "They told us if we could figure out an incentive that would improve your game, then we could name any reward we wanted for ourselves, too."

Anguished, Corgan cried, "Hiva was supposed to be for all three of us!"

"There are bigger things, Corgan," Brig said. "When They asked me what my greatest wish would be, I took a chance and said, 'If You'll let the Mutants live, I know I could work with them. I can make their lives better.'"

"That's it? That's what you asked for?"

Brig was obviously weary. "Look at me, Corgan. Do I look like I could run along a beach or go plunging into the ocean at Hiva? I don't want to spend what's left of my life lying under a tree on the sand watching *you*. Anyway, to sum it all up, They said yes. They'll let the Mutants live."

Corgan didn't know how to answer. It was almost over-whelming, that weak little Brig had been able to pull off something that big.

"It'll be the toughest strategy I'll ever have to devise, trying to make the Mutants useful. But at least I know I can improve their lives. And they'll *have* lives now. They won't be put to sleep like unwanted kittens." Brig lowered himself and stretched out on two folding chairs, saying, "Sorry, boys and girls, I really need a nap. Wake me when this is all over."

Taking the cotton dress They'd given her, Sharla spread it over Brig to keep him warm. Then, with her finger to her lips, she gestured for Corgan to follow her to the far end of the room.

"I'm seriously worried about Brig," she told Corgan. "He was never strong to begin with, and the War really wasted him." She sat on the floor, tucking her feet beneath her, and gestured for Corgan to sit beside her. But he wouldn't.

Crouched above her, wretched and disillusioned, Corgan cried, "I'm the one who feels wasted! I can't believe how you tricked me. I trusted you."

"Maybe you shouldn't have trusted me. I told you I didn't care anything about honor."

With his back against the wall, he stared down at her. "I never know what to believe about you. At least when I trusted you not to cheat, you didn't. The stats proved that."

After a moment she answered, "Everyone was worried

about your slump, Corgan. They were trying to motivate you."

"They must have thought I was pretty stupid to be jerked around like that."

"Not stupid. Just innocent." She reached up, took his hand, and pulled him, resisting, down beside her. "Think about it, Corgan—would you have tried so hard to win Hiva if you'd known I wouldn't live there? That's why They didn't tell you."

He shook his head. "So it was NNTK all over again."

"No. 'No Need To Know' is a lot different from 'Don't let him find out.' It was all part of the conspiracy of silence— don't ask, don't tell, just win the War."

Straightening his back, he said, "Yeah, well, you can just think about *this*! All your lies and scheming were for nothing. I came out of the slump, and I did it by myself."

Again she was silent. Then, "You're right. How did you do it?"

He gave a bitter, ironic laugh. "I was *motivated* because I didn't want you to have to cheat. But even more important . . ."

"What?"

"It was . . ." His voice broke. "What you said. When you told me you believe in me."

"Oh, Corgan!" She leaned forward to lay her head against his shoulder, and he didn't pull away.

Once again her presence, the scent of her, the feel of her body against his, of her hair against his skin, made his heart pound in spite of his damaged illusions. "It was easier when I lived inside a Box," he said. "Being told what to do, what to think. Real life is too messy. People are too complicated. The real world isn't worth all the trouble."

"Give it a chance," she said.

He leaned his head back against the wall and watched the room's muted colors pulse in ever-changing, fluid shapes. Beautiful reflections, and that's all they were. Not reality. "One thing's sure," he told her. "I could never stand to go back inside a Box. Not anymore. Now I'm not sure where I belong."

"On Hiva," she answered.

That made the ache come back again. "So what did you request for your reward?" he asked.

She stirred against his arm and sat up to face him. "An automated DNA sequencing machine. There's a really powerful one in a place called Nebraska, just sitting there useless because it's full of contamination."

"That means They can't get it for you, right?" In the room's indirect, pulsing luminescence, her golden hair shimmered with highlights, the way it had the first day he ever saw her.

"They promised They would. They'll send out a squad of robots to get the sequencer, decontaminate it, and find some kind of passable roads to transport it here."

"Sounds pretty major," he said.

"It'll take at least six months, They told me. But it's worth it, Corgan—it's an incredible machine. It can detect mutations at the two-cell level, before the cells even start to divide."

He asked, "Does that mean there won't be any more Mutants?"

"There'll always be some born naturally, outside the lab. Brig will have plenty of work to do. Anyway, even using the sequencer to analyze DNA, I'll need years to discover anything valuable." She smiled. "I can't wait to start. Decoding human DNA is the ultimate goal. At least for me it is." She lowered her eyes and said, "I decided I'd do anything to get it. Even lie to you, Corgan. I'm sorry."

As she moved closer to him, he winced from the pain in his twisted shoulder. "Does it still hurt that much?" Sharla asked him. "Let me rub it for you."

He leaned forward to let her get behind him and massage his shoulder. Unable to see her face, Corgan asked, "So! What are you planning to do for the six months it takes to get your machine here?"

Her strong fingers kneaded his muscles, but they stopped. Seven and nineteen hundredths seconds passed before she answered, "Well, I thought I'd . . . go with you to the Isles of Hiva. If you want me to. Do you?"

Forgetting his pain, Corgan squeezed his eyes shut. He said, "Yes."

FOURTEEN

Corgan was bloody up to his elbows. His strong hands groped inside the warm body, grasping, tugging, as the cow bellowed her outrage and pain.

"I have to twist it," he told Sharla. "I don't want to hurt it—wait! Wait. I feel the head. It's coming out now. Stand back." In a rush of fluid the calf fell into his arms.

Corgan laughed out loud as he stood the calf on its wobbly legs and pulled off what was left of the placenta. "She's alive. She's beautiful!" Pointing to his own blood-soaked blue jeans and manure-caked boots, he said, "And I'm filthy. But who cares?"

After he rubbed the calf with a rough towel, its brown and white hair stood up in little whorls.

Sharla asked, "Do you need to let the lab team know right away that the calf has been born?"

"No hurry," he told her. "They can do the blood test later. I'm going to leave her with her mother for a while."

"Look at those big brown eyes," Sharla murmured. "Even if she isn't transgenic, even if she turns out to be just a plain ordinary cow, she's darling."

But it will be a lot better if she *is* transgenic, Corgan thought. With the arrival of each new calf, the genetics team kept hoping. So far they'd created just two calves that carried a special human gene resistant to the Ebola virus. Maybe this new baby would be the third.

A blood sample and a simple genetic test would confirm—or dash—the hopes of the team. If the calf was transgenic, it meant the team had succeeded in implant-ing the human gene into the fertilized ovum, and the cow would grow up to produce milk containing a human protein. Extracted from the milk, the protein from one cow could stop an Ebola outbreak in a whole domed city. Protein from two dozen transgenic cows would be able to cure an epidemic worldwide. And Ebola was just a starter. The genetics researchers—the people who shared a laboratory on the northern end of the island—had already recombined genes to counteract every major plague virus. If their work eventually succeeded, Earth could become habitable again. But so far, only two out of sixty-one new-born calves had turned out to be transgenic.

"As long as you don't have to report the calf's birth right away," Sharla said, "let's go down to the beach. You really ought to wash all that . . . stuff . . . off you."

"What, you don't like mud, and blood, and—" Corgan grinned at her, bent his knee, and pointed to the heel of his boot. "This nice 'stuff' on my boots? Maybe you don't know the right word for it. Let me improve your vocabulary, Sharla. This 'stuff,' this cow by-product, is called—"

Her laughter rang out, that wonderful, rich, delicious laugh that Corgan loved. "Never mind. I know what it's called. Just leave the boots here."

Both of them ran barefoot from the top of the hill, where the barn stood, all the way to the beach. Corgan could easily have outraced Sharla because he was the faster runner, but he liked to stay behind her where he could watch her free, graceful movements.

Six months' worth of bleaching from the tropical sun, six months of salt spray from the ocean, six months' wear and tear from sand, and Sharla's cotton dress had become tattered. She insisted on wearing it that day even though she'd grown taller and the dress had shrunk and torn at the hem.

Corgan's blue jeans had suffered almost as much. They were torn, faded, frayed, and stained from the work he'd been doing. Since he hadn't been given a shirt to go with the jeans, he went bare-chested most of the time. His skin had turned far darker from the sun than Sharla's, because Corgan was brunette, something he'd never even thought about when he lived inside the Box where there was no real sun.

They raced into the surf and splashed each other until Corgan had completely cleaned himself of the cow's birth matter and the spatters of manure on the legs of his jeans.

Then they swam together, floating where the surf carried them.

He pulled her to her feet so he could always remember her the way she was now, as they stood there in the shallow water, the waves lapping their ankles. Sharla looked golden. Sun had streaked her hair countless different shades of gold, some of them exactly matching her skin.

Waves crashed around them, pushing them forward and then pulling them back when the water returned to its bed in the sea. This was the real roar of the real ocean they were hearing, so much more powerful than artificial noises filtered through electronic signals and aerogel.

Sharla's dress clung to her. When she shivered, Corgan took her hand and led her out of the surf.

"Look," she said, pointing at the sand.

They knelt to examine a jellyfish washed up by the waves. It lay stranded on the sand, brown, shiny, and gelatinous, like an overturned bowl with a dark fringe around the edges.

"You can see inside it," Corgan exclaimed, pointing to narrow coils of viscera, and to the thin, delicate strands of tissue that showed beneath the transparent surface membrane.

"Primitive and perfect," Sharla announced. "We've evolved, and they've stayed the same."

"Let's figure out a way to move it so we can toss it back into the ocean. It'll die here in the sun."

"No, Corgan," she said, pulling on his arm. "Don't interfere with nature. The waves washed it up, so—"

His bark of laughter was incredulous. "You don't want

me to interfere with nature? And *you're* going back to slice up DNA and engineer humans! While *I* stay here, birthing genetically altered calves that might save what's left of humanity."

Sinking down, she patted the sand for him to sit beside her. "We only have a little while before I have to leave. Let's not waste it talking shop. No ideas deeper than . . . than the foam on the surf."

Corgan sprawled on the beach and looked out at the waves. He loved the way they rolled up and melted the sand from beneath his bare feet. Taking Sharla's hand, he pressed it into the damp surface. The imprint of her palm and fingers stayed just out of reach of the foam-flecked water. Then he imprinted his own hand, with the indentations of his fingers meshing into hers.

"I'll miss you," she said.

"Your things are already packed, and the Harrier jet won't take off for about an hour," he told her. "You don't have to leave just yet." He remembered his own flight in the Harrier jet when the panels of the domed city had opened to allow the aircraft to rise, straight up, out of the only place he'd ever known till that time. At six thousand meters' altitude the aircraft had turned southwest. It was then that Corgan saw, for the first time, snow-covered mountain peaks, and actual trees, and lakes that reflected sunlight and made his breath catch with their beauty.

Sharla said, "You never even mention minutes anymore, Corgan, let alone fractions of seconds."

"Why should I? I work with cattle now. All that matters to animals is seasons, not seconds." Digging another imprint in the sand with his fingers, he said, "There's something else different about me, too. Look."

He held up his hands. They were rough and splintered, with the fingernails ragged and none too clean. "I remember," he said, "at the celebration, when I hit Jobe—all I could think of was that I didn't have to worry about my hands anymore. I could split my knuckles on his face, and no one would care."

Sharla smiled. "Jobe cared! The poor guy—he never knew what he did wrong."

After a while they stood up to walk back toward the Western Hemisphere Biotechnology Laboratory, keeping close, holding hands. The sun warmed them. He ached because he knew she was leaving him. She'd stayed with him nearly every minute for six months, cheering him when he delivered a calf, helping him learn to be comfortable with the genetic scientists in the laboratory. Sometimes he needed to get away, to go off by himself, but he was getting better at socializing, Sharla told him. Getting used to people.

"They like you," she said. "They love telling you about their work because you listen and you learn so fast."

"It's interesting stuff," he'd answered. "It's like finally understanding how and why I got started in a test tube. Me and the calves—we're mutations with a purpose."

Since both Corgan and Sharla had been born in the laboratory on the same day, they'd celebrated their fifteenth birthdays together, running on the beach. They'd played a real game of Go-ball with real racquets and a real ball, using a line drawn in the sand for their net.

Now, on her last day on the Isles of Hiva, they approached the laboratory. The roof of the narrow, single-story building had been thatched with palm fronds in the same way the natives had thatched their huts so long ago, or so he'd been told.

"Have you heard any news about Brig?" Corgan asked.

"He's in bad shape. He can't walk at all now, but he keeps working on his programs for the Mutants. I'll see him tomorrow."

"Tell him I said . . ." What message could he send to Brig? Nothing seemed adequate.

"I'll give him your love," Sharla promised. "Do you want to wait here? I'll just be a minute inside the building. I need to change into my LiteSuit and pick up my bag for the flight."

"I'll wait," he told her. The Harrier jet would leave in a few minutes from the concrete launch pad two hundred meters away. Corgan could hear the jet engines warming up. To find out if he could still do it, he tried to count the revolutions-per-second of the engines just by listening to them throb, but his ability to calculate time had fallen off. He was no longer split-second accurate.

When Sharla came out of the building, they walked toward the launch pad. "I almost hate to leave Hiva. It's so beautiful here," she murmured. "Everything is! I understand why Gauguin wanted to paint it all."

"Who's Gauguin?" he asked, raising his voice when they approached the aircraft.

"A French artist who came here two hundred years ago. These islands were called the Marquesas then. He painted the people and the ocean and these very same palm trees, or at least the ancestors of these trees."

"Ancestors," he mused. "Everything has them, one way or another. Trees, humans, cows—"

"That reminds me." Speaking loudly now, she turned toward him. "Listen, Corgan, when you're putting together your statistical data on the transgenic cattle, be careful."

"Careful? Why?"

In one hand, Sharla carried the small bag that held her clothes; in the other hand, a pink hibiscus blossom to remind her of Hiva. She backed slowly across the concrete pad, still facing Corgan. When he attempted to follow her, the pilot waved him away and shook his head, meaning Corgan couldn't come any closer.

"Don't always believe statistics," Sharla shouted. "Statistics can be tweaked to prove almost anything. Genetic stats, population stats, War-game stats!"

He frowned, trying to understand the words he had trouble hearing over the engine roar. "Wait a minute! What are you—Sharla?"

The engines revved to a higher pitch. Sharla climbed a small ladder to reach the open hatch of the cockpit, then turned and waved.

At the top of his voice Corgan cried out, "Sharla! The game stats! Did you—"

"NNTK, Corgan."

"Sharla!" Not caring about his own safety, Corgan ran toward the Harrier jet.

"'Bye, Corgan! Enjoy your Isles of Hiva that you love so much! I'll be back someday." She slid into the seat behind the pilot just before the hatch closed above her.

The aircraft rose vertically, lifting straight up into the perfect sky. Corgan ran after it until there was nothing left to see. Sharla was gone.

Alone, he stood on the empty beach.

The Clones

INTRODUCTION

By the year 2080, plague, disease, terrorism, and nuclear war had confined Earth's two million human survivors to a few domed cities, where they were governed by the Western Hemisphere Federation, the Eurasian Alliance, or the Pan-Pacific Coalition. When it was discovered that a small group of islands in the Pacific had become livable again, the three federations decided to wage a bloodless virtual war, with the winner to take possession of the Isles of Hiva.

All his life Corgan, then fourteen, had trained to be the champion of the Western Hemisphere Federation. Genetically engineered for quick reflexes, superior physical condition, and a remarkable time-splitting ability, he'd been raised in isolation inside a virtual-reality Box. Everything Corgan saw, smelled, touched, or heard reached him through electronically transmitted signals.

Only three weeks before the start of the War, Corgan met—virtually—his two teammates: Brig, a ten-year-old Mutant who was a superb strategist, and Sharla, who was the same age as Corgan. It was Sharla, with her brilliant ability to break codes, who brought him his first real human contact. She also taught him to mistrust the Supreme Council, whose orders he'd always obeyed.

Disillusioned, Corgan began to lose his perfect sense of timing. After the Supreme Council promised that he could live on the Isles of Hiva if only he would win the Virtual War, Corgan's skills improved. But during the grueling, gruesome, realistic enactment of the daylong War, Corgan's team barely managed to win, and Brig suffered real damage to his already weak body.

Corgan got the reward he wanted: to live on the Isles of Hiva. Even better, Sharla joined him there for the first six months. But just before she left to return to her laboratory in the domed city, Sharla hinted that she might have cheated to win the Virtual War.

It is now 2081. . . .

ONE

The sky was blue. A real sky, a real color, with real clouds, not a collection of pixels in a virtual-reality Box. Every once in a while, when he had a brief moment to himself, Corgan would let this real world seep into his senses, reminding him how much better even one minute of reality felt compared with the fourteen years of virtuality he'd experienced inside his Box.

He bent down to pick up a rock, a hardened piece of the lava that a couple million years earlier had spewed out of the ocean to create the Isles of Hiva. The rock filled his cupped hand with a satisfying weight. He ran his thumb across its porous surface and then, taking aim, hurled it toward the top of a tall coconut palm, smiling when he heard the *thwack* of rock hitting nut. The coconut he'd chosen fell neatly into the sand at his feet.

For no particular reason Corgan calculated the speed of his throw and the arc of its trajectory. At one time he'd been able to split microseconds in his mind, but not anymore. Glancing again at the treetop, mentally computing its height to be 11.47 meters, he happened to notice a small black dot moving in the sky above the palm fronds.

Too high for a seagull, it might be a frigatebird, but frigatebirds didn't fly that fast. As the object grew larger he heard the drone of an airplane. The Harrier jet! But the lab at Nuku Hiva wasn't scheduled to receive a flight for a couple more weeks, so why would the Harrier be coming now? Corgan ran toward the landing strip and reached it just as the jet dropped vertically onto the concrete pad.

After the engines slowed and quieted, the hatch opened, allowing the passenger seated behind the pilot to climb out. A helmet and a blue LiteSuit hid the passenger's identity until gloved hands reached up to remove the headgear, releasing a cascade of golden hair. Sharla!

Corgan's heart beat loudly enough that he could calculate its rhythm without even trying. Four months earlier he and Sharla had said good-bye, not long after celebrating their fifteenth birthdays together. Now here she was again, for whatever reason—it didn't matter. She'd come back to Nuku Hiva; that was enough.

He reached her and threw his arms around her, but she returned only a one-armed hug because her right hand clutched a flight bag. "Wait!" she told him as she carefully set the bag onto the tarmac. "Make sure you don't step on it," she said, laughing a little, and then both her arms flew around him, and she kissed him until he grew dizzy.

"Where can we go to talk?" she whispered. "Privately, I mean."

"Uh . . . you remember the barn where I work with the transgenic cattle?"

"It's only been four months—of course I remember. I'll meet you there. Take this bag, handle it very carefully, and don't look inside until I get there. I have to check in at the lab first. As soon as I can get away, I'll come to the barn."

Waiting beside the Harrier jet, Pilot called out, "Sharla, hurry," and then both of them were gone. Corgan stood there, bewildered, growing even more perplexed when he thought he saw the bag move slightly, not more than a few millimeters, but . . . no, he must have imagined it.

When he picked it up, it was heavier than he'd expected. Trudging up the hill toward the barn, he started to swing the bag, then remembered Sharla telling him to handle it carefully.

The barn smelled of hay and manure, which Corgan didn't mind. During the fourteen years he'd spent inside his virtual-reality Box, he'd never smelled anything the least bit unpleasant. Here on Nuku Hiva this pungent, earthy odor in the barnyard was just one of many signals that he had his freedom now.

He set the bag on a shelf in the back room where he stayed when he waited for the cows to give birth. The herd numbered forty-seven now; no bulls, all cows, and twenty-eight of them were pregnant. Nuku Hiva was such a lush, green, overgrown island that a hundred times as many cattle could have grazed there without depleting the forage.

Since one of the cows was due to deliver any day now, Corgan went to check her. "Hey, Fourteen, how's it going?" he asked her. "Gonna give us what we want?" They were trying to create one perfect calf with a human clotting gene, another with a gene to help diabetics, and others that would produce disease-fighting compounds in their milk. Cow pregnancies lasted two hundred eighty-four days, a long time to wait to find out whether a genetic transfer had worked.

Fourteen answered with a loud moo. Corgan never named the cows; he'd been instructed not to treat them like pets or get attached to any of them. That rule wasn't hard to follow. Cows were not especially endearing.

He kept wandering out to the brow of the hill to search for Sharla. She had to be down there in the lab with the pilot and the two scientists—except for the barn, the lab was the only building standing on Nuku Hiva. Enough of his time-calculating ability remained to let him know that seventy-two minutes and fourteen and a half seconds had gone by since she'd left him at the landing strip.

At last he saw her coming, and he ran down the hill to meet her. "Race you to the barn," she said. Sharla—always competitive. The first time he met her she'd beaten him at Go-ball. Virtually.

She was panting a little when they reached the barn. Noticing that, Corgan felt satisfaction because his breathing hadn't sped up at all—he might have lost his mental time-splitting ability, but physically he was in superb condition. Although his heart might have been beating a little faster at the moment, that was because he wanted to kiss Sharla again. She pulled away, saying, "Later. Lots to talk about now. Did you open the flight bag?"

"No. You told me not to."

She smiled. "Still Corgan the obedient. Never does anything he's told not to do, no matter how curious he is."

Flushing, he asked her, "So, what's this all about? Should I open it now?"

"No. Let me give you all the news first."

Corgan glanced at the flight bag and again thought he saw a fleeting ripple of movement against one of its sides. Whatever was in there, whether mechanical or biological, seemed to be capable of motion.

"Come sit beside me," Sharla offered, curling herself on a loose pile of straw. "You'll need to sit down to handle what I'm going to tell you."

"Is it bad?" he asked.

"Part of it." She took a deep breath. "Brig died."

It wasn't a shock; they'd known it had to happen. Still, Corgan had hoped that somehow Brig might grow strong again. Brig, the whiny, brilliant, deformed, demanding, great-hearted Mutant who'd been the third member of their Virtual War team. Brig the strategist who'd helped win the War for the Western Hemisphere Federation. The War had taken such a toll on Brig's already weak body that it was only a matter of time before his meager strength gave out.

"The only thing that kept him going toward the end was his battle to keep the Mutant alive," Sharla said. "He won that battle. At least no Mutants were terminated while Brig still lived."

"And now?"

Turning to face Corgan, Sharla shifted on the straw. "It's such a long story. Really complicated."

"Start with why you're here," he prompted.

"Do you want the official reason or the real reason?"

"Both, I guess."

"Well, as you already know," she began, "I am the most incredible code breaker the world has ever known."

"And so humble, too," he muttered wryly, even though what she'd said was true. Just as Corgan had been genetically engineered to have fast reflexes and time-splitting ability, just as Brig had been artificially created as a superstrategist, Sharla had been bred to break codes. All three of them had come out of the same laboratory, genetically engineered in the same domed city.

"DNA coding is no mystery to me," Sharla continued. "I can anticipate every step, cellular and chemical, in the creation of humans—or animals. And a few months ago I figured out a way to hurry up gestation. So now your calves can develop and get born in just three months, instead of forty-plus weeks."

"That's incredible," Corgan breathed.

"Yeah, like I said, I'm incredible. Naturally, the Supreme Council ordered me to come here to show your scientists how it's done."

The two scientists on Nuku Hiva, a woman named Delphine and a man named Grimber, shared a badly underequipped laboratory during the day and shared a bed at night. Every day and well into the evening they bent over their lab tables, probing with thin pipettes to laboriously suck the nucleus out of cows' eggs, then replacing them with a human nucleus that contained a gene for whatever trait they were trying to replicate.

In the evening Corgan would help them. He could tell to the tenth of a second when a zygote had reached eight cells, the point at which the cells had to be separated so that each could be genetically altered, one at a time. When it was time for a blastocyst to be implanted, Corgan would select a cow from the free-ranging herd and lead it down to the laboratory. After implantation the cow would be penned in the enclosure outside the barn where Corgan stayed. Eighty percent of the implanted blastocysts failed to take. Of the ones that "took," at least half were lost to miscarriage. Of the calves born, only four of them so far had carried the desired traits, and two of those had died soon after birth. The work was tedious, the equipment meager, and the success rate low. Still, Delphine and Grimber struggled on.

"So, what did they say when you told them the news?" Corgan asked.

"What do you think? They were thrilled. At least Delphine was. You know Grimber—nothing ever makes him smile. But it will mean a lot more work for them, since the cows will have to be implanted three times as often. They want to teach you the techniques so you can help them."

That sounded good to Corgan. He was growing tired of being nothing more than a cow nursemaid. Only a year ago he'd been the champion of the Western Hemisphere Federation, the player who'd won the Virtual War—with help from Brig and Sharla. After the horrible War he'd wanted to hide forever in the Isles of Hiva, the prize the three federations had been fighting over, the only uncontaminated land left on Earth. He'd won the War, and as his reward he'd chosen to live on Nuku Hiva.

At first it was everything he'd dreamed of. Now—well, peace and tranquility were good, but he was getting a little bored. On Nuku Hiva the seasons hardly changed. The temperature stayed pretty much the same, and it rained so often that the island was perpetually green. Fruit fell from the trees into his waiting hands. He could swim in the surf, slide down roaring waterfalls, sleep on warm sand. And all the while, his skills kept eroding like the island's lava rock, ground down by rain and ocean waves.

"So that's why you came here, to teach Delphine and Grimber?" he asked.

"That's the official reason," Sharla answered. "There's a much, much bigger reason, but it's only for you and me."

That excited him because he thought she meant the bond between the two of them. She was the first girl, the first *human being*, he'd ever touched. For fourteen years he'd lived without any human contact, surrounded by electronic images that to him seemed real because he'd never experienced anything different. Then Sharla broke him free, unlocked the door to his Box, and showed him a world both better and worse than he'd ever imagined. He'd been afraid to touch her, afraid of contamination, but when she laughed at him and kissed him, he'd come shock-ingly alive, aware of blood pounding in his veins and the scent of warm breath against his skin. From that moment he'd loved her, and he thought she loved him, too, yet he was never entirely sure of her.

Now she was pointing to the flight bag. "Are you ready to see inside?" she asked.

"Sure. I guess so." He lifted it from the shelf, again surprised at the weight of it. "Where should I put it?"

She knelt and gestured for him to kneel facing her on the straw. "Put it between the two of us," she said. "Like a Christmas scene."

"A Christmas scene?" As usual, he hadn't a clue what she was talking about.

Sharla opened the zipper only an inch at a time, amusing herself by teasing him. When it was open all the way, Corgan bent down to peer in.

A doll? He saw pale pink flesh and then actual movement—this time it was not his imagination. A small hand lifted no more than thirty millimeters. Corgan pulled apart the sides of the flight bag, and there lay a human baby, sound asleep.

"Where'd you get it?" he sputtered. "Whose is it?"

Sharla laughed. "For now, he's yours."

He stared at the baby; it smiled in its sleep. Corgan didn't know anything about babies, but this one didn't look like a newborn. It was pretty big, and it had tufts of bright red hair. "You mean it's been asleep in this flight bag all along?"

"Don't call him an it. He's a he. He's been asleep ever since we left the domed city. I drugged him."

"*Drugged* him! That's terrible! How could you do that to a baby?"

"I had to," she explained. "Nobody knows he exists, so no one can know that I brought him here. Since I needed to smuggle him out, I had to make sure he wouldn't wake up." Indignantly she asked, "Do you think I'd do anything that would put him in danger? Trust me—I'd never hurt him. He's my own creation."

"He's . . . he's yours?" Corgan stammered. "Your own baby?"

She laughed without inhibition, the laugh that always made him feel off balance because half the time he couldn't tell what was so funny. "Oh, Corgan, as if I could have given birth since the last time I saw you!" Then the laughter faded and she said, "But I guess in a way he *is* mine. He's Brig."

"He's Brig's?" This kept getting crazier; it was making no sense at all. Brig had been only ten years old when he died. There was no way he could have fathered a baby.

"I didn't say he's Brig's. I said he's *Brig*! Right before Brig died, I took tissue from his brain—with his blessings. The baby lying there is a clone. Of our dear, departed Brig. And now"—Sharla slid her hands beneath the sleeping baby and held him up toward Corgan—"he's yours."

T W O

Just then it started to rain—it rained a lot on Nuku Hiva—
and the roof of the barn leaked.

"Take him!" Sharla ordered. "Get him into a dry
spot."

Corgan scuttled backward on his knees like a sand crab,
then leaped to his feet and backed away even more. There
was no way he was going to touch that baby.

"Corgan!" Sharla shouted. "What's the matter with
you? It's just a baby! Does he have to moo before you'll
handle him?"

"Okay, Sharla," he answered, "you said there was an
official story and a real story. What you just told me sure
can't be the real story, because it's too fantastic for anyone

to believe. So how about giving me the truth now?"

Sighing with exasperation, Sharla scooped up the baby and asked, "Don't you have a dry area in here?"

He led her to the bunk where he'd spent many a night alone, waiting for a cow to give birth. They sat with the baby between them.

"What time is it, Corgan? I need the exact time so I'll know when Brig's drug will wear off."

"Quit calling him *Brig*! This is not Brig. This baby looks perfect—he's no Mutant. If you'd cloned Brig, the clone would be a Mutant, too, wouldn't . . . ?" The last thought slowed to a stop in Corgan's throat because he didn't know if it was true.

"Just tell me what time it is!" Sharla snapped.

"Nineteen hours, forty-eight minutes, seventeen seconds, and—"

"I can do without the seconds," she told him, still sounding testy. "Okay, he should be waking up in the next half hour, so I'll tell you everything real fast because we have to work together and we don't have much time. I'll be leaving here tomorrow."

"Tomorrow!" He felt as if he'd been punched. No matter how irritating she could be, he wanted her to stay. He never got enough of her, not even during the six months she'd spent on the island after the War.

"So here's the story," she said. "I'll give it to you fact after fact. Fact one: The Eurasian Alliance is challenging our scores on the Virtual War."

"You mean they think we cheated?" Or *you* cheated, Sharla, he said to himself. He'd suspected that, but he had no way of knowing for sure. And to tell the truth, he didn't *want* to know.

"Don't be silly. Do you think I'd have been careless enough to leave any traces, even if I'd . . . ?" She didn't finish, but her eyes showed just a hint of amusement, plus total self-assurance. Sharla was good, and nobody knew it better than she did. "No, they believe there might have been a minor miscalculation in the scoring—a mechanical error, no one's fault. They say if we can't confirm that our win was legitimate, they want to fight the War all over again."

"NO!" Corgan yelled it so loud that the baby jerked convulsively, although he didn't wake up.

"Don't worry, if we do have to fight it again, you won't be in it."

"I won't?" That calmed him for a minute, but then he began to wonder aloud, "Why not? Who would take my place?"

"There's a thirteen-year-old girl in the Western Hemisphere's domed city in Florida. They say she's even faster than you were, Corgan."

He stood up so quickly he bumped his head on the slanted ceiling. Sharla laughed and said, "So much for your great reflexes."

"A thirteen-year-old *girl*?" He would have hated to fight another Virtual War, but to be replaced by a *girl*! And one so much younger!

"Yes. She's supposed to be a real marvel. I've only met her virtually, and we haven't yet practiced together, because we're waiting for Brig-A to get old enough to be the strategist."

Corgan's head was reeling, and not just from the bump. Sharla was talking about this baby, wasn't she? It would take ten years for him to be old enough to fight another Virtual War . . . and why was she calling him Brig-A? "What do you mean, 'Brig-A'?" he asked her.

"Get ready for fact number two," Sharla answered, gently touching the baby's cheek. "This baby in front of you happens to be Brig-C. Brig-A is back in the domed city." She glanced up at Corgan, saw how agitated he was, and relented enough to tell it to him straight. "The Supreme Council ordered me to make one perfect clone of Brig. But because the technique is so unreliable, they gave me the go-ahead to create four clones, hoping I'd produce at least one good one. Then They told me that the others would have to be . . . eradicated."

She grimaced at the word but went on: "I agreed to it, Corgan, because I didn't know if I could do it at all. My DNA sequencing machine is so outdated . . . but . . ." She looked down at the baby. "I got lucky. I made two perfect clones, Brig-A and Brig-C. Brig-B and Brig-D were flawed from the beginning, so they were never placed into the artificial womb."

"You mean you let those two die." Corgan hadn't noticed it before, but Sharla looked tired. She had dark smudges under her eyes, and she kept twisting her hands.

Looking up again, she said, "One way or another, they died. You can believe whatever you want to. But there's only one artificial womb in the lab now, and I had two perfect fetuses developing. The Council said I had to choose between Brig-A and Brig-C, pick one and terminate the other. I couldn't do that! They were *Brig*!"

She knelt down and placed her cheek next to the baby's, smoothing his tufts of fiery red hair—that part of him was exactly like Brig.

"So what did you do?" Corgan asked softly.

"I put Brig-A into the artificial womb, where the Council members could see him if They came to check. With Brig-C, I . . ." She hesitated. "Maybe you won't like this next part. I implanted him into one of the Mutants, a girl about our age who has no mental capacity at all, and her arms and legs are stunted, so she can't move around much. But her reproductive system worked just fine."

"Sharla—"

"It was only for three months," she answered defensively. "And then I had two perfect babies—identical, but distinct." Smiling, she said, "Brig-A acted like a little pirate, grabbing every toy his clone-twin ever touched, so I called him Brigand. Since Brig-C loved to splash around in his bathwater like a little fish, I named him Seabrig." Sharla paused, then added, "Even with their different personalities, there's a strong psychic connection between them. Each one seems to know what the other's thinking."

"How can they be thinking anything?" Corgan asked. "They're just babies."

"For now. But not for long." Sharla really did look tired. Sighing, she pushed back the hair from her forehead and continued, "I told you I discovered this new system to speed up pregnancies. But that was just a spin-off of what I was really trying to find. The Council wanted me to clone a Brig that would turn ten years old in about half a year."

"That's impossible!"

"Nothing's impossible for me, at least when it concerns codes. Game codes, genetic codes, DNA—I can do all of it better than anyone else." The dam burst then and her words poured out so fast that Corgan had trouble understanding them all. She told him that since animals mature so much faster than humans, she decided to borrow the rapid-maturing trait from animal genes. Using frozen human egg cells from the same supply that had produced Corgan, Sharla, and Brig, she inserted Brig's cells plus the animal gene for early maturity into the healthiest eggs she could find.

"All I wanted was for these clones to grow up fast, so if we have to fight another War, Brigand will be ready. In six months."

"Six months!" Corgan exclaimed.

"Yes. Think about how fast puppies and kittens grow up. And take a look at Seabrig. He's only two weeks old, but he's as developed as a ten-month-old baby. In about another month he'll be like a three-year-old."

It was then that Seabrig began to wake up. He stirred and opened his eyes—Brig's eyes. Groping for his mouth, he stuck a thumb into it and began to suck vigorously.

"He's hungry," Sharla said. "You need to feed him."

"What do you mean *I* need to?"

"Corgan!" she cried, jumping to her feet and glaring at him. "You have a whole herd of cows out there. Can't you find some milk for one hungry baby?"

Just then Seabrig rolled over, took his thumb out of

his mouth, and grinned crookedly at Corgan. It looked so much like the real Brig that Corgan was startled.

"Okay," he muttered, and went out to milk one of the cows whose mutated calf had died a few weeks earlier. When he came back with the milk in a bucket, Seabrig was sitting up on the bunk.

"Put it in a cup," Sharla instructed. "He can already drink out of a cup. In another week he'll be walking."

"Sharla!" Corgan exploded. "How am I supposed to take care of this kid? I'm in charge of the herd, and you just told me that they want me to work more hours in the lab at night. Anyway, I don't know a thing about taking care of babies."

"Oh, Corgan, you just don't have any faith in me," she sighed, rummaging in the bottom of the flight bag. "You won't have to do anything except hide him from the Supreme Council and take him outside to play whenever you can. Mendor's going to raise him."

"Mendor!" Mendor, the computer program who'd raised Corgan for fourteen years inside his virtual-reality Box. Mendor, who could morph from a loving Mother Figure to a stern Father Figure in about four seconds flat. Mendor the teacher, the nursemaid, the comforter, the disciplinarian. When Corgan had asked Mendor after the Virtual War, what he/she was going to do when Corgan left the domed city, he/she had replied, "You won't need me anymore, Corgan, so I'll cease to exist." Now Sharla was saying that Mendor existed again.

"I reprogrammed Mendor," she said. "So right now we have to build a virtual-reality Box, up here on the hill. It won't be much like our old virtual-reality Boxes in the domed city. All I could smuggle out was a lot of LiteSuit material—we'll use it for curtains to put up a makeshift Box for Seabrig. No locks or anything, but I'm betting Mendor will keep him under such tight control, he won't even try to run away."

Helping Sharla unfold the yards and yards of shimmering LiteSuit material, which was sensitive to electronic impulses, Corgan said, "This stuff ought to work. I can't wait to see Mendor again."

"You won't," Sharla said. "The program will only react with Seabrig, not with you. Sorry about that, but it can focus on only one individual at a time." Sharla shook out the material and added, "But it's the same program that raised you, so Seabrig may turn out more like you than like the original Brig."

"Good!" Corgan blurted out, then felt a bit embarrassed for criticizing the dead. But the original Brig had been a pain in the butt most of the time, in spite of his brains and his compassion for the Mutants.

During the hour it took them to set up the makeshift Box and get the Mendor program running, Seabrig sat and watched with eyes far too knowing for a supposedly ten-month-old baby. Corgan realized he was going to have his hands full, Mendor or no Mendor.

When they'd finished, Sharla said, "Put him inside, and let Mendor do her thing, beginning with changing his diaper. Mendor knows how to atomize a dirty diaper and rearrange the molecules into a clean one."

"Really? Is that what she did with me?" Corgan asked,

making Sharla break out in that rich laugh of hers.

"What did you think—that you were potty-trained from day one?" She picked up a handful of straw and threw it at him, then ran out into the night.

The rain had stopped, and the sky was so full of stars it seemed the universe was theirs for the plucking. "Who needs sleep?" Sharla asked. "We'll stay up all night. That moon is too beautiful to waste."

At last Corgan had what he wanted—her undivided attention, her arms around him, her breath warm against his lips. And her promise to return in a few months, when Seabrig would be old enough to find out who he really was.

THREE

Seabrig grew up even faster than Sharla had predicted. Within eight weeks he'd reached the age of five. His hair was unmistakably Brig's—a thick, flame-red mop. He had Brig's crooked teeth, too, but his body was strong, straight, and lean, a total contrast to the mutated body of Brig. The original Brig had begged to be carried because it hurt him to walk; Seabrig scampered around with the speed of a lynx. And he never shut up.

"Corgan, Mendor is my mother, and Mendor is my father, too, but what are you?"

"What do you mean what am I?"

"Are you my grandfather? My uncle?"

"I'm your friend."

Seabrig weighed that in his mind—Corgan could almost see the wheels spinning. "Don't I have anyone else that belongs to me?" he asked.

"You have a . . ." Corgan stopped. He'd been about to say, "You have a twin brother," but Brigand was Seabrig's clone-twin, not exactly his brother. And neither of them knew that the other existed. He changed it to, "You have a nice life here, don't you? You get to play outside as much as you want. Why, when I was your age—"

"Yes, I know, when you were my age, you were stuck inside a Box all the time and you never got out except to go to your Clean Room, where you did your elimination and took a shower, and your hair was cut by robotic machine—"

"Stop!" Corgan cried. "You talk too much."

"Okay, I won't say any more if you take me to the beach," Seabrig said, looking sly.

Already the kid was showing signs of becoming a strategist, Corgan realized. At the moment there were no cows that needed attention, so Corgan agreed. "It's a bargain. You keep quiet for half an hour, and I'll take you to the beach."

But Seabrig couldn't stay silent for more than five minutes at a time. On the hike down the hill toward the ocean he announced, "Corgan, Mendor the Father said cannibals used to live on this island."

"How would he know about this island?" Corgan asked.

"It was in a book. Mendor the Father turned on the pages electronically, and I read them. I can read, you know," he said proudly, as though he hadn't bragged about it six times a day for the past week. "Could you read when you were my age?"

Your age? What *is* your age? Corgan wondered. And no, Corgan hadn't been able to read that young. "Tell me about the book," he said.

"It's called *Typee*, and a person named Herman Melville wrote it a long time ago, in the year 1846. That's two hundred thirty-four years ago."

"Two hundred thirty-five," Corgan corrected.

"I knew that!" Seabrig shouted with laughter, and jumped up and down. "I figured it out in my head, but I said the wrong number because I wanted to see if you were paying attention. Anyway, cannibals lived here once. Do you know what a cannibal is?"

Corgan thought hard. His vocabulary consisted mostly of terms used in mathematics and technology, since practically all his life had been devoted to preparing for the Virtual War. "I guess I don't," he admitted.

"Then pick me up," Seabrig said, lowering his voice as much as he could, "so I can tell you right into your eyes."

What a goofy kid! Corgan stopped on a terraced level of the hill and lifted Seabrig until their faces were close together. "A cannibal," the little boy declared, still using his artificially deepened voice, "is someone who *eats people*!"

"Oh, come on," Corgan said, putting him down.

"It's true! Mendor the Father said the book was true. Mendor the Father knows everything, Corgan, and you don't know hardly anything."

He's Brig, all right, Corgan thought.

"Want to know what the cannibals called human flesh when they ate it? They called it *long pig*, 'cause I guess people and pigs taste pretty much the same. So when a cannibal said he was having long pig for dinner, he really meant"—Seabrig paused dramatically, raising his hands in mock horror—"that he was eating . . . a *human being*!" Running to catch up again, he asked, "Do you think they ate the eyes, Corgan? And the fingers and toes? But no, fingers and toes would have fingernails and toenails on them, so you'd have to spit them out—"

"Oh, stop!" Corgan ordered. "You're disgusting."

"No, I'm not! Everything I said is true." They'd reached the shore, and Seabrig pulled off his LiteSuit to run into the waves.

"Come back here and put your LiteSuit on," Corgan called to him, but Seabrig answered, "It's too tight. Mendor the Mother says I keep growing out of my suits so fast she can't keep up with atomizing and reconstructing them."

"Well, wear it anyway."

"Why don't you ever have to wear a LiteSuit?" Seabrig demanded. "You're always in those raggy old denim jeans, and you don't even wear a shirt."

Was it necessary to defend himself to this mouthy kid? Corgan wondered. "It's because my skin is tougher than yours. Look at me, and then look at you." Corgan was naturally dark and had been exposed to so much sun since he'd lived on Nuku Hiva that the rays no longer bothered him. Redheaded Seabrig, though, had such pale skin that without protection, he'd get seriously sunburned. Corgan waded into the surf and grabbed the boy, yelling, "If you swim naked, you're going to get cooked till you hurt so bad you won't be able to sleep tonight!"

"Let me swim like this for just a little while," Seabrig pleaded. "I love to have the water touch all of me. I promise I'll stay in the deep part, where the sun won't get me."

"Okay, but no more than fifteen minutes," Corgan agreed, "and then it's back into your Suit."

"Fifteen minutes to the second. Right, Corgan? Mendor the Mother said you won the War because you're the greatest time calculator the world has ever known. I wish I could do that."

Yeah, I wish *I* could still do it, too, Corgan thought. A thirteen-year-old girl! Every time it crossed his mind, he bristled. He'd begun to practice calculating fractions of time again, but he was so rusty at it that he couldn't get past tenths of a second, nowhere close to hundredths.

Seabrig dived and swam like a dolphin. Walking along the beach, but always keeping an eye on Seabrig, Corgan tried to sort out his feelings for this little boy. Because he was growing so rapidly, both mentally and physically, it was hard to keep up with what he was—prodigy or pest. Usually after half an hour of his nonstop chatter, Corgan couldn't wait to take him back and dump him into his Box, where Mendor would be responsible for him.

"It's been fourteen minutes, fifty-six and eight-tenths seconds," Corgan shouted. "Out! Now!"

"I know, I know, I'm coming." Seabrig climbed, dripping, out of the ocean like a tiny Poseidon emerging from the waves. "I am Seabrig, the water warrior," he announced.

"Okay with me," Corgan told him. "Now put on your LiteSuit before you become Seabrig the fried fish."

"Oh, all right. At least it looks better than your jeans."

Corgan glanced down at his jeans, which Seabrig had called "raggy." Ever since he landed on Nuku Hiva almost a year ago, he'd worn the same pair of denim jeans, the kind everyone in the twentieth century seemed to have dressed in, back when Earth was safe and uncontaminated. Or at least that's what he'd been told. And Seabrig was right; the jeans really were raggy—threadbare in every spot where they weren't full of holes.

"Seabrig," Corgan began, "would you ask Mendor the Mother if she could atomize and then reconstruct my jeans?"

"Of course, Corgan. I'd do anything for you."

"You would?"

"Absolutely. Didn't I ever tell you, Corgan? You're my hero."

That kid! Like Brig, Seabrig could be aggravating one minute and lovable the next. Corgan picked him up and swung him around in the same rough way that the original Brig had loved. "Stop it!" Seabrig was shouting now, through gales of giggles that sounded exactly like Brig. If Corgan closed his eyes, he could almost pretend that . . . but Brig was dead.

"You *did* get sunburned," Corgan remarked. "I told you you should have kept your LiteSuit on. Come on, we'll go back to the barn a different way—along the jungle path, where the trees can shade you."

Once inside the darkness of the jungle, Corgan began

to wonder whether it had been a mistake to bring Seabrig there. Giant banyan trees towered above them, their leafy green branches blocking all but small fragments of sky, their aerial roots reaching down like stalactites toward the knife-edged, moss-coated boulders that thrust up, sharp and dangerous. A misstep between two of those jagged rocks could break a leg.

"Stay close to me," Corgan warned Seabrig, but the boy ran laughing into the thick growth. When he circled back, Corgan tried to grab him, but he darted out of reach, as quick and slippery as the moray eels that lurked inside watery caves, waiting for a victim. After a minute, when he stayed silent and hidden, Seabrig burst out from behind a tree, flapping his arms at Corgan and shouting, "Did I scare you? I bet I scared you, right?"

"Come back here," Corgan ordered, but once again Seabrig slipped past him, his running footsteps crashing through the undergrowth. Suddenly everything fell silent. Corgan waited for four and a quarter minutes before he began to worry. It would be easy to lose Seabrig in this part of the jungle. Wild boars roamed here. Corgan had never actually seen one, but on rare occasions he'd heard them rooting and snorting through the undergrowth. Once he'd caught a fleeting shadow of what must have been a very large boar, judging from the trampled leaves, broken branches, and gouged-out earth it left behind.

At last, faintly, from a distance, Seabrig called, "Come see what I found, Corgan." He no longer sounded mischievous, but subdued. "Come quick, please, Corgan. I'm over here by the biggest tree."

Corgan tried to follow the trail of trampled leaves and broken twigs left behind by Seabrig, but he couldn't fit into the narrow spaces between vines and roots the little boy had been able to wiggle through. Since Corgan always carried his knife—curved like a machete but only half as big—in a sheath tied to the belt loops of his jeans, he started to cut his way past the thick growth. When he finally reached Seabrig, he found him kneeling on the damp earth, holding . . .

"Where did you get that?" Corgan demanded.

"It was stuck in the roots of the tree behind me."

"Let me see it." Gingerly Corgan reached to take the human skull from Seabrig's hands. Every once in a while, when Corgan had explored the island, he'd come upon human long bones or bleached skulls imprisoned within the cagelike roots of the banyans. Those remains would startle him, but not frighten him—after all, since the whole population of Nuku Hiva had been wiped out in a plague seventy years earlier, there wouldn't have been anyone left to bury the last of the dead. It was no surprise they'd rotted where they fell, their bones becoming enmeshed in the tree roots that grew up around them.

This skull was different. Two long, sharply pointed boar's tusks curved from the back of the jaw to where flesh had once covered the cheeks. The eye sockets held stark white seashells painted black in the center; they stared straight into Corgan's eyes. All the teeth were intact, erect in a ghostly grin, with the boar's tusks attached so cleverly they seemed to have grown right out of the jawbone.

Seabrig announced, "He was a chief."

"How would you know that?" Corgan asked.

"I just know. See the tusks? When the spirit of a wild boar goes inside a man, it makes him a mighty chief."

"Did Mendor tell you that?"

"He didn't have to," Seabrig answered, shaking his head. "It came to me inside my eyes when I put my hands on top of this skull."

"You mean you had a vision or something?"

"I don't know what you call it—it's just . . . all at once I knew about the magic of the boars."

What an imagination, Corgan thought. "Come on, put the skull back where you found it, and let's get going," he said. "I need to check on the cows."

"I want to keep the skull. Can I keep it, Corgan?" Seabrig begged. "It will teach me secrets."

Corgan shrugged. Let the kid have his fantasies—they didn't hurt anything. "Sure, you can keep it, but no more games now—just stay beside me till we get back to the barn."

Without arguing—for a change—Seabrig followed Corgan. When the path became so overgrown it was hard to break through, Corgan picked him up and carried him, trying to protect him from the snapping branches that slapped against Corgan's bare chest and ripped a new hole in his already worn jeans. He told Seabrig, "Guess you'll really have to ask Mendor to reconstitute these jeans for me now."

"Why? Don't you like that nice breeze blowing on your butt?" Seabrig laughed uproariously, wagging the grinning skull in front of Corgan's face. "See? He thinks it's funny, too."

"Yeah, yeah. I'm glad you're both amused. You can get down and walk now."

Mendor the Mother did reconstruct the denim jeans, although so much of them had been lost to wear and tear that the cloth of the new jeans was a lot thinner. Corgan still worked bare-chested during the days. At night, when he reported to the laboratory, he wore a white coat that Delphine washed every few days in one of Nuku Hiva's streams.

So much rain fell in Nuku Hiva that rivulets cascaded constantly from the high, craggy peaks. When Seabrig got older, Corgan decided, he'd take the boy for a ride down one of the island's swift waterfalls. Sometimes Corgan put together a makeshift sled of wide leaves to ride as he shot down the fifty-meter chutes; other times he just slid down on the seat of his pants. If he took Seabrig, he'd have to hold him tightly, but the boy would love the plunge. . . .

"Concentrate!" Delphine cried sharply. "Your mind is drifting off somewhere, Corgan."

"Sorry." He pulled himself back to the moment. It was late at night, he was tired, and he found it hard to do the necessary delicate, microscopic probing with his work-roughened fingers.

"Why can't you come here earlier in the evening?" Grimber complained. "You said there aren't any cows that'll be giving birth anytime soon. What do you do up there in that barn?" Grimber raised his balding head to peer over the top of his glasses. "This part of the work is far more important than watching a cow's belly grow."

"I . . ." Corgan tried to think up any reasonable excuse.

He couldn't tell them he was hiking through the thick tropical growth with a little boy, teaching him which fruits were good to eat and which would make him sick, pointing out brightly colored birds he didn't know the names of, making sure neither of them tripped over the multitude of gnarled roots. The existence of Seabrig had to be kept secret. If Corgan had trusted Delphine and Grimber, he might have told them about Seabrig, but the two scientists were so wrapped up in their work that their human emotions seemed to have withered. Maybe permanently. Like machines, they measured, they prodded, they probed into microscopic cells hour after hour, week after week, day and night alike. Never did they bother to walk through their door into the lush tropical paradise outside, where they might have been stirred by the scent of jasmine in the star-filled night, by the moon casting its light across the restless waves, by the cooing of doves in the darkness.

"There's always a lot to do in the barn," Corgan answered lamely. "Sometimes one of the cows will wander off, and I have to go looking for her. Or sometimes a calf will get a hoof stuck between rocks—"

"Never mind the excuses," Delphine said wearily. "Just try to get here earlier." She bent over a binocular microscope, using both hands to hold back her bushy black hair so it wouldn't get in the way.

What if he told them? Corgan wondered again. What if he did, and they reported to the Supreme Council that an extra clone of Brig was alive and growing bigger by the minute on Nuku Hiva? The Supreme Council wanted only a single Brig clone—but why? Wouldn't an extra one be good insurance? What would They do if They discovered Seabrig—kill him? That made no sense, but Corgan couldn't take a chance. Sharla had said to keep the boy a secret. He just wished Sharla would hurry and come back.

FOUR

Number Nineteen. She was a very young heifer giving birth to her first calf, a situation Corgan had never dealt with before, and he was nervous. Nineteen lay on her side, her head tied to a post, the tip of her tail tied up to her neck with a piece of twine. She was taking longer than more mature cows took to birth calves—should he help her? If so, when?

She bellowed as the calf's front hooves and nose appeared. That was good, but half an hour passed after that and no more of the calf came out. Corgan lubricated his arms with an oil he'd made from the coconuts growing in abundance on Nuku Hiva. Reaching gingerly, he determined that the calf was in a normal birth position, and that was a relief, because if it hadn't been, he wouldn't have known what to do. Taking chains from a bucket of water he'd already sterilized, he placed a loop of chain around each foreleg, just above the hoof. Then, gently, he began to pull, first one leg and then the other, a few inches at a time.

"Corgan, Corgan!" Seabrig shouted. "Corgan, something happened!"

"Can't you see I'm busy?" Corgan asked, not taking his eyes from the calf.

"But Corgan—"

"Don't bother me now!" The calf had begun to emerge, one shoulder after another, but still too slowly.

"You're always too busy when I need you," Seabrig said, pouting. The catch in his voice made Corgan turn to glance at him. Seabrig's face was paler than usual, and his eyes looked huge.

"Look, this shouldn't take too long," Corgan told him. "In fact, if you wash your hands and arms real good, you can help me." Since Seabrig seemed to be somewhere around eight years old now and he was undeniably intelligent, he ought to be able to—

"*I'm* not touching any of that yucky stuff!" Seabrig exclaimed. "That's *your* job. Ee-yew! It's disgusting."

Corgan snapped, "Then you'll have to wait till I'm finished." A moment later the calf cleared the birth canal and began to breathe normally. Corgan relaxed.

"All right," he said, "I need to clean her, but that can wait for a few minutes. Now, tell me what you're so excited about."

An expression of uncertainty spread over Seabrig's face. "An airplane came," he said.

"Really?" Corgan hadn't even heard it, but then, the heifer had been bellowing a lot.

"A girl got out. And . . . someone else."

"The pilot?" Corgan asked.

"No," Seabrig stammered. "It was—" And then he stopped.

Instantly Corgan understood. Sharla had arrived with Brigand. Seabrig must have seen someone who looked exactly like him climbing out of that Harrier jet. No wonder he was spooked.

Corgan dried his arms with a piece of tapa cloth, then reached for Seabrig. He said nothing, just held the boy tight. Sharla'd probably taken Brigand to the lab, where Delphine and Grimber would see him for the first time. As scientists, they'd be interested in Brigand the clone, never dreaming that there'd been another one just like him right here on Nuku Hiva for the past few months.

"Explain, please, Corgan," Seabrig said in a small voice.

How could he explain? He'd have to wait till he heard from Sharla, who must have a reason for bringing Brigand to Nuku Hiva. "Go stay with Mendor in your Box until I call you," he told the boy.

"NO!" Seabrig stormed. "I saw something that didn't make sense, Corgan. It scares me, and I need to know what it means. Was it an image of me that bounced out of my own thought waves and got reflected back to my eyes? If it was, how could that happen? Tell me, Corgan!"

Corgan stalled. "These people that got off the plane— did they see you?"

"No. I was hiding behind a tree because you always told me that no one is supposed to see me. I need to know, Corgan. Was that . . . was that person—I don't mean the girl—was he real?"

Standing, Corgan said, "I told you I could talk to you for only a few minutes. The time is up."

"I won't go till you explain!"

"Seabrig, I've got too much to do here. Go to your Box now, or I'll—"

"You'll what?" Seabrig demanded.

"I'll grab you and drop you into this slime." The floor of the barn's birthing room had become smeared with a mixture of afterbirth, blood, and spilled coconut oil.

Seabrig detested mess, which was why the threat worked. "All right, I'm going!" he cried. "And I hate you."

"You'll get over it." Corgan untied the mother cow and helped her struggle to her feet, then went back to cleaning the baby. "Good job, Nineteen," he told the cow. "You have a nice, healthy little girl here, and she already has a name—she'll be called Fifty-two. That all right with you?"

As Corgan began the tedious job of cleanup, Nineteen twisted her head to get a look at her baby. In spite of its slowness, the birth had gone well. A few months earlier Corgan had lost a calf that tried to come out rear-feet first—he'd watched helplessly as both the mother cow and the unborn calf died after hours of agony. This birth had been much more satisfying.

It wasn't until he poured the last bucket of clean water over the barn floor that Sharla appeared on the brow of the hill, followed by a redheaded boy clutching her hand.

Corgan's breath caught. Except for the green LiteSuit the boy wore, he'd have been certain it was Seabrig. Just to make sure, he parted the curtain of Seabrig's Box to see if he was still in there. He was.

"Surprise," Sharla said softly.

For once Corgan had no urge to take her in his arms. "Why are you here?" he asked.

"I convinced the Supreme Council that Delphine and Grimber needed to see Brigand in person." Her hand rested on the back of the boy's neck; he reached up to curl his fingers around hers. "Say hello to Corgan," she told him.

"Hello to Corgan," he answered, and grinned, making Corgan swallow hard because the grin was identical to Brig's and Seabrig's, like an image reflected over again from one mirror to another.

"Well, where is he?" Sharla asked.

"Seabrig?" Corgan stalled.

"Yes, of course Seabrig. Brigand wants to meet his clone-twin."

"Brigand knows about this?" Corgan asked, incredulous.

Sharla nodded and squeezed Brigand's hand. "He and I tell each other everything. You can't imagine how brilliant he is, Corgan. More than the original Brig! But then, he's had me to teach him since he was born, unlike the original Brig, who spent the first six years of his life in the Mutant pen."

Put on the defensive because he'd never taught Seabrig anything except how to swim, Corgan answered, "Seabrig's been taught too. By Mendor. A couple of months ago he read a whole long, difficult novel about this island. He told me there used to be cannibals here."

Sharla only smiled. "Brigand read an entire twenty-volume set of encyclopedias he found in the library of the domed city."

No way was Corgan going to get caught up in a bragging contest. If he did, he'd lose. Sharla was always three steps ahead of him.

"So, where is he?" she asked again.

"Yes, bring him out," Brigand demanded. "He's my clone-twin, and I'm ready to meet him. Is that him?"

Corgan turned to see Seabrig's eyes peering from the Box. The rest of him stayed hidden behind the tightly pulled curtain. Before Corgan could stop him, Brigand ran to the Box and yanked the curtain aside. The two clones stared at each other, saying nothing.

Look at that, Corgan thought. I might have won the bragging contest after all. Seabrig had been raised on cow's milk, coconuts, breadfruit, bananas, mangoes, cashews, and all the other fruits of Nuku Hiva, plus fish they speared in the lagoons, and beef from the occasional cow that had to be sacrificed. All that abundance had made him taller than his clone-twin, broader in the shoulders. And the hours he'd spent in the sun, running across sand and through surf, had sprinkled a few freckles across his nose and cheeks.

Brigand, having lived in a domed city and been fed mostly on a diet of soybean-based synthetic foods, had paler skin and sharper bones. Corgan knew all about the monotony of synthetic food—he'd been raised on it himself. Yet in spite of the slight differences in their bodies and coloring, the boys were so strikingly alike that seen separately, they'd have been hard to tell apart.

Brigand reached out one finger and touched his clone-twin on the shoulder.

"Who are you?" Seabrig whispered. "Am I projecting you out of my imagination?"

At that Brigand burst out laughing. "Did you hear what he said, Sharla? What a funny kid!"

Frowning, Corgan knelt beside Seabrig and told him, "That boy's name is Brigand, and he's real, not imaginary. He's—you could say he's sort of your twin brother, Seabrig."

Brigand scoffed, "We're not twins. Twins come out of the same womb. I was grown in a laboratory, and you"—he pointed to Seabrig—"came out of a Mutant."

Moving toward the two boys, Sharla placed her hands on Brigand's shoulders. "Both of you were cloned from cells of a superb strategist," she added. "You and Brigand are clone-twins, Seabrig."

"I don't understand! I have to ask Mendor," Seabrig cried, and ran back into his Box.

Corgan shouted after him, "It's all right!" Then he turned to Sharla and hissed, "You should never have sprung it on us like this, Sharla. If you'd given me some warning, I could have prepared him."

"He'll be fine," she answered. Brigand scowled as Sharla came closer to Corgan and slid her arms around him. "Aren't you at least glad to see *me*, Corgan? I can stay here for a whole week before I have to go back. The two Brigs will get to know each other, and you and I can . . ." She laughed. "Renew our acquaintance."

Her nearness had the effect on him that it always had—his heart beat faster. "Sure I'm glad to see you," he admitted. "But I need to make sure Seabrig is all right. Uh . . ." He hated that he sounded so pleading—"You'll wait here, won't you?"

"Yes. I'll show Brigand the new calf. He's never seen a live animal before."

When Corgan opened the curtain to the Box, he found Seabrig huddled on the floor, curled up like a baby. "I didn't even know what a clone was, Mendor," he was saying. "That boy made me feel dumb."

At one time Mendor had been Corgan's own virtual program—his mother, his father, his teacher, all in one. Now that Mendor had been reprogrammed to care for Seabrig, Corgan couldn't even see him/her. Or hear what Mendor was saying to Seabrig.

He waited for whatever was happening to be over, torn by his desire to go back to Sharla. At last, with a sigh, Seabrig stood up. "Mendor says," he told Corgan, "that I may be a clone, but I'm still unique. And she says she loves me but she'll never love Brigand, no matter how much alike we are."

"Did she explain about cloning?"

"Yes. I understand it now. I mean, I know how it's done, Corgan. I just don't know why it happened to me."

Only Sharla can explain that, Corgan thought. But whatever her reason, he was glad she'd created Seabrig.

Putting an arm around Seabrig's shoulder, he led him outside.

FIVE

And it was all right.

Looking back later, Corgan remembered the beginning of that week as the happiest time of his life. Seabrig quickly adjusted to having a clone-twin, and to being one. Brigand turned out to be less of a brat than he'd seemed at first. And Sharla! Sharla was perfect. Happy, funny, affectionate—the girl Corgan had fallen in love with the year before.

On her fourth day on the island, Sharla decided to dress Seabrig in Brigand's LiteSuit and take him to the laboratory. "Delphine and Grimber will never suspect anything," she assured Corgan. "If they mention his rosy cheeks, I'll just say Brigand got a little too much sun yesterday."

"Why do you want to do this?" Corgan asked. "I've been so careful to keep him away from Grimber and Delphine."

"Because, don't you see? It's like a game—switching clones. And it'll give Seabrig a chance to see something new."

"A game!" Corgan protested. "That's not a good kind of game to play, Sharla."

"I want to! I want to!" Seabrig cried, jumping up and down. "Sharla will take me, and Brigand will have to stay here with you, old crabby-face Corgan."

As happened so often when Sharla was around, Corgan's objections got shot down. It was as though Sharla's ideas glowed, while Corgan's were dull as dirt. However, Brigand seemed satisfied to stay with Corgan—unlike Seabrig, Brigand was fascinated by the cows.

"So grass goes in and milk comes out," Brigand had said.

"No, grass goes in and poop comes out," Seabrig corrected him, happy to lord it over his clone-twin. "Milk is produced by an entirely different system from the digestive system that ends up with this disgusting, smelly—"

"Let it go," Corgan had ordered, a little embarrassed, but Sharla only laughed.

The visit to the laboratory turned out to be uneventful, according to Seabrig's report later that morning. "Delphine and Grimber hardly even looked at me," he said. "All they care about is the stuff they see through their microscopes. Here, Brigand, you can have your LiteSuit back."

"No, I think I'll stay in your grubby old clothes," Brigand answered. "They're nice and stinky and remind me of you."

"Stinky! I'm not stinky!" Seabrig tackled Brigand, and the two of them rolled around on the ground, laughing hard as the falling rain turned boys and ground soggy enough that they could smear each other with mud. "This isn't mud, it's cow poop!" Brigand yelled, sticking a handful of it down Seabrig's shirt. So of course Seabrig had to retaliate by chasing his clone-twin all over the hill, throwing mud balls at him, both of them shrieking with laughter.

Shaking his head, Corgan said, "I never acted like that when I was a kid."

"Maybe you should have. It wasn't till you met me that you finally began to loosen up," Sharla told him, coming up close as if to kiss him, but instead tracing a fingerful of mud across his cheeks.

"Stop that!" he ordered.

"But you really need to loosen up *more*!" She rubbed the rest of the mud into his hair and took off running, with Brigand and Seabrig whooping around her like a couple of savages.

Slowly Corgan followed in the direction they'd taken, slipping a little on the rain-slick path. "This way, this way," he heard faint voices calling from inside the thick growth of trees on the lower hillside. As he made his way through the dripping, jungle-thick stands of banyan trees, whose aerial roots snaked to the ground, as he climbed over boulders of volcanic rock coated with inch-thick green moss, he wondered why he could never get into the spirit of game playing, which came so easily to Sharla and the boys. Maybe it was because his Virtual War training had never seemed like a game. He'd played Golden Bees and Go-ball to sharpen his reflexes, to perfect his timing, to increase his stamina, and never just for fun. Maybe if he'd had another boy to play with—brother or clone-twin or just plain friend—he'd have turned out more like the two boys who were leading him on a chase through this dank jungle. He could hear their muffled giggles.

He knew they were waiting in the undergrowth to pounce on him, but they wouldn't catch him by surprise. After all, he was *Corgan*, champion of the Western Hemisphere Federation, possessor of the fastest reflexes known to humans—at least until this thirteen-year-old girl, whoever she was, had taken that title.

"Yaaaah!" From behind trees on either side of him Seabrig and Brigand leaped at Corgan. His arms shot out like whips and he caught them in midair, one in each hand. Clutching them around their necks but keeping the pressure gentle, he held them suspended, kicking and screaming, a meter above the ground. Their arms flailed out as they tried to hit him, but Corgan's arms were considerably longer, so they couldn't come close. And he was strong enough that he could have held them out there all day if Sharla hadn't stormed up shouting, "Put them down!"

"What'll you give me?" he asked, teasing, trying to "loosen up" the way she'd said he ought to.

"You better ask what I'll give you if you don't," she cried, picking up a coconut. "How about if I nail you with this thing right between your eyes?"

Still playing with her, Corgan said, "I need some instructions. Am I supposed to lower them gently to the

ground, or should I just drop them suddenly, like this?"
When he let go, both boys landed howling on the moss-
covered rocks. "That's what you get for trying to ambush
me," he told them. "Quit your whining, or I won't take you
down the water slide."

Immediately Seabrig quieted down, and Brigand stopped
whimpering long enough to ask, "What's the water slide?"
Sharla echoed, "A water slide?"

"It's great!" Seabrig shouted, jumping to his feet.

"And it'll be even better after all this rain," Corgan told
them. "Come on. First we have to find a banana tree."

"I'm not hungry," Brigand said.

"Not to eat, stupid!" Seabrig yelled. "To ride on."

Sharla's eyebrows rose. "Ride on bananas?"

Now it was Corgan's turn to smile condescendingly, to
be in command. "Come on. You'll see." Taking the lead,
he guided them through the overgrown wilderness. It
was hard going, but he'd brought his knife, and where
the vines made the path impassable, he hacked his way
through. Then the knife blade hit something that made
it ring.

"What's this?" he asked, pulling away the vines and
leafy growth that covered it. "I thought it was a rock. . . .
It *is* a rock. But it's carved."

A grotesque face peered out at them from rust-colored
volcanic rock, with two enormous eyes and a flat nose and
downward-curved mouth. It must have been meant to be
female, because the roughly sculpted arms held a baby
with an equally grotesque head, and beneath that clung
another child, standing.

"I know what it is!" Seabrig cried. "It was in that book I read. It's a tiki. A god."

"This one's obviously a goddess," Sharla said. "Whew, is she ugly! Her face looks like a cross between a turtle and a lizard." When a roll of thunder broke right over their heads, Sharla looked up at the sky and joked, "Sorry, Goddess, I didn't mean to insult you. Please, no lightning bolts."

"Look how weathered the rock is," Corgan said. "This statue must have been here a long time."

"Forget the statue. I see a banana tree," Brigand announced. "So show me how we're supposed to ride on a banana."

Seabrig howled with laughter again—he'd been doing that every few minutes, it seemed, since he became friends with his clone-twin. "We don't ride the bananas, dummy, we ride on the leaves!"

Swinging his knife, Corgan reached high into the tree and cut several of the wide, long, shiny green leaves. "Each of you carry some," he instructed. "We don't have far to go."

They'd been hearing the dull rush of water somewhere, and the closer they came to it, the louder the sound grew, until they reached a high waterfall cascading over a cliff. It dropped freely for ten meters or so, then hit a slope of rock that had been polished slick by years of water erosion. "That's the slide," Corgan said. "First we have to swim across this little pool to the other side. Then we climb to the top of the slope."

"And after that we slide down on the banana leaves. It's

so much fun!" Seabrig enthused, but Brigand's face turned gloomy.

"I can't swim," he said.

"You can't?" Seabrig hurried toward his clone-twin and took his hand. "I can, and if I can do it, you can too, because we're the same person. If we go into the water together, my thought waves will beam right into your head and you'll know how to swim."

Sharla scoffed, "That is so silly, Seabrig. I don't want Brigand to drown because he thinks he's going to—Brigand, come back here!" But the two boys were already splashing at the edge of the water. They eased themselves into the pool, and then, amazingly, Brigand began to swim. "How did he do that?" Sharla exclaimed. "I never taught him. There's no place to swim inside the domed city."

"Maybe there really is some kind of mental or psychic connection between the two of them," Corgan answered. "I don't know much about clones, but I did notice something odd this morning. When you took Seabrig to the lab and Brigand stayed with me, all of a sudden Brigand started to laugh. I asked him what was funny, and he said Seabrig had just knocked over a test tube and Grimber was mad at him. I kind of forgot about it, so I never did ask Seabrig if it really happened."

"Weird," Sharla said.

"Anyway, they're over on the other side now, so let's follow."

Once across the pond, the four of them climbed up the rock face beside the waterfall until they reached a ledge at the halfway point, where the sleek slope began. "I'll go first," Corgan announced, "to show you how it's done."

"No, *I'll* go first," Seabrig declared. Before Corgan could stop him, he slipped two of the broad banana leaves beneath his bottom. Holding on to the edges of them, he shot down the cascade, yelling the whole distance, until he plunged into the pool below.

"Well, since you've already seen how it's done," Corgan said wryly, "who's next?"

"Me!" Brigand did exactly what his clone had done. To Corgan, it looked as though a virtual image had been replayed. Brigand's movements were exact duplicates of Seabrig's.

"More thought waves?" Sharla asked, and Corgan answered, "I wonder."

For the first time in three days Corgan and Sharla found themselves alone, up there on the precarious ridge. "We don't have to hurry, do we?" she asked. "The boys are playing down in the pool."

"There's a cave a little way above here but we'd have to climb up to it. We could do that, unless you'd rather not leave Brigand on his own, considering that he just learned to swim fourteen minutes and thirty-seven seconds ago."

"Know what? I'm willing to take a chance. We'll hear them yell if anything's wrong," she answered.

Corgan climbed first, showing Sharla which rocks were solid enough to hold weight and which ones might crumble underfoot and perhaps cause a rockfall, crashing down into the pool where the boys were playing. Shrubs grew out of cracks in the rocks, with their roots hanging naked and ropelike for Corgan and Sharla to clutch for support. They were able to steal only a few minutes inside the cave before the boys started yelling for them, but those minutes were worth the climb.

"We're coming!" Corgan shouted from the mouth of the cave. "You two get out of the pool. I'm going to dive."

From the cave to the pool was twelve-meter drop, but Corgan had done it before. He knew the pool was deepest right in the center. With a quick glance back at Sharla, he leaned over the edge and pushed off, free-falling like a frigatebird diving into the ocean for fish, cutting through the glassy water in exactly the right spot. When he surfaced, he waved to Sharla and then began to swim toward the edge of the pool.

As he pulled himself onto the rocks he glanced upward and yelled, "Sharla, no!" but she was already in motion, curving gracefully and then straightening through the long descent until her fingers split the water's veneer and her body, in its pale blue LiteSuit, became lost in the deeper blue of the pool. Terrified, Corgan waited for her to surface. She came up grinning, her hair clinging to her shoulders.

"Why did you do that?" he demanded harshly. "It's dangerous if you've never tried it before."

"There's got to be a first time to try something," she answered. "Otherwise there can never be a before. I just followed you and aimed for the exact place you dived into."

"You scare me sometimes," he said. "No, not just sometimes. You scare me a lot."

The boys were already climbing the rock wall, carrying their banana leaves to repeat the slide. "They'll only be able to come down once more before the leaves get shredded," Corgan said.

"That'll be enough for today anyway," Sharla decided. "Do you want to go back up again?"

"No, let's just stay here and talk. What do you think of Brigand?"

"He's fine," Corgan said. "Only I like my kid better."

At first murmuring, "That's kind of biased, isn't it?" she then admitted, "Though I guess Brigand can be a little bossy."

"Hmmm, I wonder who he gets it from." Corgan ducked as she flicked water from her fingertips into his eyes.

"It's just . . ." She paused. "It's just that Brigand is mine, all mine. I created him. Oh, I know I created Seabrig, too, but you're the one who's raised Seabrig. With Brigand, I've been with him every minute since he emerged from the artificial womb, except for the two days when I brought Seabrig here to you." Smiling, she said softly, "I love the way Brigand clings to me. He sleeps in a little cot right next to mine, and every night he holds my hand until he falls asleep. It's so sweet—he won't even go to sleep unless I'm there beside him."

"Yeah, real sweet." Corgan didn't like the images those words were putting into his head. Brigand was like an eight-year-old now, not a baby!

"And he's incredibly smart. I teach him something once and he learns it right away. Not only that, he's perceptive—he has an amazing way of guessing what everyone is thinking." She began to laugh then, a little embarrassed. "I must be sounding like a proud parent. But you know . . ." Another pause. "Maybe I'll never have a child of my own, and this is the closest I'll get to being a mother."

Uncomfortable, not knowing how to answer that, Corgan sputtered, "Hey, like I said, Brigand is fine." He wanted to turn the conversation away from talk about childbearing (after all, if Sharla became a mother in some future time, Corgan hoped he'd be the male involved in the process). "Seabrig's fine, too," he added. "I'm fond of the little guy, but it's nothing like what you're describing. I guess yours is a female thing."

"I guess. Something like that."

"But it's funny," he went on, "the older Seabrig gets, the less he reminds me of Brig. I mean, he's just turning into himself. Just plain Seabrig."

At that moment the two boys came shooting down the sheer slope and hit the pool with such a big splash that Corgan got drenched all over again. Sharla'd had the foresight to move out of the way.

"We're going exploring now," Brigand announced.

"You better not go too far," Corgan warned them, but as usual, Sharla challenged him.

"Let them run around and see things," she said. "You said there aren't many snakes on the island."

"Hardly any. But there are a few wild boars."

"Really?"

It was Brigand who answered her, saying, "Think about it, Sharla. There have to be wild boars. Those tusks in the skull Seabrig found are boar tusks. From a big, big,

big animal." He curved his two index fingers upward on either side of his mouth and lunged at Sharla, snorting like a boar, pretending to gore her, boring his head into her neck. She laughed and pushed him away.

"Don't worry about it," Corgan told her, wanting to get rid of Brigand. "They'll be safe enough. I've never come face-to-face with a boar—I think they avoid contact with humans." To the boys, he added, "Just don't go so far that we can't hear you if you yell. And that is an order."

"Yes, master," they both said, bowing and giggling. And then they were gone.

"Alone at last," Sharla sighed. "For maybe five minutes."

Corgan took off the shirt he'd put on to keep himself from getting scratched by the jungle branches, and wrung the water out of it. "There's something I'd like to ask you, and it's not about the clone-twins," he said, avoiding her eyes as he pulled the wet shirt over his head. "I want to know about this thirteen-year-old girl you mentioned, the one in the other domed city who's supposed to take my place if there's another War. Tell me about her."

Stretching out on a smooth boulder, her face to the sun, Sharla answered, "Well, I've only met her virtually, but I'll tell you what I know. She's had a birthday—she's fourteen now—and she's not only lightning fast in virtual practice games, she's an athlete, too. She can run a faster mile than almost all the male athletes."

"Is she pretty?" Corgan wanted to know.

Sharla raised her head, shaded her eyes with her hand to look directly at him, and asked, "Why should you care?"

"Hey! I don't know. Just curious. Is she pretty?"

"Yes. She's tall and thin, but she has muscles and long black hair that swings across her shoulders when she races. There! Satisfied?"

Corgan grinned. "I think I'm starting to like her. What's her name?"

"Ananda." Sharla drew it out as if the word tasted a little sour on her tongue. "Ananda the Awesome, they call her."

"And they used to call me Corgan the Champion." He couldn't keep a hint of bitterness out of his voice. "Now I guess they call me Corgan the Calf Catcher."

Sharla shifted to look at a rainbow that arced overhead now that the rain had stopped and the sun had returned to send fingers of light through the crowded leaves above them. Without turning toward him, she told him, "This was your decision. You chose Nuku Hiva as your reward for winning the War. The Supreme Council would have liked you to stay in the domed city, but you were the hero of the Federation, so They let you do what you wanted. Do you think you made the wrong choice?"

He couldn't answer that straight off, because he didn't know. He regretted the loss of his time-splitting ability, yet his reflexes seemed just as fast as ever. Thinking back on life in the domed city, where he'd been confined to a virtual-reality Box, eating synthetic food, running on synthetic tracks, being deceived by the Supreme Council, which had controlled his life—no, he didn't miss that. Nuku Hiva was almost unbearably beautiful. If only Sharla would stay there with him, he'd never ask for more.

His thoughtful mood was shattered by high-pitched screams.

"Corgan! Hurry! Something's wrong with Brigand!"

six

SIX

Corgan and Sharla raced toward—where? Seabrig's terrified voice kept calling them, but the jungle's thick growth masked the cries, scattering them shrilly one minute and muting them the next. "Over there!" Sharla cried, but when they turned in that direction, the shrieks seemed to come from the opposite direction. The tangled roots of the banyan trees caught them, tripped them, tore at their hair, and all the while Seabrig kept screaming.

Or was it Brigand? Did they hear one child crying, or two? With his knife Corgan hacked through the thick undergrowth. His timekeeping ability meant nothing now because every minute felt as long as an hour.

"Look!" Sharla cried, snatching a torn piece of green

LiteSuit from a branch. "It's Brigand's. He came this way."

"They changed clothes, remember?" Corgan reminded her. "Seabrig wore that."

When they broke through and found a boy sprawled on the ground wearing a green LiteSuit, Corgan couldn't tell which clone it was because his face and hands were smeared with dirt. "Seabrig?" Sharla cried. "Where's Brigand?"

"He's . . . he's—"

"Where! Stop bawling and tell us," Sharla yelled, shaking Seabrig so hard his head bounced. "Is Brigand hurt?"

Seabrig pointed through the twisted mass of trees. Twenty meters away, barely visible, they could see a shock of red hair. Not on the ground. Whatever was wrong with Brigand, he was at least standing upright.

When they reached him, Sharla threw her arms around the boy, but he stood motionless, expressionless. In his hand he held a bamboo spear taller than he was, carved with odd designs: squares within squares; circles divided into four sections, each with a different symbol; figures that could have been humans or lizards.

"Look at his eyes," Corgan said. "He's in some kind of trance."

Brigand stared vacantly, his eyelids as wide as it was physiologically possible to open them, his pupils enlarged almost to the rims of his irises. Corgan passed his hand across the boy's face, but there was no response.

"Brigand, wake up!" Sharla begged. "Can you hear me?"

Nothing. Not a muscle twitch, not a blink of those staring eyes.

"What happened to him?" Corgan asked Seabrig, who was still whimpering.

Wiping his nose with his sleeve, Seabrig answered, "We were exploring. We pretended to be cannibals. Brigand went ahead of me and I couldn't find him, but I heard him laughing, so I followed the laugh. Over there." He pointed through the trees. "It's like a . . . a house. No, not exactly . . . it's made of shiny black stone. . . . It's a . . ."

Seabrig, who had never seen any buildings except the barn and the laboratory on Nuku Hiva, had no words to describe whatever was "over there."

"Show me," Corgan told him. "Sharla, come on."

"I can't leave Brigand. Not when he's like this—wait a minute! I think he's coming out of it."

Brigand had begun to move. He dropped the spear, shook his head as if to clear it, and began to mumble a long flow of unintelligible sounds. "Sharla" was the first word they could understand.

"I'm here, baby," she answered.

"Not a baby," Brigand muttered. "Chief."

"Yes. Right. Can you walk?" she asked him. "Can you tell me what happened?"

"My spear. Where's my spear?"

When Seabrig picked it up and handed it to him, Brigand leaned on the spear and took a few stumbling steps. Sharla tried to help him, but he brushed her aside. Straightening himself to his full height, he breathed deeply a few times, said some more of the words they couldn't understand, then strode forward so rapidly he seemed to melt through the tangle of trees and overhanging foliage.

"Wait for me," Sharla called, but he paid no attention. Seabrig hurried to catch up to his clone-twin as Corgan took Sharla's hand and helped her across the treacherous snarl of naked roots.

This part of the island was new to Corgan. Whenever he'd gone to the water slide, he'd always been able to follow a barely noticeable path, but this area was mostly thick, impenetrable jungle growth. Although it was invisible from where they'd found Brigand, less than five meters ahead of them stood the structure of gleaming stones that Seabrig had described.

Cut to matching sizes and polished to a high gloss, the blocks had been piled one on top of the other to form an oblong building three meters wide and two meters high. "Come around to the other side," Seabrig called out. "We're over here."

Through treetops meshed overhead, one thin ray of sunlight shone directly on Brigand. With the spear held upright in his hand, he stood on a circular piece of polished black rock. As he struck the round rock with the bottom of his spear, he boasted in a voice that was still a bit shaky, "I pulled down this big stone all by myself. Seabrig didn't think I could do it, because it looked too heavy and it was really stuck, but I did it anyway!"

"It was a door," Seabrig explained, pointing to an opening in the structure. "I tried to help him move the rock, but it was too hard, so I went to find a stick to pry it open with, and that's when I found the spear. Brigand took it from me and said it was his, and then he stuck the end of it behind the round door like a lever."

"Give me a lever and a place to stand and I will move the earth," Brigand declared.

"Archimedes said that," Seabrig told them. "Anyway, Brigand said I should back off, because whatever he was going to find when he opened the door would be his, not mine."

"That's right. And it *is* mine."

"Go on, Seabrig. What happened next?" Corgan asked.

Seabrig's dirty face wore a look of uncertainty. "Well . . . well, I got mad when he said that about everything being his."

"Yes?"

"So I backed off pretty far. Then . . ."

"Then what?" Corgan urged him.

"Then there was this sound like a big wind, sort of like that cyclone that almost hit us before it blew out to sea—do you remember, Corgan? And after the wind I heard a moan, or maybe a groan. When I came back, Brigand was crawling through the round hole—I mean, he'd been inside, and he was coming out. He stood up and took a couple of steps to where you found him, but then he got all stiff like that and he couldn't move or talk. That's when I started yelling for you."

"I better find out what's in that place," Corgan said.

"I already know what's in there, but I'm not telling anyone," Brigand announced, "because everything in there is mine. So you better not touch it, Corgan."

Corgan knelt to peer through the opening into the gloom inside. At first glance he thought he saw a bird with colorful tail feathers spread out like a fan. On his

228

hands and knees, he crawled farther into the vault and then recoiled. The feathers made up a headdress worn by a corpse.

As his eyes adjusted to the darkness he saw the reclining figure of a man at least six feet tall, dressed only in a loincloth and a necklace of boars' tusks. Every inch of the dead man's skin had been tattooed with animal and human figures, with crosses, coils, sharks' teeth, ferns, and faces that looked like the one on the tiki they'd found earlier that day.

"It's a tomb," he called out to Sharla. "There's a body in here."

"Let me in." She crawled through the opening to kneel beside Corgan and said, "Look at that! He's perfectly preserved." Reaching out as though to touch him, she hesitated, then pulled back, saying, "With that crown of feathers, he must have been an important chief or a high priest or something. And that necklace—all those boars' tusks—they're ugly, but the necklace itself is beautiful."

Brigand yelled out again, "I told you, everything in there belongs to me. The necklace, the feathers on his head, the bowls . . ."

Corgan hadn't noticed the bowls at first, but now he saw them everywhere—at the head and the feet of the corpse, lining the walls of the tomb, and set side by side in every available space. Running his finger around the inside of one of the bowls, he said, "Oil. Probably burned for light. There's enough of a smell that I'm sure it wasn't coconut oil. Something else—I don't know what."

As Corgan handed a bowl to Sharla, Seabrig yelled

through the opening, "Brigand can have all that stuff, Corgan. I don't want it. I don't even want to see the body. How long do you think it's been there?"

Sharla moved a little closer to the corpse, sniffed it, and murmured, "There's no odor of death. It looks like he died only today, but that's impossible. No one has lived on these islands for seventy or eighty years, we were told."

"What if the tomb was sealed long ago by a vacuum?" Corgan speculated. "That would have kept the body from deteriorating." It could also account for the "wind" Seabrig said he'd heard: air rushing into the tomb when Brigand broke the seal. "If Brigand crawled in here as soon as he opened it, he would have inhaled whatever vapor was left from the burned oil. That's probably what made him blank out."

"Mmm, maybe." Sharla didn't look convinced.

"So, what should we do with the corpse now?" Corgan asked her. "It won't look this good for long." Whenever one of Corgan's cattle died, the flesh decayed quickly, almost before the scavengers arrived—the rats, feral cats, and owls, drawn by the scent of rotting meat.

Sharla answered, "Just put back the stone the way it was."

"Not before I get what belongs to me!" Brigand shouted from just beyond the opening.

"You can forget that," Corgan told him. "I'm not letting you rob any tomb!"

Crawling out into the daylight, Corgan had to shield his eyes from the sun, which haloed Brigand in silhouette: He loomed above Corgan like an evil omen, spear in hand, appearing to Corgan's sun-dazzled eyes to be taller than he really was.

Sharla emerged right behind Corgan, and as she stood up to brush dust and dry leaves from her LiteSuit she argued, "What difference would it make if Brigand took a few souvenirs? The guy in there isn't going to miss his necklace and his feathers. In a few days he won't even look human any longer—we're in the tropics, remember? He'll turn to mush. Go ahead, Brigand, you can have the things you found. Do you want me to go back in and get them for you, or do you want to get them yourself?"

Overruled again! Corgan was tired of it. Positioning himself in front of the tomb to bar the way, he ordered, "All right. I will permit you to remove one thing, and one thing only, from this tomb. But you better get it fast, because I'm going to cover up the opening in about forty-five seconds, and if you're still in there, you'll get sealed inside with the big chief's rotting carcass." To add to the threat, Corgan walked over to the round stone and stood with his hand on the edge, ready to roll it toward the tomb.

Annoyed, Sharla murmured, "Really, Corgan, that's a horrible thing to say to a little boy."

"Yeah, well, it worked." He pointed to Brigand, who was counting as he hurried out of the tomb, "Forty-two, forty-three, forty-four seconds—and I'm out. So you can't seal me up, Corgan, no matter how much you'd love to get rid of me."

The ivory white necklace of wild boars' tusks hung around Brigand's neck and reached all the way to his belly button, which showed through his torn shirt. Lifting the necklace with both hands, he shouted, "I am the powerful cannibal chief of Nuku Hiva! Every living creature on this island will obey me!"

"You sure got that wrong," Corgan told him, no longer trying to hold back his irritation. Raising his head so that his voice rang out through the trees, he shouted, "If anyone's in charge of this island—*I* am! I won the right to that when I fought the Virtual War. So I make the rules around here! Does everyone understand that?"

Eyes wide, Seabrig nodded, while Brigand scowled. Sharla smiled a little and said, "You're pretty impressive when you're angry, Corgan. I like it. Go ahead, tell us— we're waiting to hear the rules."

He threw her a quick glance to find out if she was mocking him, but saw that she wasn't. Holding both boys by the hand, she waited for Corgan to speak.

"Just this," he said. "Brigand seems to be feeling fine now—whatever knocked him out isn't bothering him anymore. I say we leave this place and forget we were ever here, and let the chief's corpse rot in peace."

He expected a response, but there was none—maybe because he stood facing them with his fists clenched and his jaw thrust forward. "All right!" he declared. "The rain has stopped, and I plan to salvage what's left of this day. We'll go back to the pool to enjoy the two hours and forty-seven minutes of daylight before the sun drops behind the peaks."

Sharla nodded. "So be it! Let's go, clone-twins. Corgan has spoken, and he is master of the island. For now."

seven

Brigand dawdled all the way back to the waterfall, dragging the spear. He lagged so far behind the rest of them that they had to keep yelling at him to catch up, but he followed at a distance of at least ten meters, his boars'-tusk necklace swaying from side to side on his narrow chest.

The sight of the waterfall in sunlight was so striking that even Brigand paused in wonderment. Rainbows spanned the pool and the crest of the falls, where the cascading stream splashed against porous volcanic rock.

"Let's go!" Seabrig called.

"Wait a minute." Corgan reached the clone-twins, who'd already begun to climb, and pulled them down by their ankles. "You can't use those banana leaves—they're so shredded they'd tear through and you'd lose control. Take the ones Sharla and I had—they're in better shape. We'll stay down here while you slide."

"Not acceptable!" Brigand said. "Sharla belongs with me. You and Seabrig can stay down here."

Corgan picked up Brigand until their eyes were level and their faces were only inches apart, and said, "If you want to go down the water slide with Seabrig, fine. But Sharla's going to be here with me. Got it?"

Tugging Corgan's arm, Sharla said, "Let me handle this. Listen, sweetie," she told Brigand, "you're turning into the world's best strategist, so you need to understand other people's strategy, too. What I mean is—Corgan and I would like a little time alone together."

"Why?" Brigand demanded.

"Because we hardly ever get to see each other. But you and I are together practically every minute in the domed city, aren't we? And we'll be back there in just a few days—"

"Oh, all right. But I don't like it!" Brigand stamped his foot in the shallow edge of the pool, splashing all of them, before he started to climb the cliff again. Seabrig followed, carrying the banana leaves for both of them.

Smiling apologetically, Sharla said, "He's usually fine when it's just the two of us together. It's only when he's around you that he gets a little bratty. I think he's jealous."

"Jealous? You mean he's jealous that you and I are . . ."

Corgan didn't finish the sentence, because he didn't know exactly what he and Sharla really *were*. Not lovers, like Delphine and Grimber, although Corgan had loved

Sharla from the moment they first met in the darkened hall outside his virtual-reality Box. Yet they were much more than friends. Since they so rarely saw one another, though, it was hard for them to *be* anything, to have any kind of relationship that could be defined by a simple term.

"Brigand won't keep on being a little kid for much longer," Sharla said. "Neither will Seabrig. In a couple more months they should be as old as you and I are right now. Then both you and Brigand will *really* have something to be jealous about," she teased.

Corgan didn't want to think about that. He already disliked Brigand—what would happen if the boy turned into an actual rival for Sharla? Brigand would keep on aging, fast—both boys seemed to be picking up two years' maturity for every month they lived, which was what Sharla had genetically programmed them to do.

"And then what will you do?" Still teasing, she slipped Corgan's knife from its sheath and asked, "Will you and Brigand have a sword fight over me?" Posing with a hand on one hip, she thrust the knife in midair as if she were fencing.

"Put that thing down!" he ordered her. "It's not a toy— it's sharp!"

They were interrupted by Brigand's cry from the edge of the cliff. "Yaaaah! Sharla, look up here. Watch me, Sharla. Sharla, look at *me*!"

Corgan groaned, "Oh no, they went all the way to the top. If they try to slide from there, they'll get hurt. It's too far and too steep." He yelled, "Climb back down to the slope and start your slide from where we did before."

Neither boy answered. Side by side they squatted on the edge of the cliff, with the wide banana leaves underneath them. Water surged around their hips and rushed down their legs, free-falling from their feet to the slope ten meters below.

"Did you hear me? Don't do that!" Corgan shouted. When neither boy paid attention to him, he said, "You tell them, Sharla. They'll break their necks if they push off from the top."

"Brigand—" Sharla called, but at that moment both boys leaned forward to slip into the falls.

The waterfall was narrow, barely wide enough for the two of them to fit together side by side. To gain more space for himself, Brigand thrust out his elbows, knocking Seabrig sideways into the loose pile of volcanic rock that edged the falls.

As Brigand hit the water, plunging through the stream that gushed around him in glistening sun-sprayed sheets, Seabrig scrambled for a hold on the wet rocks, grabbing a boulder to keep from sliding down the volcanic rubble that edged the falls. Pebbles and small debris broke away beneath him to bounce down the face of the cliff.

"He'll start a rockfall!" Sharla screamed. "Brigand will get hurt!"

But Brigand was not the one in danger. He'd barreled safely along the center of the falls to crash into the pool, surfacing almost immediately.

Far above, Seabrig hugged his boulder tightly as Corgan yelled at him, "Hang on! Don't try to climb back up to the rim. I'll come and get you."

Seabrig shouted back, "No, I'm all right. Brigand did it, and so can I! If I can just get a good foothold, I can jump into the falls from here." He stretched an arm toward the cascading water, a good meter beyond his reach.

"Are you crazy? Stay right there!" Corgan had already begun to climb the slope toward the boy.

"Don't come up—I'm okay!" Still clutching the boulder, Seabrig tensed himself for a leap into the waterfall. Suddenly the large boulder began to give way, peeling loose from the crumbling volcanic matrix that held it. Panicked, Seabrig clung to the boulder until it nearly rolled on top of him. Only then did he hurl himself loose, kicking away from the wall of rock to hurtle into the waterfall headfirst.

Arms spread, fingers splayed, he tumbled in a wild spiral toward the pool, hitting the surface hard as chunks of rubble and slabs of broken rock fell around him. Instantly Corgan dove into the depths of the pool to get him, but the boulders that kept crashing onto the muddy bottom churned up silt, turning the water murky. Corgan felt his way through the dimness, getting hit by rubble that was still falling, bumping into slabs of stone that might have been on the bottom forever or might have just fallen from the rockslide. He was swimming blind now, fighting both the murky water and the unfamiliar pool bottom.

He surfaced to breathe, panicking because he'd been underwater for three minutes and fourteen seconds, and so had Seabrig. Shaking the water out of his eyes, he yelled to Sharla, "Did Seabrig come up yet?" But he could see that he hadn't.

Just before he turned back, he saw Brigand dive into the pool, the boars'-tusk necklace still around his neck, and his teeth clamped around Corgan's knife.

"What's he doing?" Corgan shouted.

"He thinks Seabrig might be buried down there, and he's going to dig him out," Sharla shouted back.

"With my *knife*?" Not waiting for an answer, Corgan dived again into the murk. If he couldn't see underwater, how could Brigand? Unless . . . if the boys did actually have some kind of mental connection, maybe Brigand *would* be able to find his clone-twin when Corgan could not.

Corgan groped around futilely until his head began to pound and his eyesight grew dim. His panic escalated. Since his own lungs were about to burst from lack of air, could Seabrig still be alive?

He came up just in time to see Brigand push an unconscious Seabrig toward the edge of the pool.

"You found him!" Corgan yelled, relief flooding him— until he rubbed the water from his eyes and got a better look.

Seabrig's head hung back. Both his arms dangled lifelessly in the water, and as Sharla waded toward him, the water around Seabrig turned red. When she lifted him, a horrible gush of blood spurted from the boy's right arm.

"I had to do it. I had to cut it off!" Brigand was babbling, crying. "A big rock pinned him and I couldn't pull him loose! If I hadn't cut off his hand, he would have drowned."

Corgan's head reeled from oxygen deprivation, and his pulse pounded so loud in his ears that he doubted the words he'd just heard. They were wrong words, they were mistaken words, and his eyes deceived him too, because it looked as though Seabrig's bleeding arm ended at the wrist. That couldn't be true. . . .

"You cut off his hand?" he bawled. His horror began to mount as his head cleared. Seabrig was the child he had promised to take care of, and now here he was, drowned and bleeding. All because of Brigand! First Brigand had pushed Seabrig into the avalanche, then he'd mutilated him! For no reason! He could have called Corgan to rescue Seabrig—no matter how big a rock trapped him, Corgan could have pulled him loose.

He fought the urge to grab Brigand and beat him senseless. He had to concentrate on Seabrig. Corgan had seen blood before—every time a cow gave birth to a calf, he dealt with blood—but this was human blood, great quantities of it, and how much blood could a little body like Seabrig's stand to lose before none was left? He leaped to where the boy lay on the ground, and clasped his own hand tightly around the severed stump, pressing with all his strength to make the bleeding stop. "Hold it this way, as tight as you can," he instructed Sharla, while quickly, with shaking fingers, he tore strips from his own shirt and wrapped them around the bloody wrist.

Trying to remain calm, although her voice trembled, Sharla said, "I'll go into the pool and try to find the hand. If I can find it, it can be sewn back on. Come with me, Brigand. Show me where it happened."

The two of them sank into the water then, and Corgan was left with Seabrig, not even sure if he was alive. He rolled him over, then lifted him by this midriff, facedown in a desperate embrace, trying to squeeze water out of the boy's lungs. Behind him Sharla and Brigand splashed in the pool, surfacing and diving again, but Corgan paid them little attention—what did it matter whether they found the hand, if Seabrig was dead?

Corgan's entire being focused on the boy in his arms. Green tendrils of moss trailed, dripping, from Seabrig's body, from the hair that looked even redder now that the skin was so gray and cold. "Don't die, don't die," Corgan begged. "Come back! You can have anything you want. I'll never be too busy for you. . . ."

No motion. No sound. Not the flicker of an eyelash. *I've lost him,* Corgan mourned, not knowing whether the drops that ran from his own cheeks were pond water or tears.

Suddenly Seabrig's body spasmed and a gush of filthy fluid spewed out of his mouth. "Yes!" Corgan yelled, his hope rising. *"Come on, breathe!"* He covered Seabrig's mouth with his own and forced air into the boy's lungs.

Seabrig choked then, and coughed, and finally breathed, one ragged breath after another. But he remained unconscious, which was just as well, Corgan realized. What would he say when he came to and discovered his hand missing? Sharla broke through the pond's surface then and cried, "I can't move any of the boulders, and Brigand isn't even sure which one it was."

"You stay with Seabrig, and keep those strips of cloth wrapped tight," Corgan ordered her, shouting it even though she'd climbed out of the pool and was standing right next to him. "I'll swim down with Brigand to look for the hand."

The water had cleared a bit but not enough; it was still hard to see through the dimness. Corgan followed Brigand to the bottom, where a mass of rocks and debris lay piled. For a boy who claimed he'd never learned to swim before that morning, Brigand managed to glide through the water like a seal. When he pointed, Corgan pulled the smaller rocks from the pile to get to the base. Twice he had to go up for air and for a quick check on Seabrig, who lay moaning, his head on Sharla's lap.

By the third time he dived, Corgan had removed most of the smaller rocks and was able to push against the boulder Brigand kept pointing to. Even though things weigh less in water, the boulder was massive. He could tilt it only a few inches, then it would settle back again, raising more mud to obscure his vision. Grabbing Brigand by the neck, he propelled the boy to the surface and told him, "Next time when I move it, you look underneath for the hand. If it's there, grab it."

Brigand nodded, and the two of them dived again. Corgan used all his strength and was able to tip the rock farther than he had before, but when Brigand peered underneath, he just shook his head. If only Corgan could roll the rock all the way over, to knock it on its side, he could look for the hand himself. But he had to trust Brigand to do it. And he didn't trust him. Not a bit.

There was no more time. He couldn't let Seabrig lie there bleeding. Corgan had to get Seabrig to Delphine and Grimber—they were scientists, they had a laboratory and instruments, so they ought to know how to cauterize and sterilize the wound.

When he told his plan to Sharla, she said, "No! We can't let them find out that I made two clones of Brig."

"Sharla! What are you planning to do—let Seabrig bleed to death? Then for sure there'll be only one clone! Forget that—I'm taking him to the laboratory."

"Wait! If you do that, tell them he's Brigand," she instructed.

"Why? Why keep up the deception? This is an emergency! Who cares if Delphine and Grimber find out?"

"I care! The Supreme Council—"

"Sharla, you've defied authority your whole life. Why start worrying about it *now*?" This was no time to argue—Corgan picked Seabrig up in his arms and began to run. Let Sharla and Brigand find their way back on their own.

His mind flashed back to the time in the domed city when he'd carried Brig, racing through the corridor to get him back inside his Box before the code kicked in and the Box became locked for the night. Brig's big, awkward head had bounced against Corgan's chest the way Seabrig's perfectly formed head was doing now. He couldn't let this child die! It didn't matter that Corgan had him for only a few months; didn't matter that the boy could be a royal pest. Corgan had to make him live!

When he reached the laboratory, Delphine screamed, "What happened to Brigand?"

That was Corgan's chance to tell her about the clone-twin, but he didn't. "He got caught under a rockfall in the pool," he answered. "There was no other way to free him."

"Who did this to him?" Grimber demanded. "Who cut off his hand?"

Corgan's mind raced. He couldn't say "Brigand"—they believed the unconscious boy on the table was Brigand. He stalled, trying to decide what to answer. Blame the amputation on Sharla? If not Sharla, there was only one other person who could take the blame—Corgan himself. "I did it," he finally said.

Grimber stared suspiciously and asked, "Where's the hand? What happened to it?"

"Still under the rock. I couldn't get it."

"Never mind that now! Put him on the table," Delphine ordered. "Clean him quickly. I've got to suture those exposed veins and arteries."

"First we need to stabilize him," Grimber declared. "Looks like he's in shock. Check his pulse." Without thinking, Delphine reached for the boy's right wrist but realized there was nothing there to lift.

Trembling, she picked up his left wrist and said, "Pulse is weak and rapid. Eyes are dull, pupils dilated. You're right, Grimber, he's in shock."

"Of course I'm right. Rip open his LiteSuit so he can breathe," Grimber ordered. "How did it get so tight on him? It's as if he's grown since he was here this morning. Raise his feet. Don't stand there like an idiot, Corgan! Put something under his feet."

"Can you hear me, Brigand?" Delphine asked.

In a weak voice Seabrig began, "I'm not—" Then he stopped.

How much of that conversation back at the pool had he

understood, when Sharla told Corgan to lie about the boys' identities?

"You're not what, dear?" Delphine asked, but Grimber broke in, "Get to work on those sutures. You've got to stop the bleeding. Anesthetize him. We don't have anything except chloroform, but if you're careful, that will work. Corgan, you get out of here. You're in the way."

"Let me stay at least until you put him under," Corgan pleaded, but Grimber yelled, "I said get out!"

Outside the laboratory Corgan paced. One small part of him wondered where Sharla and Brigand might be, but he was too worried about Seabrig to really care. At the very worst, they could climb down the mountain to the seacoast and follow the beach back to the landing strip. The sun had set and a huge moon rose, casting enough light that Sharla and Brigand should be able to see where they were going once they descended out of the jungle.

After fifty-seven minutes and thirty-two seconds had passed, Corgan quietly opened the door to the lab and crept inside. Both Delphine and Grimber were bent over Seabrig's unconscious form. His bloody wrist lay on the base of one of their microscopes; Grimber was peering through a microscope that magnified the tiny blood vessels to twenty times their size. Carefully he was sealing them against further bleeding. Not making a sound, Corgan went back outside and headed toward the beach.

He was right: Sharla and Brigand had followed the coast rather than trekking through the thick jungle growth in the darkness. When Corgan ran to meet them, Sharla leaned against him and asked, "Is he alive?"

"Yes. They're working on his wrist. And—they believe he's Brigand."

She heaved a deep sigh. "That's good. I've been thinking and thinking. I've got to take him back with me to the domed city, and I'll have to keep up the pretense that he really is Brigand."

"No!" Brigand said. "I don't want him to be me."

"Just for a while," she soothed him, "because this is a really complicated situation, and I need to work out all the angles."

"Why can't he just stay here?" Brigand asked.

Sharla knelt in the sand, put her arms around Brigand's waist, and looked up at him. "Seabrig will need an artificial hand. A robotic hand. There's no way to build one for him here on Nuku Hiva—no technicians, no electronic parts, no delicate machine tools. It can only be done in the domed city, where I'm friends with a lot of the engineers, and they'll keep quiet about it if I ask them to."

"But when we fly back to the domed city, Pilot will see that there are two boys instead of one, won't he?" Brigand asked. "So it won't work."

Brigand was right. There was no way to cram Seabrig into a flight bag now, the way Sharla had done when he was a baby. And even if Pilot stayed silent, the ground crew that met the flight at its destination would notice. . . .

Then Corgan got it. And at the same moment Brigand got it, too. *"No!"* he cried to Sharla. "You want me to stay here on Nuku Hiva with Corgan while you take Seabrig back with you."

"Just till we work things out—"

"I won't do it! I can stop this right now. I'm gonna tell Delphine and Grimber there are two clones."

Brigand turned to run across the beach and the landing strip toward the laboratory, where light still shone through the windows. He was fast, but Corgan was faster.

EIGHT

Corgan tackled Brigand with plenty of yardage to spare between the boy and the laboratory. As he threw him onto the ground he fought hard to resist the urge to grind Brigand's face into the dirt. This was the boy who'd hacked off Seabrig's hand, supposedly to keep him from drowning, but was that the truth? How could an eight-year-old—if that's what he was—make a judgment call like that? What was he really up to? And come to think of it, what had happened to the knife?

Brigand was shrieking, "Let me up! I hate you, Corgan." By then Sharla had caught up with them.

Clamping his arms around the boy even more tightly, Corgan said, "Sharla, I'm handling this. You stay out of it.

Go to the laboratory and find out how Seabrig is doing. By the way, I told them I was the one who cut off his hand."

In shadows cast by the moonlight Sharla's face was hard to read. Corgan thought her lips trembled, but he couldn't be sure. "I—I'm grateful," she said. "Somehow I'll make it up to you." After hesitating, she asked, "But would you please go easy on Brigand?"

"I'll do whatever I have to."

As she started toward the laboratory Brigand cried out beseechingly, "Sharla, don't leave me. Sharla!"

She began to run. Away from him.

"Come back! Please!" he sobbed, but she didn't turn around.

Wrestling the sobbing boy off the ground, Corgan dragged him a good quarter mile along the beach, then into the coconut palms, which stood deep in shadow. All the while Brigand kept kicking and insisting, "I saved Seabrig's life. He was stuck under a boulder. I had to get him loose. He'd have drowned, Corgan. I saved his life."

"Shut up!" Corgan found what he was looking for: a long, sturdy vine. Now Brigand became submissive, docile, but Corgan knew that was as much of a sham as his lies about Seabrig; at the first chance Brigand would bolt away and run to Sharla.

"Don't, Corgan! What are you doing? Please don't leave me here," he begged. "I'm scared of the dark."

Shoving him against the trunk of a tree, Corgan began to wrap the vine around both boy and tree, around and around, talking to him all the while. "You're staying here until the Harrier jet comes to take Sharla and Seabrig away

248

from the island. Once they're gone, I'll cut you loose, but you'd better keep away from the laboratory, because if I catch you telling any of this to Delphine and Grimber, I'll tie you up again and leave you out here in the jungle forever. And if I do that, you can yell as much as you want to, and nobody will ever hear you."

Tears ran down Brigand's cheeks; they reflected the moonlight. His voice, though, stayed under tight control. Almost matter-of-factly he said, "You're gonna be so sorry you did this, Corgan. From now on you and I are enemies. I have the power of the chiefs in me—"

"Where'd you get this sudden power? From that boars'-tusk necklace? How 'bout if I pull the necklace off you right now and throw it into the ocean?"

"No!" Brigand cried piteously, and all at once Corgan felt ashamed of himself. Brigand was half his age and less than half his size. Why was he bullying him this way? What if Brigand was telling the truth, and he really had saved Seabrig's life by cutting off his hand?

Abruptly Corgan turned away and left the boy, calling back to him, "I'll bring you something to eat later tonight."

"Don't bother!" Brigand yelled defiantly.

Corgan took off his shoes because it was easier to run barefoot along the sandy beach. His worry about Seabrig's condition impelled him to run faster and faster; when he reached the laboratory, he found that the surgery had been completed and Sharla was cradling Seabrig in her arms, trying to get him to sip water from a spoon. "Come on, Brigand," she crooned, "drink a little water."

Seabrig stared up at her through half-lowered lids.

"Brigand?" he whispered, either questioning why she called him by the wrong name, or perhaps wondering what had happened to his clone-twin.

"Don't try to talk now," she quieted him. "I'll stay here beside you all night."

"I want Corgan," he murmured.

"Corgan has other things to do, but I'm here for you, Brigand," she told him.

"And I am, too," Delphine said, bending over to check Seabrig's pulse, adding to Sharla, "You know, I always wanted a child of my own, but when I was a baby, my parents hadn't yet been evacuated from the radiation zone, and as a result I grew up to be sterile."

Corgan was surprised that Delphine—who seemed to be the ultimate dedicated scientist—had maternal feelings. As he watched from across the room she laid her hand tenderly on Seabrig's forehead and asked, "Do you feel cold, Brigand? I could bring you another blanket."

"He's fine," Sharla said quickly. "I can take care of him—oh, here's Corgan."

Corgan approached the lab table Seabrig had to lie on since there were no cots or hospital beds in the building. "Hey, friend," he said, "how do you feel?"

"My hand hurts," Seabrig complained.

Taken aback, Corgan didn't know how to respond, since he couldn't imagine how a hand could hurt if it wasn't there. Still groggy from the chloroform, Seabrig apparently wasn't yet aware of what had happened to him. "I'll stay with him for a while," Corgan told Sharla.

"No, I already explained to Brigand that you have other

things to take care of," she insisted, giving him a deliberate look. Obviously she wanted Corgan out of the way—just as she wanted Delphine and Grimber out of the way—so she could tell Seabrig about the switched identities, that he was now supposed to be his clone-twin instead of himself, that he was going to be taken away from Nuku Hiva.

"I know what you're planning, Sharla," Corgan murmured, "but before you talk to him, I want to talk to him first. He doesn't yet realize . . ." Corgan glanced toward the bandaged wrist. "Does he? Has anyone told him?"

Sharla shook her head.

"Then give me some time with him so I can take care of it."

Without answering, Sharla got up and left the room.

Corgan knelt beside the table on Seabrig's right side, then carefully lifted the blanket that covered the boy. Blood stained the bandages, but Seabrig wasn't looking; he kept his eyes on Corgan.

"Why am I here?" he wanted to know. "What happened to me?"

"Do you remember anything?" Corgan asked. "Think back. What's the last thing you remember?"

"The waterfall. The top of the cliff. Did we—make it?"

"Brigand did." Corgan spoke softly in case Grimber or Delphine might be within earshot. "When you slid down, there was a rockfall. A boulder landed on you. On your hand. In the pool."

"Did it break my hand? Is that why it hurts so much?" Seabrig's eyes looked so trusting. . . .

In an instant Corgan made up his mind. Why burden

this boy with suspicions about his clone-twin? Seabrig would have enough to suffer now—taking on a new identity, learning to use an artificial hand, living in an even more artificial, unfamiliar, unfriendly world.

"Here's what happened," he said. "Your hand got pinned under a huge boulder, and I couldn't find you because the water was all muddy from the rockfall. But Brigand, your clone-twin—he was a real hero. He dived to the bottom and saved your life by . . . by . . ."

"By what, Corgan?"

"He had to amputate your hand to free you. Otherwise you would have drowned."

It was only then that Seabrig raised his arm to look at his bandaged wrist. As the disbelief on his face turned to fear, then horror, Corgan got to his feet—he couldn't bear it any longer. "Everything's going to be all right," he said brokenly. "Sharla will tell you the rest. You've got a lot of exciting things ahead of you. You and I will talk more tomorrow."

As he turned to leave, Seabrig called out to him, "Corgan! It's lucky I taught Brigand to swim, isn't it? So he could save my life."

Delphine and Sharla had approached, Delphine carrying a thermometer. "Did you hear that?" she asked. "He sounds a little delusional. He may be running a fever."

It was all Corgan could do to keep from hurling himself past Delphine and out of the laboratory. On his way to the barn the tears he'd tried to hold back began to flow freely. With every step he took, his own guilt grew inside him, expanding, consuming him. *He* was the one who'd taken the boys to the dangerous water slide. *He'd* let them climb to the top by themselves because he'd wanted to be with Sharla. If only he'd been able to find Seabrig in that murky water, to reach him before Brigand did. Now Seabrig was maimed. He would be taken away from Nuku Hiva, the only place he'd ever really known, and sent to the domed city, where everything would be strangely different.

Not until Corgan had almost reached the barn did he realize he hadn't taken any food to Brigand as he'd promised. The moon was gone now, hidden behind the volcanic peak; in that kind of darkness he'd have a devil of a time finding the tree he'd tied Brigand to. And Brigand had told him not to bother bringing any food, so why should he trek all the way down the mountain again?

Besides, he had to make certain all the cattle were accounted for—after all, he'd been gone from them all day. Half a dozen other practical excuses occurred to him, justifications for not going to Brigand, but he knew the real reason was his fury over what Brigand had done to Seabrig. Even though Corgan's conscience kept delivering sharp stabs to his brain, he decided to ignore Brigand until dawn.

The events of the day should have exhausted him, but he couldn't sleep. In just two more days the Harrier jet was due to arrive. Sharla would leave then, Seabrig would go with her, and Corgan would stay behind with his doubts and with Brigand. He got out of his bunk and went to the tent they'd fashioned as a makeshift virtual reality Box for Seabrig. If only he could reach Mendor! Mendor the Mother would comfort him; Mendor the Father would advise him on whether he was doing the right thing.

Inside the tent a pale glow suffused the curtains as though they slumbered, awaiting a call from Seabrig. Corgan sat on the little bench he'd carved for Seabrig out of sandalwood.

"Mendor," he said aloud, like a prayer. "Mendor." That was all. His mind began to fill with images of his childhood: Mendor the Mother hovering over him to make sure he ate all the carefully manufactured food on his plate— mainly soybeans doctored with nutritious additives that were supposed to help him grow stronger and perform faster. Mendor the Father, stern with Corgan whenever he was careless in a practice session, later becoming a benign, steadfast Father Figure who praised Corgan, telling him how important he was to the Western Hemisphere Federations.

He had been so protected! Never had he been required to make a decision, make a choice. Never had he been responsible for the life of a child or even the life of a pet, because all his pet dogs and cats and turtles and birds had been virtual, made of electronic signals.

Then he'd chosen to live free on Nuku Hiva, and he'd suddenly become responsible for two lives—first Seabrig's, and now Brigand's.

For a moment he deluded himself that the glow on the walls of the virtual-reality Box had turned a little brighter. But no, Mendor wasn't going to help him. Corgan was on his own.

He had options: the first, to betray Sharla by telling Delphine and Grimber what had really happened. That way he might be able to keep Seabrig here, but then

Seabrig wouldn't get an artificial hand. And what if—as Sharla believed—the Supreme Council should decide to terminate Seabrig?

Strike out that option.

Or he could find the tree, right now, where he'd tied Brigand and bring him up here to the relative comfort of the barn, thus quieting Corgan's own conscience about treating the boy so harshly. But even here Corgan would have to keep Brigand tied up if he wanted him to stay quiet. The first chance Brigand got, he would be out of there, spilling everything to Grimber and Delphine. So option two would end the same way as option one, with Seabrig in danger of extermination.

Or they could follow Sharla's plan. But Sharla was not a strategist, she was a code breaker. So maybe her plan wasn't all that good. If only the clone-twins, who'd been bred as strategists, were a little older, they might have come up with better ideas. But they couldn't, not the way they were now: Brigand spoiled and fixated on Sharla, and Seabrig in no condition to suggest anything.

As Corgan lay rigid on his bunk, knowing sleep would never come to him, he heard noises he couldn't identify— snorting, grunting. The cows shifted in the pen and mooed restlessly, then began to run, their hooves shaking the ground.

Corgan leaped out of his bunk to rush outside. At the edge of the pen he saw a shadow of tremendous size, grunting, moving, pawing the ground. In the darkness he couldn't tell what it was, but he grabbed the lantern hanging on the outside of the barn and managed to light it with trembling fingers.

He turned and stared at the ugliest creature he'd ever seen. From pictures in old books he recognized it—a wild boar. Five-inch-long tusks curved upward from its lower jaw; a second set of smaller tusks curled up from its upper jaw. The creature must have weighed 135 kilograms at least. Its hide, a revolting mixture of drab grays, had bristles sticking out all over. Its snout, long and flat with two large nostrils protruding forward, looked slimy in the lantern light. Its mouth opened wide to reveal a curling, dripping tongue.

But worst of all were the eyes. Small and yellow, they glowed with malevolence.

If the boar attacked him, it could rip him apart with those tusks. Corgan would have no defense except to swing the lantern at it and hope the burning coconut oil would spill on the beast, driving it away. Yet it made no move to attack. Snuffling, snarling, it glared at Corgan for a full, long, awful minute, its eyes fierce with hatred. Then it turned to run, crashing through the trees.

nine

Early the next morning Corgan carried mangoes, bananas, and fresh milk to Brigand, who was easy enough to find in daylight.

"How am I supposed to eat with my arms tied up?" he asked.

"I'll untie your arm," Corgan answered, doing just that as he spoke. "And while you're eating, you can give thanks that you still have a right hand to feed yourself with."

But as soon as his arm was free, Brigand knocked the food right out of Corgan's grasp: Bananas dropped, mangoes rolled on the ground, and milk spilled all over the place.

Trying to suppress his anger, Corgan said, "I hope you weren't too hungry, because I'm not picking up that stuff." After yanking down a second, smaller vine, he wrapped one end of it around Brigand's wrist, then circled the tree trunk with the other end, tying both securely. "There. Now you have some motion with that arm, but you're still not going anywhere." Relenting, but only a little, he thrust a banana into Brigand's fingers and told him, "That's all you get until later. Maybe you'll be lucky and a coconut will land on you and crack itself open on your skull."

As Corgan hurried away he wondered why Brigand managed to aggravate him so much. Normally Corgan was polite to the few people he ever came in contact with; he was kind to animals; and he'd been pretty affectionate with Seabrig most of the time. But Brigand made irritation rise inside him like bile, in a way he'd never experienced with anyone else.

He reached the laboratory before Grimber and Delphine were out of bed, and that was good, because it gave him a chance to talk to Sharla. "Where did you sleep?" he asked her.

"On the floor. Here, beside him." She reached up to pat Seabrig's arm. "That is, the little I slept at all. He moaned all night. It made me cry."

It seemed that during that interminable night, tears had been shed all over the island.

Seabrig raised himself a little on his left elbow and then fell back because the effort was too tiring. "Where is my clone-twin who saved my life?"

Corgan answered, "He's staying out of the way. We can't let anyone find the two of you together."

"But I have to see him before we go," Seabrig pleaded. "I need to thank him."

Sharla and Corgan exchanged glances. No doubt she was wondering too where Corgan was keeping Brigand. "Don't worry, I'll work out something," he said. "Now, tell me what else I can do for you . . . Brigand." It was the first time he'd used the name, and he shuddered because it jarred his teeth to say it. Seabrig, though, seemed pleased.

"It's like a game, isn't it?" he asked softly. "We're all playing a game where we fool anyone who doesn't know the secret. Anyway, Corgan"—and he lowered his voice to a whisper again—"from now on you'll be able to tell us apart, because I'll have a superhand that's made of titanium, with stainless-steel finger pads so it can be magnetized. Sharla explained to me how wonderful it will be. She says it will do things that no real hand ever could—did you know that, Corgan?"

Though Seabrig was weak, his enthusiasm rose and his voice grew louder as he went on: "It'll have four fingers and a thumb, and it'll be able to lift twice as much weight as you can, Corgan. It won't be able to feel anything, though, and that's good, because it means it will never hurt me if it touches something hot or if it gets hit hard, like by a hammer. And if I do need to feel something, I can touch it with my left hand."

Corgan gave a brief nod to Sharla, enormously grateful that she'd managed not only to console Seabrig, but to convince him that an artificial hand was an advantage, not a tragedy.

"When can I leave here?" Seabrig asked. "When can I see . . . you know?"

Corgan figured that the less time the clone-twins spent with each other the better, since the situation had turned so risky. "I think you need to stay here a while longer," he answered. "It's up to Delphine. She's the doctor."

"Not really, Corgan. She's taking care of me, but she isn't a real doctor. She just knows how to poke genetic material into eggs borrowed from cows. Sharla," he asked, turning toward her, "when you created me, where did you get the genes to make me grow up so fast?"

Looking uncomfortable, Sharla hesitated. "Uh . . . why don't we talk about that another time?"

"No! I want to know now!" Like his clone-twin, Seabrig had an obstinate streak, and like the original Brig, he could whine when he didn't get his way. "You have to tell me what I want to know, or I'll get upset. And then my stump will take longer to heal, and it'll be your fault."

"Don't call it a stump!" Corgan ordered.

"All right, I won't if Sharla tells me the truth," Seabrig answered. "Where did she get the genetic material that makes . . . the *other one* and me grow up faster than anyone else?"

"From animals, right?" Corgan looked inquiringly at Sharla.

"*What* animal?" Seabrig demanded.

"Go ahead, Sharla, tell him. I'd like to know too. Let's see—which animals would mature really fast compared to humans?" Corgan wondered. "Mice? Dogs? Cats?"

"If you must know," Sharla murmured, "it's pigs."

"Pigs!" Both Seabrig and Corgan cried in disbelief.

"Yes, pigs. They're really close to humans in their genetic material. Even a hundred years ago doctors were implanting pig valves into humans with heart problems—it's called xenotransplantation. Pigs make ideal donors because their organs are about the same size as human organs, and they weigh close to the same as humans. . . ."

While Sharla went on to list all the advantages of pigs as organ donors and genetic donors, Corgan's mind slipped back to that horrible ugly boar that had visited him last night. Boars, pigs, swine—all names for the same species. The natives of Nuku Hiva must have had some special reverence for wild boars, judging from the tusks fused to the human skull Seabrig had found a few weeks ago, and from the body in the tomb, which wore an elaborate boars'-tusk necklace. It flashed into his memory that the first thing Brigand had done this morning when Corgan freed his arm was to clutch that necklace, as if to assure himself that it was still there. That was right before he knocked away the food Corgan offered him.

If Brigand had received genetic material from a boar—and the males of domestic pigs, as well as wild ones, were called boars—would that make him feel connected to . . . ? That was crazy! If it were true, Seabrig would have developed the same feelings, and Seabrig hadn't cared a bit about the boars'-tusk necklace. He was happy for Brigand to have it.

But where had that wild boar come from last night? And why last night of all nights? In the year Corgan had lived on the island, that was the first boar he'd actually seen.

Sharla was still explaining: "A change made to just one of the one hundred thousand pig genes means that proteins on the surface of the pig's organs will be recognized as human—"

Corgan interrupted, "Did both boys receive genetic material from the same animal?"

She sighed. "From the same species. What difference does it make?"

"But—from the same animal?"

"I don't know. The tissue was frozen. I used two separate cryo-vials."

Corgan shook his head to clear it. Maybe because he hadn't slept last night, his mind raced with ludicrous thoughts about the clone-twins, about donor pigs and wild boars. Just then the bedroom door opened and Delphine came rushing out, asking, "How is he this morning? Is his temperature normal? Do you think you could eat something, Brigand?"

Following her, Grimber said, "If he's going to eat, I'd prefer that you move him off my lab table. Children spill things. Especially since he's not used to eating with his left hand."

With a stricken expression Delphine cried, "That was terribly cruel for you to say!" but Grimber ignored her, muttering, "I'll move him myself. There's no reason he can't sit up in a chair to eat."

"Never mind!" Corgan commanded, cutting off Grimber as he moved toward the lab table. "Sharla and I will take care of . . . of Brigand . . . now. I'll carry him to my quarters in the barn."

Delphine's eyes filled with tears as she begged, "Don't take him away, please! I can find a place for him. His bandages will need changing, and I have to do it—you can't. That barn is a filthy place; there's no way to make it sterile—"

Gently, Corgan told her, "Just tell me when to bring him back and I will. I promise you'll see him before he leaves Nuku Hiva." And then to Sharla, "Let's go. Take the blanket."

Seabrig used his one hand to clutch Corgan's neck as he was lifted from the table. His body felt lighter than it had before, and his face looked strained from the pain of being moved, but he didn't complain—he just bit his lower lip with his teeth and squeezed his eyes shut. Sharla trailed them, trying to wrap the blanket around Seabrig as Corgan walked quickly through the door. Behind them Delphine reached toward Seabrig. She looked anguished.

"Do you think this is wise?" Sharla asked Corgan. "To move him?"

"We had to get him out of there. Delphine's all right, but I don't trust Grimber. Since we have to keep this a secret, we'll take care of him ourselves."

"Anyway," Seabrig said, grimacing with pain even though Corgan was trying to walk as smoothly as he could, "now I can see my clone-twin, right?"

"Sure," Corgan answered, wondering how he was going to arrange that without Brigand wrecking all their plans. "But first we have to get you settled in."

Carrying Seabrig up the side of the mountain was easy for Corgan but hard on Seabrig. Sharla tried to comfort the boy by keeping him covered, and tried to distract him by telling him about the hover cars that transported people through the domed city, about the hydroponic gardens that grew all their food, about how exciting it was to be lifted straight up off the ground in the Harrier jet and then to see the Earth from ten thousand meters above its surface. Seabrig tried to smile, but his eyes were shadowed with deep, dark circles and his skin looked leaden, except for a ring of deathly paleness around his mouth.

"Mm-hmm," he answered. "Corgan told me about some of those things. Corgan, when I'm gone, will you still be my best friend?"

"I will. Nothing can change that."

"When will we see each other again?"

"That's hard to say right now." Certainly Corgan didn't know the answer—unless the answer was "Never." Seabrig would most likely stay in the domed city, at least until it was decided whether the Virtual War was to be refought. As soon as he regained his stamina, he would need to be trained for that. Brigand had already been in training; Seabrig would have a long way to go to catch up.

And if there weren't another Virtual War, what then? Would Seabrig ever be able to leave the domed city? Would Corgan have to hide Brigand on Nuku Hiva for the rest of both their lives? That brought up another possibility. The clone-twins aged at the rate of two years for every month they lived. By the end of a year they'd be the equivalent of twenty-four years old; after two years, forty-eight; after three years, seventy-two. And after that, how long would they live?

When they reached the barn, Sharla ripped down the LiteSuit material on the makeshift Virtual Box, using it as sheets on Corgan's rather messy bunk. "At least they'll be clean," she said, wrinkling her nose. "This whole place smells like cows."

"What would you expect it to smell like?" Corgan snapped.

"Don't fight," Seabrig pleaded, his voice weak. "Corgan, can I see Brigand now?"

"All right, I'll go get him," Corgan said grudgingly. "Sharla, while I'm gone, will you find some food for all of us?"

"Oh. Find some food. What am I supposed to be—your sweet little housewife?"

Corgan's jaw worked. "Do you want me to get food and let you go for Brigand? Only one problem with that—you don't know where he is. So how will you manage to find him?" *Stop it,* he told himself. They had only one more day together and then she'd be gone, and he didn't know when he'd see her again. He realized that fatigue and worry were taking a toll on all of them. No, that wasn't true—Seabrig was trying to keep the peace: He looked at them pleadingly and begged in a weak voice, "Don't! Please be nice."

"Sorry." Corgan knelt beside the bunk and with his fingertips brushed Seabrig's pale cheek. "I know how much you want to see your clone-twin," he said softly, "so I'll bring him here as quickly as I can. You rest until we get back, will you? Promise me." When Seabrig nodded and closed his eyes, Corgan came close to losing control.

Abruptly he stood up and hurried to the shed where he kept his equipment. From hooks on the wall he took down the meter-long cattle prod he used when any of the cows got balky, although that rarely happened. Fingering the trigger, he made sure the batteries had enough power to shoot sparks from the double prong on the end of the rod. Just let Brigand try to bolt!

Jogging down the side of the mountain, he quickly reached the stand of coconut palms where he'd tied Brigand. Brigand's eyes reminded Corgan of the wild boar's of the night before—radiating hostility. "See this thing?" Corgan asked, brandishing the cattle prod. "Let me show you what it can do."

He fired it off so close to Brigand's ear that some hair on the boy's neck got singed. Brigand jerked away but kept his disdainful expression.

"You think that was bad? You should feel it when it hits you head-on," Corgan said, trying to scare him. "Now, here's the deal. I'll untie you from the tree, but I'll keep the vines wrapped around you till we get close to the barn. That's where Seabrig is. He wants to see you. For some reason he seems really fond of you."

"Of course he is. He loves me," Brigand said. "We're clone-twins. We're the same."

"No, you're not the same, and I'm sure glad of that. Now, when we get to the barn, you'll be nice to Seabrig, or . . ." Again Corgan pulled the trigger of the cattle prod, this time charring the bark of a tree. "You'll be nice to him for as long as he's here."

"And then what?"

"Then, after Seabrig and Sharla leave this island, you can do whatever you want."

"Stay as far away from you as I can," Brigand shot back. "That's what I want."

"Good. You'll be doing me a favor. Now, let's get going."

TEN

At the door of the barn Corgan hung the cattle prod back on its hooks, whispering to Brigand, "You'll be surprised how fast I can reach this if I need it."

Scowling, Brigand entered the part of the barn where Seabrig lay on Corgan's bunk.

"Brigand!" Seabrig cried, his face lighting up. He raised his right arm in greeting, then selfconsciously lowered it again to lift his left hand instead, mumbling, "Sometimes I forget. *Usually* I forget."

Brigand's scowl disappeared as he sat down cross-legged at the foot of the bed. "Does it hurt bad?" he asked.

"Brigand, you didn't even say hello to me," Sharla told him. "I've missed you."

Slowly Brigand turned to stare at her, his gaze accusing. "You'd better get used to missing me, since this whole plan to separate us was your idea. Yours and Corgan's."

Sharla stammered, "I . . . we have to do this. There's no other way."

In the stony silence that followed, Seabrig rested his left hand on his clone-twin's arm and asked, "What's the matter, Brigand? Don't you want to go ahead with all this? If you don't, it's fine—I can get along without an artificial hand. Anything you want to do is fine with me. After all, you saved my life."

Corgan wanted to blurt out, "The decision is not up to Brigand," but he held back, waiting for what Brigand would answer, ready to reach for the cattle prod if Brigand started to upset Seabrig.

Instead Brigand clasped Seabrig's good hand and said, "From now on, it's you and me. We're warriors together. We don't need anybody but each other. As soon as I can get away from this island, I'll come to you in the domed city."

"Don't make promises you can't keep," Corgan warned him. At the same moment he heard a commotion outside: The cattle had become restless again, mooing and crashing into the rails of the pen. As he ran out he grabbed the cattle prod, and there, in almost the same spot as the night before, stood the wild boar.

"What is it?" Brigand came out to see and then rushed forward to knock the prod out of Corgan's hands, yelling, "Let him alone!" Fearlessly he ran toward the boar, his arms spread wide as if to protect it from Corgan.

"Get away from him!" Corgan shouted. "He'll kill you."

"No, he won't." Completely without fear, Brigand faced the boar and held out his hand, almost touching the hideous snout. The boar snorted, attempted to rear on its hind legs, and then, unexpectedly, turned and trotted off. With a brief glance at Corgan, Brigand called out, "Why don't you stick yourself with that prod, Corgan, and see how you like it. I'm going back to my clone-twin."

Standing motionless, Corgan tried to make sense of what he'd just witnessed. In some unfathomable way Brigand had calmed the boar, almost as if he'd communicated with it. It had to be a matter of chance, nothing but random chance—if Brigand tried anything like that again, he'd surely be maimed or killed. Corgan had read, or heard of, or been taught by Mendor—he couldn't remember which—that killer wolves and bears and even poisonous snakes would sometimes back away from an attack if the human showed no fear. Maybe that's what had happened. He turned that over in his mind as he went into the pen to try and quiet the cows.

Back inside the barn he found Brigand with his hand gripping Seabrig's arm just above the severed stump. "I have the power of the chiefs inside me now, and I'm sharing my strength with you," Brigand was telling him. "Do you feel it? Come on, get up. You're stronger than you think."

Focusing intently on Brigand, Seabrig raised himself to sit on the edge of the bunk.

"Now I'm going to tell you what will happen to you," Brigand announced. "You will receive a new hand, one made of metal and wire and springs. The new hand will give you power, although not as much power as the power of the chiefs that I have in me." Tightening his grip on the damaged arm, Brigand added, "Plus, I'm giving you a new name."

"What is it?" Seabrig asked, never taking his eyes from his clone-twin.

"Seabrig the Cyborg."

Corgan flinched, hating it. A cyborg was part human and part machine. Just because Seabrig would have an artificial hand, that didn't make him a cyborg.

Seabrig smiled, accepting the name. "Cyborg. I like it. I have something to give you, too, Brigand," he said. "Corgan, would you get it for me? It's up there." He pointed to the human skull, which rested on a shelf above the smaller bunk where Seabrig usually slept. When Corgan handed it to him, Seabrig held it out to Brigand. "See?" he asked. "It has tusks like the ones in your necklace."

"The sign of the chiefs," Brigand answered. "Wild boars give cannibal chiefs their powers."

Annoyed, Corgan ordered, "Don't fill his head with that kind of foolishness! You're getting him all worked up, and he needs to rest. I think you'd better go now, Brigand."

"I'm going." After Brigand gave his clone-twin a quick hug, he promised, "We'll grow up fast. Stay brave, Cyborg." Then he stalked through the door, cradling the skull in his arms.

Running after him, Sharla cried, "Brigand, come back! I need to talk to you, to say good-bye." That left Corgan alone with Seabrig, who glanced up at him a bit shyly.

"I know you don't like him, Corgan, but I wish you

hadn't chased him away," Seabrig said. "Oh, well. We'll stay connected." Seabrig tapped his temple with the index finger of his left hand. "We communicate up here."

Suddenly weary, Corgan sat down on a pile of hay. "Seabrig," he asked, "on the days you were out playing by yourself and I wasn't around, did you ever see a wild boar on the island?"

Seabrig shook his head. "I never saw him, but I heard him in the jungle. Making noises. Pawing around."

"How did you know it was a boar if you didn't see him?"

Shrugging, Seabrig answered, "I knew. And Mendor said I was right."

"How would Mendor know?"

Seabrig just shrugged again, not bothering to answer.

Hours went by and Sharla didn't return. Corgan wished he could go to find her, but he couldn't leave Seabrig alone. Yet Seabrig seemed much stronger. He ate all the fruit Corgan piled on a plate for him, drank a whole liter of fresh milk, and then got up to walk around the confined space of Corgan's quarters.

"Tell me about Sharla, Corgan," he requested. "Will she like having me with her all the time, or will she miss Brigand too much?"

"Believe me, Sharla's going to be coming out way ahead of the game. By having you, I mean, while I get stuck with your clone-twin."

Sharply, Seabrig said, "Don't talk about Brigand that way. He saved my life."

Again Corgan felt tempted to tell Seabrig of his suspicion that Brigand had unnecessarily mutilated him for some unimaginable reason. Again he decided against it. Instead he said, "I don't know how you and I will be able to stay in touch after you leave. There's no radio contact between here and the domed city. All the communication satellites have failed, or burned up crashing back to Earth."

"The Harrier jet comes every so often," Seabrig reminded him. "I'll give Pilot messages for you. And you'll write back. Please?"

"I will. I promise. And you be sure to study hard. Learn everything they can teach you in the domed city. You'll be an even greater strategist than your . . . your . . ." He wanted to mention Brig, but he didn't know what to call him. Seabrig's cell donor?

After Seabrig fell asleep, Corgan went outside to pace back and forth on the brow of the slope, waiting for Sharla to return. The sky was at its most magnificent: cloudless, with the moon and Venus shining brilliantly against a background of bold stars and softer galaxies.

When at last she came to him, a little breathless from the climb, Corgan asked her, "Do you remember when we lived in the domed city together and I saw the real sky for the first time?"

"I remember."

"The sky that night was almost as clear as this one, with the Milky Way spread overhead like a carpet. I remember how it amazed me. Now we're here in the Southern Hemisphere, and there are galaxies up there that we could never see from the domed city." He pointed. "They're called the Magellanic Clouds. See them?"

"Uh-huh," she agreed, barely looking at the sky. "Everything's all right now. It's all settled."

"Between you and Brigand, you mean. What about between you and me?"

In answer, she came to him and raised her face for his kiss. As much as he wanted to fight against it—this need of his to love Sharla—he couldn't. Not tonight. And why should he fight her? What had happened to Seabrig couldn't be undone. And her solution—to take Seabrig to the domed city—was the only right one.

"Brigand says he's not coming back here to the barn," she told him. "At least not until after I leave, and maybe not then, either. He found himself a little cove between the seashore and the jungle, and he says he'll live there."

"He'll be back," Corgan assured her. "If only because he loves to aggravate me."

Sharla looked unhappy. "There was something I wanted to do for him—reprogram Mendor so Brigand would have at least one friend, since you dislike him so much."

"I don't—"

"Sure you do. It's obvious. He told me some of the things you said to him."

Corgan felt his cheeks grow hot with embarrassment. He could just imagine how Brigand would have distorted Corgan's threats.

"Anyway, I can't reprogram Mendor for Brigand if he's not here. It's a matter of iris identification. The dots and whorls in the colored part of each person's eyes are unique. I mean, really unique—not even the left and right irises match each other in the same person," she explained, and added, "Even identical twins have different iris patterns from each other. And our clone-twins do, too, which is why Brigand wouldn't be able to use Mendor unless I could recode the program with an image of Brigand's iris."

The idea hit Corgan instantly. "Uh . . . if you can't do it for Brigand . . ."

"Yes?"

"Could you reprogram Mendor for me? I feel like I really need Mendor right now."

Sharla sighed. "It'll take me half the night, but yes, I can do it. It won't be complete, though, until we rehang that LiteSuit fabric that Seabrig is using for bunk sheets."

Corgan felt torn. There was so little time left before the Harrier jet would arrive to take Sharla back to the domed city. Did he want her to waste these final hours reprogramming Mendor just so he could get advice to deal with his mounting problems? But he had to admit he felt a need for the comfort of Mendor the Mother Figure, although he could do without the discipline of Mendor the Father Figure.

"Do you mind?" he asked her.

"Since it was my boy Brigand who caused all this trouble, I guess I owe it to you."

Now was the time to be manly, to tell her that taking blame for things that couldn't be changed was a waste of time. That she owed him nothing. But he remained silent.

"All right, come on," she said. "I need you for the iris-imaging part. After that, I work alone."

He meant to stay awake until she'd finished reprogramming Mendor, but as the night wore on, his weariness caught up with him. Since Seabrig was in Corgan's bunk, Corgan slept on the floor, on a bed of straw. Even when he heard the cattle lowing restlessly, probably because the boar had come back, he couldn't manage to pull himself awake.

But when he sensed Sharla beside him, he came vibrantly awake. After she'd kissed him, she said, "It's finished. All you have to do is hang up the LiteSuit fabric and Mendor will recognize you."

"Stay with me," he pleaded. "For what's left of the night. In one hour, twenty-seven minutes, and fourteen and ninety-three hundredths seconds, the sun will come up."

"Oh, Corgan, you make everything so romantic," she answered. "Nothing softens a girl's heart like a whole string of fractions." But she lay beside him, warm against him, raising his roughened hands to her lips. Was this what she'd meant when she said she'd make it up to him for the lie about Seabrig's hand? If so, the lie was worth it.

Less than three minutes had gone by when they heard Seabrig's sleepy voice. "What's happening?" he asked. "Is that you, Sharla? Did Brigand come back?"

"No, he didn't," Corgan answered. "Go back to sleep."

"I can't. I'm wide awake now. Maybe I should go in and say good-bye to Mendor."

"I'm afraid Mendor won't work for you anymore," Corgan told him. "Sharla has reprogrammed Mendor for me. I hope you don't mind too much."

"It's all right. I'll just go outside and see my island for the last time," Seabrig said, but when he tried to get up, he stumbled in the darkness. "Whoops! I guess I'm not as strong as I thought I was."

"Here, let me help you." By then Sharla was on her feet, her arms supporting Seabrig as he walked toward the door. "I don't think you should be outside by yourself anyway," she said. "Brigand told me that right before he left, a wild boar came here."

Corgan gave up. Standing, he said, "I think it was here a little while ago, too."

"I'm not afraid of it. It wouldn't hurt me," Seabrig told them.

How do you know? Corgan wanted to ask, but he didn't dare to drag that whole weird uncertainty back into his own thoughts. He'd thrash it out later. Instead he sat with Sharla and Seabrig—Seabrig between the two of them so they could keep him warm—to watch the sun rise over the ocean.

"I'll miss it," Seabrig said. "But I'll miss you even more, Corgan."

"And I'm going to miss you, too. A whole lot." He put his hand on Seabrig's head, on that bright red hair that had always given him away when they played hiding games among the trees. Corgan hoped the Harrier jet might be delayed, by bad weather or by lack of fuel or anything not too catastrophic, something that would keep Seabrig—and Sharla—on Nuku Hiva for another day, another week. He'd be grateful for even a few extra hours.

"Will you say good-bye to Mendor for me, Corgan?" Seabrig asked.

"I will."

"Tell Mendor about my new name. Cyborg. And will you please try to like my clone-twin, Brigand?"

Lie to him, Corgan told himself, and answered, "That won't be a problem."

Seabrig laid his bandaged arm across Corgan's knees. "I trust you, Corgan," he said. "Because we're friends."

ELEVEN

Corgan couldn't even say good-bye to Sharla the way he wanted to, because Delphine had come to the landing strip. She crouched before Seabrig, hugging him and weeping over him.

"Dear, dear Brigand," Delphine cried.

"Call me Cyborg," he said. "That's my new name. From now on, everybody must call me Cyborg."

"Oh. Well, I just want to tell you how much I'll miss you . . . Cyborg. Please send me letters about the progress you make, and just to . . . just to . . ." She dabbed her eyes. "Just to say hello. Remember me in your thoughts, dear boy."

Gravely Cyborg answered, "I will. Both. Send you letters and remember you."

Corgan and Sharla could only hug each other briefly before Pilot called out, "Load up. It's going to be tight with three people in here." That was true. This particular Harrier jet was a trainer, with seats for an instructor and a student, modified to hold just enough fuel to fly the distance from Nuku Hiva to the domed city. The extra weight of a third passenger would strain the fuel capacity—still, Cyborg wasn't very big.

"You flew us here a week ago; what's different about taking us back?" Sharla asked Pilot.

The difference—though neither Delphine nor Pilot knew it—was that the boy now boarding the Harrier jet was not the child who'd flown to Nuku Hiva the week before. Corgan knew it, Sharla knew it, and Brigand, who might be peering out from the jungle watching all this, knew it too; in fact Brigand might be ready to spring out at them and blow the whole deception sky-high.

"Hurry," Corgan urged. Cyborg had trouble climbing the ladder of the aircraft. Sharla had to stand right behind him, giving him a boost each time he jerked his hand upward from one rung to the next. The exertion left him panting, but he didn't complain.

Once they were inside, Cyborg grinned and waved at Corgan. Then Pilot slammed the canopy into place and fired up the engines to full power. From the wings, balls of vapor shot downward as the aircraft accelerated, lifting itself straight up from the landing strip. With its wheels retracting as it rose, the aircraft hovered for seven and three-tenths seconds, then turned north and flew off into the distance.

So they were gone.

Delphine turned toward Corgan to accuse him, "You didn't come to the laboratory last night. Work is piling up. We need you to spend more hours with us."

Corgan nodded. Maybe he should, now that Cyborg was gone. He didn't feel particularly responsible for the well-being of Brigand, who'd boasted to Sharla that he could live on his own in the jungle. That was probably true. Food was plentiful, predators nonexistent—except for the wild boars. And Brigand clearly wasn't afraid of the huge boar that seemed to be stalking Corgan.

Therefore, with no clone-twin to look after, Corgan should be able to spare extra time for the laboratory. But he'd much rather spend that time with Mendor, mulling over all the things that had happened in the past few months, trying to find answers to the questions that kept plaguing him.

"Why don't you sleep in the laboratory at night instead of going up to the barn?" Delphine was asking.

"Where? On the floor? You didn't even have a bed for . . . uh, Cyborg when he was hurt." Corgan had to stop stumbling over the name. Once Cyborg received his mechanical hand, people in the domed city would easily remember the new name and no one would suspect that he was not Brigand.

"I could find something to make a bed for you in the lab," Delphine was saying.

"No, thanks. I prefer my bunk in the barn."

"Suit yourself." She tossed her mane of bushy black hair and walked away, leaving Corgan alone for the first time in—how long had it been since Sharla'd brought Cyborg to him in a flight bag?

Instead of heading straight back to the barn, he decided to return to the pool where the amputation had happened. Last night he'd been thinking about the spear Brigand had found near the tomb, and about Corgan's own knife, which had disappeared. If Brigand had brought either of those things back with him to the beach that night, after the accident, Corgan had failed to see them. And the spear would have been hard to miss. By logic, therefore, both the knife and the spear should still be at the pool.

The path he'd cut through the jungle foliage two days ago remained visible, although green tendrils had already begun to snake back across the cleavage. Just as he had before, Corgan climbed over the aerial roots of the banyan trees and across the boulders of moss-covered volcanic rock, all the time wondering what had ever possessed him to lead two little boys into this jungle, which now seemed dark and dangerous. Parrots shrieked harshly at him, as if in accusation. Water dripped onto his head and ran down his cheeks like tears. The severed ends of the branches he'd cut pointed at him as though blaming him. By the time he came upon the waterfall, regret had engulfed Corgan as completely as the spray from the cataract.

He had to avert his eyes from the bloodstained rocks beside the pool. Then he forced himself to look at them, searching for his knife. It wasn't there. Knowing it would be futile, he dived deep into the pool anyway, where the mud had settled now and the water was no longer murky.

Again and again he dived, but it was no use. He couldn't find the knife.

Back at the surface he circled the perimeter of the pool, then expanded the diameter of the circle by two meters at a time, scouring the rocky ground for the spear. Again, nothing. The spear had disappeared as thoroughly as Corgan's knife.

Giving up, he started back through the jungle. Although Corgan's inner clock told him it was barely fourteen minutes and eight and a quarter seconds past four in the afternoon, the jungle had darkened as the towering mountain peaks hid the lowering sun. Again he heard the birds: Owls hooted, cuckoos screeched, mynas berated him with their noisy, grating cries.

"Who's there?" he called out. Beneath the bird clamor he heard something else: a rustling in the foliage at ground level. Corgan stopped to peer around him but saw nothing. When he moved forward again, the rustling started up once more. Something or someone was following him, not at a distance but close, although the thick foliage hid anything farther than a meter away.

Since he had no weapon to defend himself, he began to scan the ground for a broken branch heavy enough for protection, but in this lush tropical growth branches never dried out and broke off. When Corgan tried jumping on a low-hanging one, it whipped back like a spring; without a knife he couldn't cut it.

He strained his ears to listen. If it was the wild boar following him, he should be able to hear the animal's snuffling breath. He heard nothing. Should he run? Boars were fast; it could probably outrace him. He remembered those long, curved tusks; boars used them to rip open the belly of their prey. Better not run. Better head for the beach, where everything was out in the open and at least he might discover who or what was stalking him.

When he reached the beach at last, his heart slowed to normal. As far as he could see in any direction, the beach looked deserted. Except for the footprints. Boy-sized footprints. Brigand's. Heading in the direction Corgan had just come from.

To the left of the footprints a long, thin line had been traced in the sand. Corgan could visualize it as if he'd seen it: Brigand walking the beach before he headed into the jungle, holding the spear in his right hand, dragging its end through the sand, which meant he'd been to the pool ahead of Corgan. He'd probably found the knife, too.

Mendor. Corgan needed to consult with Mendor. The rain began then, one of the sudden downpours that hit Nuku Hiva so frequently. He ran the rest of the distance along the beach toward the path that climbed the slope to the barn.

Inside he whipped the LiteSuit material off the bunk and hung it on the sides of the makeshift Box Seabrig had used to communicate with Mendor. If only this would work! Although the stool he'd built for Seabrig was too short for him, he jack-knifed himself into a sitting position and waited.

Before him the shimmering material took on a shape and color that became a face, the loving, familiar face of Mendor the Mother Figure. "Corgan, dear boy," she said. "How long has it been since we said farewell?"

"Fourteen months, twelve days, twenty-one hours, sixteen minutes, and thirty-eight and forty-seven one-hundredths seconds," he answered.

"Excellent," Mendor praised him. "You've kept up your time-splitting ability."

Corgan realized that it had come back, maybe not as perfect as before, but better than it had been in months. "It seems like it," he answered.

"Are you eating properly?" she asked. "Are you practicing your speed drills?"

Smiling, Corgan answered, "Mendor, I think Sharla forgot to adjust you for the new situation I'm in. I'm here on Nuku Hiva, tending cows. I don't do any speed drills. If there's another Virtual War, I won't be fighting it."

Mendor's face sparkled with golden static as it morphed halfway between the Mother Figure and the Father Figure. In a deeper voice he/she said, "Don't count on that."

"Why? Sharla told me there's a girl named Ananda who'll take my place if the Virtual War is fought again."

"Events may intervene," Mendor said. "Always be prepared for the unexpected. Beginning tomorrow, you will practice Golden Bees once again."

Corgan shrugged. He was no longer living full-time in a Virtual Box where Mendor ruled his life; he could choose to practice Golden Bees if he felt like it, or choose not to. As for the girl Ananda, since according to Sharla she was so much more skilled than Corgan, of course she'd be chosen to perform in the replay of the War, if it took place.

"For now, Mendor," he said, "I need information. How would I go about killing a wild boar?"

He heard a whirring as the image of Mendor faded. That always happened when Mendor searched the database for any kind of information. Very shortly she was back, once again the Mother Figure, saying, "There is no large cache of information about killing wild boars. This is all I found: A wild boar is the only animal that no other animal will confront. It will attack without provocation. It is fast, it can jump, it will disembowel its victims with its long tusks."

Corgan took a deep breath. "Keep going," he said. "Anything else?"

"Long, long ago, before Earth became ruined, men hunted wild boars with spears, both in Europe and in a country named India. They called the sport pig-sticking. Unless the spear could be thrust into the boar at a vital spot, it did not kill the beast, but only infuriated it. Wild boars were killed, yes; back then, in the nineteenth century, this was known as sport. But many of the so-called civilized men who hunted the boars died too, slit into shreds by those deadly tusks."

Corgan got to his feet. "Thanks, Mendor. I'll see you later."

"Corgan, come back. You must practice your Precision and Sensitivity drills."

"Later, Mendor," he answered, pushing through the LiteSuit material. This freedom to go and come as he pleased suited him. What a difference from two years ago, before he met Sharla, when he'd obeyed every single command that Mendor issued. Back then Corgan had never been outside his virtual-reality Box; had never seen or touched a human being, a rock, an animal, or an ocean wave; had lived, breathed, eaten, and slept entirely sur-rounded by virtual images and sensations.

Now he could choose how much time he spent with Mendor. Still, he didn't want to antagonize either the Mother Figure or the Father Figure, because they were excellent sources of information. About the pig-sticking, for instance. Tonight he'd learned that it was possible to hunt boars with spears. All he had to do was find the spear. Which meant finding Brigand.

That proved to be more difficult than he'd expected. Each day when he had a fragment of time between caring for the cows, delivering the calves that were being born more frequently now, working long hours in the labora-tory in the evening, and indulging Mendor by practic-ing finger exercises and Precision and Sensitivity drills, Corgan searched the island for Brigand. Signs of him were everywhere—footprints, discarded coconut shells and banana peels, fish guts being picked at by terns and gulls on the beach. To gut those fish, Brigand had to be using something sharp. Corgan's knife, no doubt.

Weeks passed. No matter how hard Corgan searched, Brigand eluded him. And every few nights, Corgan would hear the sound of the wild boar snuffling around the cattle pen, although by the time he ran outside, the boar would have vanished into the darkness. The restlessness of the cows made Corgan's work even harder, trying to calm them. Two of them gave birth to their calves prematurely, and the calves died.

Grimber was furious over the loss, since one of the dead calves tested positive for a trait they'd been trying to transgenerate. "What kind of idiot are you that you can't even tend a herd of cows?" Grimber stormed at Corgan. "Go after that boar and kill it!"

With what? If only Corgan could find the spear, he could wait under cover of darkness to ambush the wild boar. But locating a slender spear in a wild, dark jungle was an order of magnitude harder than finding a boy—fair skinned, red haired, and who must be as tall as a ten-year-old now—and Corgan couldn't even manage to do that.

A month after Sharla and Cyborg left Nuku Hiva, the Harrier jet returned to the island for the first time. Seeing the aircraft approach, Corgan rushed to the landing strip and reached it just as Pilot climbed down the ladder from the cockpit.

"Corgan, here's a couple of things for you," Pilot said. "Cyborg sent you a letter, and your girlfriend, Sharla, sent you some new clothes." He handed over a package wrapped in heavy paper and sealed with tape.

Surprised and pleased at the word *girlfriend*, Corgan smiled as he accepted the package. "Any news about refighting the Virtual War?" he asked.

"None that I've heard," Pilot answered. "Gotta go—I need to unload these supplies and take them to the laboratory. Then Grimber will chew me out because the stuff I bring him is never exactly what he ordered. I tell him I'm not the person who packed it, but he doesn't care. And I don't give a damn that he doesn't get what he wants." Pilot curled his lip to show his disdain for Grimber. "Delphine, though, she's all right. I feel bad for that woman, stuck here with that mean son of a . . ."

Corgan ran partway up the slope before he tore open the envelope Pilot had handed him. He felt a small disappointment when he saw that the letter was from Cyborg, not Sharla. But maybe Sharla had put a note inside the package. He began to read:

Dear Corgan,

You should see my new hand. The fingers and thumb are jointed, so I can move them just the way my real hand moves. But it's even better than my real hand. For one thing, I can press a switch and the hand turns into a magnet. For another thing, when I grip something, the grip can't be broken. I can lift three times my own weight. If I wanted to, I could punch a hole through a wall and it wouldn't hurt my hand.

When you write back, be sure to address the letter to Cyborg. That's what everyone around here calls me, even though they think I'm Brigand. It's because of the hand, you know.

P.S. Tell Brigand I miss him.
P.P.S. Sharla says hi.

"Sharla says hi." That was all? Still hoping for a message inside the package, Corgan carried it into his quarters inside the barn. Carefully, trying to keep it from ripping, he pulled the tape off the paper wrapper. So few supplies reached him on the island that everything, even a crumpled piece of wrapping paper, had value.

Inside the package lay a shirt with a note pinned to it:

"To replace the one you tore up for bandages." The shirt was handsome, made of a stronger LiteSuit cloth than Corgan had ever seen before. Beneath the shirt lay—blue jeans! Where had she found them? Blue jeans were as rare and as priceless as diamonds. The pair Corgan had worn to shreds had been given to him as a reward for winning the Virtual War. In the pocket of the new pair he found another short note: "These were manufactured in the year 2012. Never worn. I got them in payment from a member of the Supreme Council when I replicated a DNA code to cure his genetic disease. Wish I could see you wearing them. Love, Sharla."

Just a few lines, but that was sufficient. She cared enough about him to spend her reward on a gift for him, rather than on something for herself. He held the note to his face, hoping for the scent of her, but it only smelled like paper.

Then, at the bottom of the package, he noticed an envelope he'd missed earlier. He turned it over; on the back was written, "For Brigand. So you won't forget me."

Lifting the flap, which was unsealed, he found a picture of Sharla—Sharla smiling, holding in her arms a baby Brigand, who looked about two years old, which meant the picture had been taken only a month after Brigand's birth.

Why should he give this picture to Brigand, when he himself didn't own a single picture of Sharla? Anyway, he'd been unable to find Brigand; in fact he'd almost given up the search—would have, except that he wanted the spear. And wanted his knife back.

Corgan propped the picture on a small shelf above his bunk, where he could see it just before he went to sleep at night and again the moment he woke up in the morning. The notes he kept under his pillow.

TWELVE

More weeks passed, but the seasons never changed much on Nuku Hiva. The only variation was the amount of rainfall: a lot, a lot more, and a deluge. Corgan wondered how Brigand kept himself dry, wherever he was.

One morning, inside the Virtual Box, Corgan said, "Mendor, I need your help."

"With what, child?" The kind, golden face of Mendor the Mother Figure shimmered benignly upon the drape. Sitting on that low stool, with his knees almost under his chin, Corgan felt like a little boy again, basking in Mendor's warmth.

"I need to find Brigand," he said. "You never met Brigand. I brought this picture to see if you could reconstruct his features from the image." He held up the photograph Sharla had sent. "Brigand was small when this was taken, but you can extrapolate, can't you? You knew Seabrig—he's now called Cyborg. Brigand and Cyborg are clones. Both of them were made from Brig's brain cells."

"Of course. I know all that." Corgan could feel a minuscule vibration in his fingertips as Mendor the Mother scanned the image he was holding and projected it onto one of the drapes beside him. As Corgan watched, the image changed rapidly—Brigand was growing up right in front of his eyes.

"Is that what he looks like now?" Corgan asked, surprised. This was a much bigger boy than he'd expected.

"I factored in all the variables," Mendor answered. "The rapid maturing that was genetically built into him, his recent diet, the exposure to the elements here on Nuku Hiva—I'm certain this is how he appears today."

"Thanks, Mendor. That will help, I hope. He's smart, though—he always manages to keep hidden from me."

"What do you expect, Corgan? This boy was bred to be a strategist. Tell me, why do you dislike him so much?"

Corgan lowered his eyes. "What makes you think I dislike him?"

"It's in your face. Dislike and distrust."

No sense trying to deceive Mendor. "It's never stopped bothering me—I think he cut off Cyborg's hand and lied about it, but I can't figure out why he'd want to mutilate his clone-twin. He seems to like Cyborg a lot. If I find Brigand, maybe I can make him tell me. Or beat it out of him."

Mendor morphed completely. As Mendor the Father Figure took over, the golden face darkened to bronze, the features grew masculine and commanding, and the voice deepened. "Violence will be futile, Corgan. Remember that," he said. Then, softening a little, "Where have you looked for the boy?"

"I've gone over the whole island, Mendor, meter by meter. I've seen his footprints, I've found bits of food he's left, I've scoured the bushes and the undergrowth, and I've searched every cove and cave. I even went back to the tomb and looked inside that, but it was pretty disgusting. He wouldn't go in there with all that rotted flesh."

Mendor asked, "Have you ever looked up?"

"Up?"

"You're assuming, Corgan, that the boy is on the ground. Hasn't it occurred to you that he might be living in the treetops?"

No, that hadn't occurred to Corgan at all. "Thanks, Mendor," he called, and pushed his way through the drapes into the barn. Stopping at his bunk, he put on the new pair of sandals he'd made out of cowhide after dampness had deteriorated his old shoes far beyond Mendor's ability to reconstitute them. Then he took off, running. He was all the way to the bottom of the slope when he realized he should have brought the cattle prod with him, but he decided not to go back for it.

Mercifully the rain had stopped falling, although everything in the jungle still dripped with moisture. *Look up,* he kept telling himself. *Why didn't I think of that?* For weeks he'd been following all the signs Brigand had left behind, often wondering why Brigand had shown such carelessness by not bothering to hide the remains of his meals. Sometimes it seemed as though he was deliberately leaving clues to taunt Corgan. Brigand, the strategist, might be setting a trap. Corgan, bred for fast reflexes, too often missed the obvious.

Look up, Mendor had said, but today when Corgan looked up, drops of rainwater fell off leaves into his eyes. Standing at the base of a tree, wiping his eyes with the edge of his new shirt, he felt the hair rising on the back of his neck. He spun around to see the carved spear lying on the ground near him, like a gift that had arrived just in time, because emerging from a bush directly in front of him was a huge wild boar, the same one that had spooked the cattle so many nights. This time there was no mistaking the boar's intent—it was not after cattle. It stood poised to attack Corgan.

Corgan grabbed the spear from the ground. Holding it in his right hand, he circled the boar, feeling a rush of excitement even greater than his fear. Nothing virtual about this encounter—the boar was an actual, physical threat. Never before had Corgan been in a conflict like this, one that might end in a real death.

Occasionally he'd had to kill a living creature— smashing the heads of fish with rocks, or knifing a cow that had to be destroyed. But this was different. The boar was a worthy adversary. It could kill him. Corgan needed to defend himself, but there was more to it than that. Bloodlust began to rise in him—he *wanted* this horrible, ugly, grotesque, ferocious animal to die. He wanted revenge for all the nights this beast had disturbed the cows, for the miscarriages of valuable baby calves it had caused, for the sleep Corgan had lost because of the boar's midnight stalkings.

When it charged, Corgan's fast reflexes served him well, letting him leap out of the boar's path. He could have thrust the spear at the exact moment of the charge, but with so much adrenaline pumping through his body, he decided to prolong the battle for the sheer thrill of it.

"Come on, come on, come and get me," he goaded the boar. Raising the spear, he picked out the spot where a thrust would surely kill it—right into the neck, severing the jugular vein. When it charged him a second time, Corgan again leaped out of the way, playing with the beast, whirling to face it as it circled, keeping it a spear's distance away from him, thwarting every thrust until it began to tire.

Perhaps Corgan grew careless then, feeling invulnerable in this dance of death. Finally deciding to end it, he lowered the spear as the boar rushed at him for the seventh time. The spear didn't hit the jugular, but instead slid deep into the animal's chest. The impact of that 135-kilogram body hurling at full force into the shaft of the spear flung Corgan onto his back. Pulse throbbing, he held tightly to the spear's shaft while the boar hung over him, trying to rake him with those blade-sharp tusks.

With each surge forward, the boar impaled itself more deeply on the spear, but it wouldn't die, and Corgan's muscles began to burn from exertion. Blood gushed out and sprayed over both of them, while those hate-filled yellow eyes kept glaring.

Straining every tendon, Corgan managed to bend his knees and slip first one leg underneath himself, then the other, raising his body centimeter by centimeter until he was standing again. Then, pushing forward with all his weight, he shoved the spear farther into the animal. Deeper and deeper he thrust it, feeling it grind against bone. Corgan's arms ran with blood up to the elbows, and his hands felt welded to the shaft of the spear, as though they would never peel free again, but his eyes stayed locked on the malevolent yellow eyes that were now beginning to dim. When at last the boar sank lifeless onto the ground, Corgan felt the intoxicating triumph of victory.

"I won! Me! Corgan!" From somewhere inside his core a wild yell poured out of his throat, the cry of a primitive hunter gloating over his kill. It penetrated the dense growth until every other jungle sound, every caw, screech, shriek, and growl, dwindled into silence. Corgan had become a savage—unthinking, possessed by instinct alone. He raised both arms, with his bloody hands open and his fingers splayed as though he could catch the burning sky, as his cries of triumph rang out through the jungle.

Suddenly something dropped from the treetops to the ground in front of Corgan. Brigand! The knife blade flashed as Brigand crouched in a fighting stance, ready to do battle. Corgan didn't even feel surprise, because the whole scene seemed a natural continuation of the battle he'd just finished.

Brigand had the knife, but Corgan's only weapon, the spear, was embedded deep inside the boar. When Brigand feinted with the knife, Corgan danced out of the way.

Instinct became useless now; he needed to think, because here was a human adversary who could strategize far better than Corgan could.

Mendor had pictured him exactly right—the height, the weight, the strong build. The only thing Mendor hadn't predicted was the filth. Brigand's hair, full of bright feathers that he'd stuck into it at random angles, was so encrusted with dirt that the red color hardly showed through. Using mud, he'd painted his face and body with the same strange symbols that decorated the spear—whorls, squares, zigzags that looked like lightning bolts. Naked except for the tattered rags that remained from the clothes Seabrig had loaned him, Brigand had turned bronze from the sun. The boars'-tusk necklace that swung from his neck held more tusks than the last time Corgan had seen it.

Brigand, the strategist, had planned it well: Although Corgan was bigger and older, he'd used up a lot of his strength in his battle with the boar. That made the two of them close to equal. When Brigand rushed him, Corgan dodged, demanding, "What do you want?"

"You'll find out later," Brigand answered.

"You mean after you kill me?"

Brigand just laughed, then lunged again. As the edge of the knife whizzed past Corgan's ear, Corgan whirled and kicked Brigand's leg below the knees, sending him sprawling. While Brigand scrambled to get up, Corgan tried to wrest the spear out of the boar's body. Side-kicking at Brigand to hold him at bay, he pulled on the end of the spear with all his strength until he felt it break loose.

Then he misjudged and tugged too hard, making the spear slide out so fast its momentum knocked Corgan onto his back. Brigand took advantage of the opening and charged toward him.

With the blunt end of the spear Corgan hit Brigand in the chest. This time when Brigand fell, Corgan leaped to his feet and then backed off, waiting for the boy to get up again, enjoying the game just as he'd enjoyed playing with the boar. "Come on, if you want to fight, then do it," Corgan goaded him.

Studying his adversary, Brigand took his time climbing to his feet. He tried to find a point where he could thrust at Corgan, but Corgan held the spear crosswise in both hands, and for every one of Brigand's thrusts, Corgan parried. The next time Brigand lunged with the knife, he swung his arm a little too hard and threw himself off balance. Using the spear as a staff, Corgan flipped it upward so it hit Brigand's arm from beneath with enough force that the knife flew high in an arc, landing somewhere behind them in the thick growth. Then, with the blunt end of the spear, Corgan knocked Brigand flat on the ground and jumped forward to stand with his foot on Brigand's chest.

"If I were you," Brigand said, "I'd kill me right now, because if you don't, you'll never be safe. But you won't kill me, Corgan. You're too weak." Brigand's gaze, as he stared up at Corgan, was cold and calculating. Cold, calculating, and insolent—he even grinned. It was the insolence that enraged Corgan; as he gripped the spear anger rose in him until everything he saw turned the color of blood.

"You think I'm weak? Think again." Lifting the spear

high, Corgan knew that if he plunged it in, the force of the thrust would skewer Brigand all the way through his body into the blood-drenched ground beneath him. He shifted his foot, in its now bloody sandal, to expose the part of Brigand's chest where the boy's heart beat.

As he stood there, poised to inflict death, images began to flood Corgan's brain. Images of the Virtual War. In a flashback he saw the blood, the gore, the soldiers blown apart, the innocent civilians—men, women, and children—lying decapitated, their limbs missing. Even though the victims were only electronic signals and not real, even though the War had been fought virtually to prevent the actual bloodshed that had devastated Earth in the beginning of the century, all that virtual carnage had sickened Corgan so badly that he still had nightmares about it.

Brigand, trapped on the ground beneath Corgan's foot, was no virtual image. He was human, a flesh-and-blood person who would die a real death if Corgan thrust that spear into him.

As Corgan stared down at him, the face that he saw emerging from beneath the filth and blood was not Brigand's but the face of the baby Sharla had brought to Corgan, of the little boy Corgan had taken care of for all those months, watching him grow, teaching him, talking to him . . . Corgan blinked and shook his head, but it didn't make any difference: In Corgan's eyes Brigand's hostile face was turning into Cyborg's innocent one. The same blue eyes, the flame-colored hair, the crooked teeth . . .

He couldn't do it.

"I told you, didn't I?" Brigand asked, his voice maddeningly calm. "You're too weak, Corgan. You'd never become a cannibal chief."

"Who would want to?" Wearily Corgan sank down onto the ground. Head bowed, he held the useless spear with its blunt end down and its point straight up.

Brigand rolled over to sit up, crossing his arms on his knees. "I knew you couldn't kill me," he said. "But if I'd won, I could have killed you. I'm not saying I would have, but I could have. The power of the chiefs is in me. With each boar I slaughter, I get more power. And more tusks." He lifted the necklace.

"How many have you slaughtered?" Corgan asked dully.

"All the ones on the island. There were three. This was the last."

"You didn't kill it. I did," Corgan reminded him.

"Yes, but I masterminded the whole thing. I left the spear where you would find it."

Again Corgan felt no surprise, but he asked, "How could you be sure the boar would show up at exactly that time and place? How could you be sure *I* would?"

"Why should I tell you? You never believe me about anything, Corgan," Brigand answered. "You didn't believe it when I told you I had to cut off Cyborg's hand to save him from drowning, but that was the truth." Crawling forward on his filthy knees to kneel in front of Corgan, he went on, "And I'll tell you why you don't believe me. It's because you don't trust Sharla, but you can't deal with that because you love her. It's easier for you to shove all your doubts and mistrust on me, since you hate me. And you know why you hate me so much? Because Sharla loves *me*."

Jumping up, Corgan shot back, "That's what you fig-ure. But here's what I figure: When you got this crazy idea in your head that you'd been zapped with the power of the cannibal chiefs, you were afraid Cyborg might tap into it, since the two of you have some weird connection—like when you could suddenly swim because he could. You didn't want to share that power with anyone, especially your clone-twin, so you cut off his hand, crippling him. That way you'd always be superior."

The insolence was gone; underneath the dirt and blood on his face Brigand went pale. In a whimper that sounded like the original Brig, he said, "Corgan, no matter what I say, it doesn't make any difference to you. So I won't even bother telling you again that I did it to save Cyborg's life."

"Then what more do we have to say to each other?" Corgan demanded. "What's next? What do you plan to do now?"

"I'm going to look for the knife."

"Oh, no!" Corgan groaned. "Do you think because I didn't kill you the first time, I won't do it if you come at me again?"

Softly Brigand answered, "You can have the knife back after I finish cutting out the boar's tusks. You're holding the spear—why should you feel threatened?"

Did Corgan feel threatened? He wasn't sure. If he did, it was not because of the knife, it was because he couldn't figure out how Brigand had made all this happen.

What kind of power *did* Brigand possess?

THIRTEEN

Brigand found the knife quickly enough. Bending over, he used its edge as a lever to pry first the huge tusks from the boar's lower jaw, then the smaller ones from the upper jaw. When he finished, he placed the bloody things into the waistband of his ragged pants.

"What next, strategist?" Corgan asked warily.

"You and I should declare a truce and go down to the beach to wash the blood off ourselves."

That sounded reasonable. The stink of congealing boar's blood was making Corgan sick anyway. Walking with a distance of three meters between them, glancing frequently at each other because neither trusted the other, they quickly covered the distance to the concealed cove where Brigand had evidently been living, the one Corgan had never been able to find. It was strewn with refuse. "I've got soap here somewhere," Brigand said.

"Where'd you get soap?"

"You left it on the beach once when I was spying on you. I picked it up while you were in the water."

Irritated again, Corgan said, "So that's where it went. I thought it got washed out in the waves. I've been doing without soap, waiting for the Harrier jet to come again with supplies."

"Which is when?" Brigand asked.

"In about two days." Why did he have the feeling that Brigand already knew that?

Standing in the water, Brigand scrubbed every inch of his body, including his hair. He was now about one and a half meters tall, thin and wiry, but muscular in the shoulders. "Why are you doing that?" Corgan demanded as the boy kept rubbing his feet through the damp sand.

"I'm scouring my feet clean. I want to go with you to the barn now so you can ask Mendor to reconstitute my clothes."

"What makes you think I'd ask her? What makes you think I'd do anything for you? Ever?"

Brigand smiled. "Because when you look at me, you see Cyborg. That's why you couldn't kill me. That's why you'll never be able to kill me."

Once—and it seemed long ago—Sharla had told Corgan that Brigand could tell what people were thinking. Perhaps that was one of the benefits of having been bred as a strategist. Corgan wished he'd been given even a little of that ability when they'd genetically engineered him, but he'd been bred to fight a Virtual War, not to figure out maneuvers.

Walking beside Brigand up the slope toward the barn, Corgan had to adjust his perception of the boy's height, because now Brigand was only about eighteen centimeters shorter than Corgan. Cleaned up, he looked—Corgan would never use the word *handsome* to describe him, but he didn't look too bad.

"Ask Mendor right away about the clothes, will you?" Brigand insisted when they reach the barn.

"What's your big hurry?"

"I'm clean now. I don't want to put those rags back on me."

The answer had logic to it, but coming from Brigand, it could be just another tactic. After the stress of two battles, after the emotional and physical drain and letdown that followed them, nothing seemed clear to Corgan. Neither he nor Brigand had killed the other, and now, thinking back on it, it seemed that neither of them had tried very hard.

Corgan took the clothes to Mendor in the virtual Box, while Brigand, naked except for the boars'-tusk necklace, stood leaning against the rails of the cattle pen, watching a new calf nurse. His hands clutched the fresh, bloody boar's tusks.

"So, you found the boy," Mendor the Mother said.

"He wants you to fix his clothes."

"A reasonable request, since what you're giving me is nothing but rags. Come back in a little while. I'll have new clothes for Brigand."

When Corgan returned to his bunk room, he found

Brigand holding the photograph Sharla had sent, staring at it hungrily.

"Put that down!" Corgan demanded.

"Why? It's mine."

Corgan's face burned. What Brigand said was true—Sharla had intended that picture to go to him. He must have seen the envelope with his name on it, which meant he'd been rooting around in Corgan's things.

"I'll go away as soon as my clothes are ready," he said.

"Go where?"

"Anywhere."

"Suit yourself," Corgan told him.

With the little amount of material available to her, Mendor the Mother made Brigand a pair of shorts that showed his scabby knees, and a sleeveless shirt that emphasized his wiry biceps. He was still barefoot, but at least the feet were relatively clean. "I'm going now," he announced, and disappeared into the lengthening shadows.

Corgan checked the cows inside the pen, glad he no longer had to worry about the great boar harassing them. The newest calf looked healthy enough. Corgan scraped a few skin cells from her ear to take to the laboratory that evening, where they would be checked for transgenic qualities.

In no particular hurry because he still felt as though he was moving in a cloud of unreality, Corgan stumbled down the slope. When he opened the door to the lab, he jumped backward in astonishment. In the middle of the room sat Brigand, tied to a chair.

"You!" Grimber shrieked, whirling on Corgan. "You knew about this!"

"About what?" Corgan answered, trying to gather his wits.

"About this boy. This *clone*. This *extra* clone, who admitted he's been living here right under our noses, hidden by you, when you were well aware the Supreme Council has forbidden the existence of more than one clone of Brig."

"Grimber, please," Delphine begged, trying to calm him.

"And this . . . this *clone* went walking right past the laboratory this evening, as bold as you please. It's lucky I happened to step outside just at that minute."

Corgan felt positive that the encounter had nothing to do with luck. This was obviously what Brigand had been planning.

The color kept building in Grimber's face as his eyes grew wilder. "When the Harrier jet comes the day after tomorrow, I'm sending this clone back to the domed city, where he will be terminated."

So that was it! Brigand's plan all along had been to find a way back to Sharla. But why had he bothered with all that elaborate subterfuge—the boar attack, then the battle between the two of them? Even though Corgan's victory had turned out to be a hollow one, if it had ended differently, Brigand might have been hurt or killed. Maybe Brigand had been trying to discover just how far he could manipulate Corgan.

Grimber kept ranting: "And you deserve punishment, too, Corgan, for your deliberate disobedience to the Supreme Council. I'll report you—and I'll report Sharla as well, because she had to be a part of this."

"Grimber!" Delphine put her arms around him, trying

to restrain him. "This little boy is identical to my dear, sweet Brigand, and I love Brigand. I won't allow you to send him to his death."

"*You* won't allow! *You* won't allow! You have nothing to say about it!" Grimber's voice rose to a scream as he shook Delphine away from him, knocking her to the floor.

"Hey—stop that!" Corgan yelled, rushing to help Delphine.

"Don't tell me what to do in my own laboratory!" Picking up a heavy tank of propane, Grimber began to swing it at Corgan, who ducked out of the way.

Suddenly Grimber gasped and started to choke. The propane tank fell to the floor as he dropped to his knees, clutching his head. "Help me," he whispered.

Corgan didn't know how to help him, and Delphine stayed sprawled on the floor, not attempting to get up. "Should I get him some water?" Corgan asked, but Delphine didn't answer.

By then Grimber had turned purple, his eyes rolling backward, his hands clutching air, his legs jerking. "Delphine, what should I do?" Corgan yelled.

"Nothing," she answered. "He's having either a stroke or a heart attack. Funny, I never thought he had a heart."

Corgan ran to a drawer where he'd seen syringes, and found them inside, but he didn't know how to use them. Although several bottles of compounds stood on the shelves, properly labeled, the labels meant nothing to Corgan. Now Grimber lay still, no longer twitching. "Is he dead?" Corgan asked.

"I sincerely hope so," Delphine answered.

Corgan slumped against the lab table, stunned and shaken.

"He was a miserable man, and he was going to have this little boy terminated," Delphine said, her voice expressionless. "Cover his body with a lab coat, Corgan. We need to make plans now. When it's light tomorrow, we can bury him."

Corgan did as she said. "Now, untie the boy," she ordered him, "and I shall get us some drinks." A moment later she came back from the bedroom she'd shared with Grimber. "Mango juice for you two, and for me, something a little stronger. I make it myself here in the laboratory."

Brigand had been following all of this with high interest. Part of the night's drama had been orchestrated by him, but he certainly couldn't have known that Grimber would die.

"Now, dear boys," Delphine asked, "what do you think we should do? Go on as before, except without Grimber?"

"I'll be heading back to the domed city," Brigand announced. "After Pilot drops off your supplies, Delphine, I'll fly back with him."

"He'll turn you in," Corgan said.

"No, he won't. I flew down here with him, remember, two months ago? He's a rebel, like me. He'll keep me hidden. I'm going back to be with Cyborg and Sharla."

Jumping to his feet so fast he knocked over the mango juice, Corgan yelled, "If you're going, I'm going too!" Then he remembered Delphine. "What about you?" he asked.

"If you leave here, Corgan," she answered, "my work will double. I'll have to do your job of tending the cattle, plus my own very important projects here in the laboratory. But I don't really care!" she cried, throwing her arms toward the ceiling. "I no longer need to answer the demands of that tyrant!"

Corgan's mind was racing. "Listen, Delphine, the Harrier jet comes here every month or so. Can you manage by yourself for a month? If I don't come back by then, I'll send someone else to tend the cattle. In the meantime," he said, gesturing to the corpse on the floor, "let me at least drag him out of here."

"I'll help you," Brigand offered, surprising Corgan.

Outside in the darkness Corgan muttered, "If we don't cover him with something, the birds will pick him clean by morning."

It had been a long, desperate day, and digging a grave with nothing more than the small hand trowel Corgan found outside the lab added to his depression and exhaustion. But Brigand didn't seem tired at all.

"How long have you been planning this escape, Brigand?" Corgan asked him.

"NNTK, Corgan," he answered.

Corgan froze. NNTK—that was what Sharla always said when she didn't want Corgan to know what she'd been up to. NNTK—No Need To Know.

"I don't mind you flying back on the jet with me," Brigand told Corgan. "But when we get there, just remember—Sharla is mine."

FOURTEEN

Once again Delphine stood on the landing strip waving good-bye to Brigand, this time to the real Brigand. Almost as an afterthought she waved to Corgan, who was inside the Harrier jet in the seat behind the pilot, with Brigand jammed between them and the spear lying on the floor, pointing to the front. Next to it lay the tusk-adorned human skull. Only Pilot wore a helmet—there were none available for the passengers. To shield them from the noise, Pilot had managed to find some bulky headsets that kept slipping off their ears.

Almost sixteen months earlier Corgan had landed on Nuku Hiva in this same Harrier jet. As the aircraft rose now he gazed through the canopy at the lush volcanic island, remembering how much he'd wanted to live there, to spend the rest of his life roaming its sandy beaches and swimming in the surf. Freedom—that was what he'd once desired above everything else. And now, of his own free will, he was departing Nuku Hiva, maybe forever.

All because of Sharla. If she hadn't (possibly) cheated in the Virtual War, the Eurasian Alliance wouldn't be challenging the results, and there'd have been no need for Sharla to create a clone to replace Brig. Then all the other events wouldn't have kept building up so rapidly, one after the other, that now Corgan found himself leaving his beloved island. As always, Sharla was there at the core of his existence, dominating his life.

The Harrier turned north, still flying low enough that Corgan could look down on the waterfall that had cost Cyborg his hand. From above it looked beautiful, splashing into the pool beneath the rocks. Corgan turned away. No time for regrets. He'd need to use these flight hours to plan what to do when he reached the domed city. The drone of the engines quieted some as they attained cruising altitude. "Corgan, do you read me?" Brigand's voice, sounding tinny, came through the headset. "How about you, Pilot? Can you read me, too?"

Assured that both of them could hear him, Brigand announced, "When we reach the domed city, I'll go into hiding. Pilot says he can keep me inside the hangar for a while, but then we'll have to figure out something more permanent. Otherwise the Supreme Council will discover me and have me terminated." He said that so casually, it was as if he were talking about having a splinter removed. "Now, here's what I want you to do, Corgan—"

"*You* want *me*? What makes you think I'd help you?"

"Because you care about Sharla," Brigand answered, "and I control Sharla."

"Not in your wildest dreams!" Corgan scoffed. "Forget it." Corgan let the headset slide down around his neck so he wouldn't have to hear anything more from Brigand.

This was the second time he'd ever flown. The first time, on the way to Nuku Hiva, Sharla had been sitting close in front of him, where Brigand was sitting now, and for the whole duration of the flight Corgan had been too caught up in her nearness to pay much attention to the feeling of flying.

Now he stared through the jet's canopy at the surface of Earth. Strange—from the beaches of Nuku Hiva the ocean had appeared dynamic, with waves crashing against rocks at high tide. Here, from high above the borderless expanse of the Pacific, the ocean looked almost smooth, except for a few whitecaps barely visible far below. He felt his spirits rise. Flying was exciting! He wished he could pilot an aircraft. The sense of freedom he'd get from soaring through the sky would be even greater than the freedom of Nuku Hiva. As the hours passed he watched the sun move from in front of the plane to beside it to behind it, spreading brilliant russet and gold along the horizon. When the plane crept into darkness, Corgan dozed, lulled by the drone of the engines.

In his sleep he heard Brigand's voice. At first he thought he was dreaming, but as he pulled himself into awareness he realized that his head had slumped sideways, pressing against one of the earphones. Still talking to Pilot, Brigand was saying, ". . . and after Corgan finally untied me, I said good-bye to Sharla and Cyborg. Then I went back to the pond, and I dived and dived until I found Cyborg's hand."

Jerking wide awake, Corgan pressed the headset against both ears.

"It was under a rock, like I knew it was, but this time the power of the chiefs let me move the rock and I got the hand out. By then it was too late to reattach it."

"So what did you do?" Pilot asked.

"I ate it. It was the only way the cannibal chiefs would grant me total power."

Corgan cupped his hands over the earphones, pushing them closer to both ears. Surely he couldn't have heard what he thought he'd just heard.

"Ate it?" Pilot asked.

"Yes. Why not? It wasn't helping anyone just lying there on the bottom of the pond."

He'd eaten it! Disbelief, then horror, then rage, exploded behind Corgan's eyes. He lunged for the boars'-tusk necklace and twisted it hard around Brigand's throat, choking him. With fingers like claws, Brigand tried to pull the sharp tusks away from his windpipe, but Corgan tightened the necklace until Brigand could no longer even gasp.

Pilot was screaming, "Corgan, let him go! Your seat has an eject device, and I control it. If you don't stop choking the kid, I'll dump you into the Pacific!"

To restrain himself, to beat down the fury that consumed him, took all the effort Corgan had, but finally he dropped his hands. Once Brigand got his breath back, he croaked, "I had to, Corgan! To get the full power of the chiefs, I had to become a cannibal too—for just a little while."

"You ate the hand!" Sick from shock, Corgan recoiled from Brigand.

"Not all of it. The fish had already started on it, so there wasn't a lot left."

"What kind of monster are you?" Corgan yelled. His revulsion grew like lava swelling inside a volcano, burning hot and foul inside him. "You cut off the hand just for that reason, didn't you? Because you thought you needed human flesh to eat. You're either deluded or completely insane."

Turning as far as he could in the seat, Brigand tried to meet Corgan's eyes. "I've sworn to you again and again that it was the only way to save his life. It was only afterward, when it got too late to attach the hand, that I decided to eat it. By then it wasn't good for anything else, so what was so bad about that? I think you're overreacting, Corgan."

"Get away from me!" Corgan yelled, pushing Brigand as far forward as he could, but there was no place for him to go.

"Control yourself, Corgan," Pilot ordered. "We'll be landing in less than an hour."

By then the Harrier jet had reached the western coast of a large land mass. At one time, Corgan had been told by Mendor, persons flying above this continent were able to see the lights of dozens of huge cities glowing up at them, like a star-filled sky mirrored below. After Earth was destroyed by plagues, terrorist attacks, nuclear wars, and the depletion of natural resources, the land turned completely dark. The planet, once home to ten billion people, now supported little more than two million. There were no longer any livable cities, no more houses and no more humans, except in the few domed cities.

The domed city. For the first fourteen years of his life Corgan had lived there without knowing where it was. When he finally thought to ask Mendor, he'd been told that in the years before Earth's surface became unlivable, the area around what was now the domed city had been called Wyoming. Wyoming used to be a state, Mendor had said, in a country once called the United States of America, on a continent once named North America. All of that was now part of the Western Hemisphere Federation, ruled by a Supreme Council in each domed city.

"Listen up, Corgan," Pilot announced through the headset. He must have raised the volume, because Corgan's ears rang. "When this aircraft lands, two people get out—Corgan and Pilot. As far as anyone will know, only the two of us made this trip from Nuku Hiva. Got that?"

"What about—?"

"*Only two of us flew here from Nuku Hiva. You and me.* If you say anything else, I'll report that you became delusional from altitude sickness."

Corgan shrugged. All he wanted was to get as far away as possible from Brigand. Apparently Pilot was going to hide Brigand somewhere. Below in the distance Corgan could see low to the horizon, early morning rays of sun reflecting off the dome of the city. Soon the jet was above the dome. It hovered there while large, curved doors in the top of the dome retracted to create a space ten meters wide and fifteen meters long, just barely enough room for the Harrier to descend.

Once the aircraft settled onto the concrete pad, Pilot shut down the engines and pulled open the canopy. Since Brigand had curled himself into a tight ball on the floor next to his spear and the human skull, Corgan had trouble climbing over him to exit the cockpit. Resisting the urge to kick him senseless, Corgan slid down the side of the jet and, to his surprise, landed in the waiting arms of Cyborg.

This was a much older Cyborg than Corgan had last seen: tall, strong, dressed in a shimmering LiteSuit, and with his bright red hair nicely groomed—no more cowlicks sticking up. Grinning, Cyborg held up his multi-jointed titanium-and-stainless-steel artificial hand and said, "Greetings, Corgan. I've been waiting for you."

"You have? How did you know I'd be coming?"

"Brigand told me."

"He did? *How*?" There'd been no radio transmission that Corgan knew of between the aircraft and the city.

With a mysterious smile Cyborg tapped the side of his forehead. Then he said, "Look over there. Someone else has been waiting for you."

Sharla! Instead of rushing toward Corgan with smiles of welcome, she stood in the shadows, her head tilted close to Pilot's, both of them deep in whispered conversation.

"Yeah, well, it doesn't look like she's been holding her breath until I got here," Corgan answered. At the moment he didn't really care; he was still too filled with disgust over what Brigand had revealed. Did Cyborg know about the hand? Did he have any idea what his perverted clone-twin had done? Did *Sharla* know?

Getting a close look at the artificial hand for the first time, Corgan asked Cyborg, "Are you still happy with your . . . uh . . ."

"Definitely! Go ahead, examine it if you want to." Cyborg held up the shiny, fully articulated metal hand and waggled its fingers in front of Corgan's eyes.

Corgan cautiously reached out to touch the stainless-steel palm, and felt an unexpected electrical shock. Cyborg laughed and said, "I only do that to my closest friends." Before Corgan could pull away, the metal hand clasped his wrist like a lobster's claw, holding him fast. "You can't escape till I'm ready to set you free," Cyborg told him, still laughing. "I mean, this hand is so powerful it astonishes even me. I've been wearing it for months, and I'm still finding new things it can do."

"That's great. I'm really impressed," Corgan said, and meant it. It was comforting to know that Cyborg, now twelve years old like his clone-twin, had adapted so perfectly to his replacement hand—which was still gripping Corgan like a vise. After Cyborg released him, Corgan rubbed his tingling wrist.

Sharla finally came to greet Corgan, but her embrace felt a little stiff, her smile looked a little forced, and she didn't exactly meet his eyes. "What's it like to be coming home?" she asked him.

"Is this home? I don't think so," Corgan answered. "Why were you talking to Pilot like that?"

"Like what?"

"Like a conspiracy."

She smiled the same mysterious smile he had just seen on Cyborg's face. "NNTK, Corgan," she answered.

"No Need to Know! For six solid months," Corgan hissed, "I never heard that stupid acronym, and now I've heard it twice in two days, first from—"

Before he could say "Brigand," Sharla stopped his mouth with a kiss. Usually when she came close to him, his anger would melt, but not this time. "Come inside," she told him. "There's a surprise waiting for you."

She led him through the shadows in the dark periphery of the hangar toward a door that connected to the domed city. Once he stepped inside, Corgan immediately felt penned in, confined, imprisoned. Here he was again, back where he'd started, in a city closed off to reality, and he had no idea if or when he'd ever get out of it.

"What's the surprise?" Corgan asked after they boarded a hover car that floated just above the electronic tracks. "That nothing around here has changed?"

Cyborg—this taller, older Cyborg that Corgan still wasn't used to—took his hand to answer, "I told you I knew you were coming, Corgan, so I announced it to the Supreme Council. They didn't ask me how I knew, because to them I'm the Supreme Strategist, and they expect me to figure out things that other people wouldn't know."

"Oh, really? One of these times I'd like to learn just how this communication works."

"To the Supreme Council," Cyborg went on, not caring

that Corgan wasn't really listening, "you're still a hero, Corgan."

By then they'd reached their stop, and they exited into a stainless-steel corridor. Corgan knew this place well. When they arrived at a certain spot in the wall, which looked no different from any other, flat double doors suddenly became visible, rolling back soundlessly to reveal a large room beneath a shiny dome. He heard, "Enter, please," the same as he'd heard more than a year ago, right after Sharla, Corgan, and Brig had won the Virtual War. Just as they had on that night he remembered so well, members of the Supreme Council now sat on an elevated dais at the end of the room, waiting for them.

Only this time it was Sharla, Corgan, and Brig's clone, Cyborg, who entered beneath a dome filled with virtual images of cheering crowds. As they approached the dais, one of the Supreme Council members—the nearly bald one—stood up to say, "We're glad to see you again, Corgan. You may stay here as long as you wish. Forever, if you desire. Your old virtual-reality Box has been refurbished for you to live in. We have also reactivated Mendor, your caretaker."

Corgan shot a look at Sharla, wondering how Mendor could be here and at the same time back in the makeshift Box on Nuku Hiva, but then he remembered that Mendor was nothing more than a computer program that could be duplicated and installed anywhere.

The woman Council member with the pleasant voice stood up to say, "Tomorrow, Pilot will return to Nuku Hiva with a young man who will take your place tending the cattle and working in the laboratory with Delphine. Thus, you have no worries, Corgan. If you choose to stay in our city, you can work at whatever you please. Or you can choose not to work at all." After giving him a brief smile, she sat down again.

Corgan was expected to make some comment, he realized, something polite, something grateful, to show that he appreciated their hospitality. Yet all he could think to say was, "Those cheering people on the dome—is that happening now in the rest of the city, or is it a recording from the night you honored us for winning the War?"

Before They answered, the Council members put Their heads together to discuss the question. Why couldn't They just say yes or no? But that wasn't the way the Council functioned. Every thing had to be discussed and deliberated.

"That's irrelevant, Corgan," They finally announced. "All those cheering people are showing you how glad we are to have you back. If you will excuse Us now, We will allow the three of you to stay here, where dinner will be served to you."

One by one, the six Council members rose from their chairs and left the room. Immediately the image of cheering people disappeared from the dome overhead. It had been a recording. So much for Corgan the Champion's return.

"Hey, what does it matter?" Cyborg asked, slapping Corgan on the back with the titanium hand, which stung. "We'll get a decent meal out of it, anyway."

"You two can have it," Corgan said. "I'm going to my Box." He knew how to get there, and Mendor would be waiting.

FIFTEEN

Mendor hardly ever morphed into the Father Figure these days; it was always Mendor the Mother, warm and loving, fussing over Corgan's well-being the way she had from the time of his birth. She offered him the best food available in the domed city, although compared with the real food on Nuku Hiva, synthetic food had little appeal. "You seem so morose, Corgan," she worried. "Would you like to play a game? Would you like to read a digital book? I can create any scene you'd like to fit into. Just tell Mendor what you want, and I'll get it for you."

What he really wanted was someone to talk to about Brigand, about the sickening revelation he'd heard on that plane ride. But who? Should he tell the Supreme Council that a deviate named Brigand was hiding somewhere in the city? If They found him, They'd know there were two clones, and one clone would be terminated. Maybe it would be Cyborg—after all, Brigand was already partway trained as a strategist. Corgan couldn't chance it.

He couldn't spill everything to Mendor, either, because Mendor would be obliged to inform the Supreme Council. It had taken Corgan only twelve and a quarter minutes to realize that this Mendor possessed none of the information stored in the Mendor on Nuku Hiva—when he left the island, he hadn't thought to bring Mendor's memory with him. Therefore, the current Mendor knew nothing about the existence of a second clone.

Definitely he could not discuss this with Cyborg. Corgan had made the mistake of telling him that Brigand had saved his life—if Corgan now said it was all a lie, that Brigand was dangerous, deluded, and maybe even deadly, would Cyborg believe him? It might force Cyborg to choose between Corgan and Brigand. In that case . . . Corgan didn't want to think about it.

Mosdy he wanted to talk to Sharla. Yet whenever he approached her, she had some excuse. "My work is piling up, Corgan," she'd say. "Unlike you, I have a job to do. The DNA machine broke down, and I'm processing a lot of the sequencing by hand now, and then there's Cyborg—he needs hours of tutoring. I just don't have time." And she would walk away from him, leaving him standing there feeling stupid.

The days dragged. Corgan began to roam the stainless-steel corridors of the part of the city reserved for officials.

That was where he lived, too, even though he had no status now except as a once-upon-a-time War hero. On a few occasions he rode the hover car with Cyborg, looking through windows at the hydroponic gardens where drab workers slaved away growing crops—mostly soybeans that could be converted to look and taste like something more appealing. Beyond that, the hover car would pass the even more drab, beehivelike structures where the ordinary workers lived with no luxuries at all. All too soon Cyborg would say, "Gotta go. I shouldn't have taken all this time off to goof around with you. Now I'll have to stay up all night studying."

"What are you studying?" Corgan asked.

"Codes. Encryption. I know that's not what I was bred for, but Sharla's teaching me and I like it."

Back inside his Box, Corgan would sink into the aerogel seat and talk to Mendor, the only person who was always available for him, although Mendor wasn't a person. Together they reminisced about the years he'd spent training for the Virtual War: the reflex practices, the Precision and Sensitivity drills, the time-splitting exercises, and all the rest. Remembering it, Corgan felt a pang of regret: If the Virtual War were to be refought today, he would not be a part of it.

There never seemed to be any news about whether the Virtual War was actually going to be refought. One day, after Corgan had been back in the city for about a month, he asked Mendor, "Tell me about Ananda."

Mendor whirred and clicked, causing her electronic face to fade and flicker the way it always did when she was trying to find out from the Supreme Council how much information Corgan would be permitted to receive. Then she answered, "Ananda is fourteen years of age. She lives in the domed city in the state that was once called Florida. She is considered by everyone to be a phenomenon. Her reflexes are faster than any ever measured in the Western Hemisphere Federation."

"Oh, great!" That meant she was not only better than Corgan was now, she was better than he'd ever been. He slumped in his seat. With his head in his hands and his eyes cast down, he didn't see Mendor morph from the kind Mother Figure into the stern Father Figure, didn't notice it until the deep voice commanded, "Corgan, straighten up!"

"What!"

"I'm the one who should be asking 'what.' What has happened to you?"

"I don't know what you're talking about."

The irises of Mendor's eyes narrowed into intense black dots as the whites expanded and gleamed fluorescent. "Ever since your return you have moped around doing nothing, feeling sorry for yourself the way you're doing now, not trying to improve your skills or finding any other way to contribute to the life of this city."

"Give it up, Mendor. You don't understand."

"I would like to understand. You may proceed to explain."

"Forget it." Corgan got up and slouched to the door of his Box, but when he pushed the door, it didn't budge. "Open it, Mendor," he ordered, trying again. This time the door disappeared entirely, fading to invisibility in the tough aerogel wall. "What the—? What are you doing, Mendor? Let me out!" Corgan began kicking the wall. Suddenly his leg froze in midkick.

He struggled, but it was useless. His leg didn't respond, not even when he used both hands to try to flex his locked knee.

"Now," Mendor declared, "you may continue to stand there in that ridiculous posture until you fall over from fatigue, or you may return to your chair and listen to what I have to say."

For six minutes, eleven and thirteen-hundredths seconds Corgan stood in that "ridiculous posture," as Mendor had called it, feeling not only like a failure, but like a fool. Then he gave in. "All right, I'll sit down and listen to you. But make it quick."

"Good." When Corgan again slumped in the chair, Mendor said, "Stare at the screen on your left. That is your face, Corgan. Do you see the petulant expression? It requires me to describe you in a way I never thought I would have to. Corgan, you have been acting like a moody, whiny, spoiled teenager."

"A what? What's a teenager?" he asked.

"It was a term commonly used at the end of the twentieth century and the beginning of this century, before Earth died. It refers to someone about your age. Back then *moody* and *whiny* and *spoiled* were words often connected with the term *teenager*." Mendor's voice swelled until the Box resonated with it. "Look at yourself, Corgan. You've been given every advantage. You were once the champion of the Western Hemisphere Federation. And here you sit now, pouting, brooding, accomplishing absolutely nothing. This must stop! You will stay in that chair until you decide on something useful to do."

"You just don't understand!" Corgan cried out to the glowering face of Mendor the Stern Authoritarian.

"Then I will listen while you explain it to me."

"I can't!"

Mendor's silence was even worse than his tirade. Well, Corgan could be just as silent. He started to count off the seconds in hundredths, then stopped when Mendor said softly, "You were only fourteen when you left me—too young to be on your own. You needed more fathering. I begged the Supreme Council to send me with you to the Isles of Hiva, but They refused. They said you were mature enough to live alone. I should have begged harder. You've gone adrift, and I feel responsible."

"Mendor . . ." Corgan rose from his chair. If Mendor had been a person, Corgan would have touched him to comfort him, but Mendor was a program, a collection of electronic impulses. "None of this is your fault, Mendor," he said. "You've done everything the right way. You made me a champion, and I won the War. But as you said, that's all in the past, and I need to do something useful now, so I've got an idea. I've been thinking about it for a month. I want to learn to fly the Harrier jet."

"Impossible." Mendor's features clouded. "We have only two Harriers, one of them seriously in need of repair. And we already have a pilot to fly the aircraft that works."

"Mendor, you were the one who taught me about redundancy. Remember? You said, 'Redundancy means having a backup in case something goes wrong.' So, what if something happened to Pilot? I could be the backup pilot."

"The Supreme Council would never permit it." Then, like sunlight breaking through a curtain, Mendor brightened. "But you can learn to fly on a flight simulator. That would be almost the real thing."

Corgan's spirits sank. Training in a simulator was not the same as flying a real jet aircraft, where he would feel the power of the engines as he climbed higher and higher into the sky with Pilot in the front seat to instruct him. In a simulator he'd be all alone in a virtual cockpit, which wouldn't do much to quell the loneliness that kept gnawing at him because of his isolation from Sharla and Cyborg.

Another idea came to him. "Fine, Mendor, get me the simulator. But there's something else—I'd like to meet this Ananda. Could you arrange for me to meet her virtually?" That way he could see for himself just how great this girl was. If he discovered she was less extraordinary than everyone claimed, if he could see one crack in her armor, he might feel a little better about himself. And maybe, in Ananda, he would find someone he could help, someone going through the same difficult training Corgan had endured before the Virtual War.

Again Mendor whirred, clicked, then morphed to half Mother, half Father. In a lighter voice he/she answered, "I'm afraid you don't understand the new regulations, Corgan. After the final communications satellite failed, all long-distance connections had to be made through underground fiber-optic cables. These cables break down often and must be repaired by dedicated workers who brave pos-

sible contamination from plague viruses and nuclear radiation. . . ." Mendor's voice droned on in lecture mode, as it
always did when supplying more information than Corgan
ever wanted or had actually asked for. Finally Mendor got
to the point. "So without permission from the Supreme
Council, you would not be able to meet Ananda virtually.
Since you have no real reason to meet her, that permission
will most likely be denied—"

"Mendor! You tell me to quit moping around, but
everything I ask for you say I can't have."

"You didn't let me finish," Mendor said. "I was about to
add, 'However, I will do my best.'"

"Thanks," Corgan said. "I'd like to go out now." He had
no difficulty opening his door this time, and he began to
run along the tunnel that connected the part of the city
where he lived to the work area. He could still run fast—
he'd kept up that ability, at least, by running every day on
the sandy beaches of Nuku Hiva. He wondered if he could
outrace Ananda, but that would have to be on a virtual-
reality track, quite a comedown after running in the real
world.

At nine o'clock the next morning Mendor was in mid-
sentence when his/her program suddenly shut down, the
image fading out into a sputtering, sparking rainbow followed by darkness. Two and a tenth seconds after that a
girl stood before Corgan, projected in three dimensions,
not only visually, but also with sound, touch, and smell—
and the smell was of good, clean sweat. "What happened?"
she asked. "I was running. . . ."

Virtually, she stood no more than an arm's length from

Corgan. She breathed heavily, perspiration darkening her gray sleeveless shirt, her arms and face glistening with sweat. "Who are you?" she asked.

"I'm Corgan."

"Corgan, the champion of the Western Hemisphere Federation?"

"Once known as."

"Wow!" Her voice was deep, and at the moment a little raspy, probably from the strenuous exercise. "I can't believe this. I've always wanted to meet you, Corgan. You're a hero."

"Not anymore."

"Yes! Always! Do you have a towel or something? I'm dripping on your floor, and I might short-circuit the electronics. This is a virtual Box, isn't it? I mean—how else would I be here talking to you?" Unselfconsciously she raised the hem of her shirt to wipe her forehead, revealing a tightly muscled midriff. In fact, muscles rippled all over her body, yet at the same time she looked entirely feminine.

"You're Ananda, right?" Corgan said. "I hear that you're the new champion."

"That's only because you quit training. Hey, if you started again, we could train together. There's a lot you could teach me."

"I don't know if They'd let me—"

"I'll fix it from my end," she broke in. "My Supreme Council gives me anything I ask for."

Once it had been that way for Corgan, too—anything he'd asked for, he got. But did he really want to work out with this girl? He studied her, starting with her hair, which was as black and thick as Delphine's, but sleek instead of fuzzy, even now, when it was damp from exertion. Her eyes, too, were dark—lively and warm, and with an innocence that reminded him of Cyborg's. Her skin glowed bronze from sunlight. Somehow she must be able to train outside her domed city, where real sun shone, because that deep color couldn't have come from artificial indoor lighting—unless she was naturally dark-skinned.

Although just fourteen, Ananda stood nearly as tall as Corgan. He could imagine running with her, their long, powerful legs pounding against the virtual track. "If you can arrange it," he said, "it's fine with me."

"I'll have my Council talk to your Council," she said. "We can start this afternoon. Golden Bees?"

"You mean you want to do more than just run?" Golden Bees was a training game he'd once had to play against himself because no competition could keep up with him. "You'll beat me at Golden Bees," he told her.

"If I'm lucky. I'll fix everything. See you later." Her virtual image disappeared gradually, becoming transparent until nothing was left but her outline, which vanished in a puff when Mendor reappeared.

"—and transformed the Western world into . . . ," Mendor continued, starting to speak at the exact spot in the sentence where he/she had shut down when Ananda appeared.

As promised, Ananda arranged things with her own Supreme Council. From then on she appeared in Corgan's Box every day. Even though the track they ran on was virtual, Mendor programmed the surroundings to look like the beaches at Nuku Hiva, or an arctic ice floe, or a forest of enormous trees, whatever Corgan asked for or Mendor imagined. Ananda seemed uninterested in the surroundings; her interest focused totally on Corgan. Once she accidentally crashed against him. In the real world they would have hit hard; in the virtual world the force of an impact was always controlled so that it wouldn't cause injury. Still, there was a definite physical sensation when they hit, and Ananda's eyes grew wide.

"Did you get hurt?" he asked her.

"No." But she stared at him as she rubbed her side all the way down to her knee. "Did you . . . uh . . . feel anything?"

"I felt something," he answered, and then turned away because he didn't want her to know just how much he'd felt.

SIXTEEN

Twice Corgan had flown in the Harrier jet as a passenger, but now, inside the flight simulator, he was the pilot. The cockpit of the virtual Harrier that materialized in his Box was made entirely of aerogel, the lightest-weight solid substance known on Earth—strong, but so much like air that it was called frozen smoke. On the Harrier's control panel, dials and gauges measured speed and fuel, while a flat-panel color display simulated an ever-changing digital-terrain map. Mendor could program the map for any type of terrain, from desert to mountain to jungle to ocean. Since Harriers took off straight up from the ground, Corgan called the simulator "vertical reality."

"That's a very clever play on words," Mendor told

him. "If I had been programmed with the ability to laugh, Corgan, I would have done so at the joke you just made—*'vertical reality.'* But alas, laughter was not built into my functional specifications."

Too bad, Corgan thought. As a buddy, Mendor definitely had shortcomings.

While he practiced in the simulator, instructions were fed into Corgan's ears through a headset, by a voice that stayed expressionless unless Corgan made a mistake and nearly crashed the aircraft. Then the voice would increase to a deafening volume and yell, "Pull *up*! Pull *up*!" Sometimes Corgan pretended to ditch the plane just for the fun of hearing that frantic "Pull *up*!"

Weeks of reflex practice with Ananda had brought him up to speed, so that his hand on the control stick reacted in only two hundredths of a second after the display panel changed. But Ananda was starting to get unhappy about all the hours Corgan spent practicing flight maneuvers.

"I need you! My performance improves when you and I compete," she told him. "I want you with me all the time."

"All the time?" he teased, but he felt flattered.

He could outscore her in the simple exercise of Golden Bees. That game consisted of nothing more than swatting at points of golden laser light that came at them faster and faster, like a swarm of attacking insects. It relied on sheer speed rather than on control. The first time Corgan and Ananda played it together, the virtual images of their four hands had got so tangled on the screen that the electronics shorted out, making both of them laugh too hard to keep going.

In Precision and Sensitivity training, Ananda was better than Corgan. She could bring her hand to within 197 microns of a square of laser light without touching it, then move the laser square using only the electromagnetic energy from her fingertips. A year ago Corgan had been able to do that, too, but now his hands were too rough, and the skin too thick, to have that kind of sensitivity. Yet he still knew enough about the drill to help her polish her technique.

He discovered that he liked the role of coach, liked working harder to train Ananda than he'd ever worked on his own Virtual War training. He was using his knowledge to help someone else become a champion, even though she'd get all the glory—and that was fine. For the first time in months he was involved in something he was good at. And it turned out that the more he coached her, the more his own skills sharpened.

"You're getting it all together again," Ananda enthused. "They're going to put you back on the team and kick me off."

"Fat chance! You're forgetting something," Corgan told her. "I don't want to fight the War again. I did it once, and that was enough."

In athletic ability they matched pretty evenly. Corgan could keep up with her when they raced, whether it was 100 meters or 1,000 meters, but he never came close to challenging her in the long jump. In that sport Ananda was magnificent to watch. She would run toward the take-off point, gaining more and more speed until she soared into the air like a bird, landing 9.75 meters from takeoff.

Her distance was unbelievable, beyond anything a human, male or female, should have been able to perform.

After one of her leaps Ananda patted the virtual sand for Corgan to come and sit beside her. "How did I look?" she asked, and Corgan answered, "Like an angel in flight. Or maybe like this Harrier jet I'm learning to fly—when its wheels and nozzles retract, it's as sleek as the frigatebirds that swoop over the shore at Nuku Hiva. Sleek, fast, and graceful—and that's how you look."

"Wow!" she exclaimed. "You sure know how to compliment a girl. Tell me more."

"No. Now it's your turn to tell me something. What do you hear about the War being refought?"

She shook her head. "All I hear from my Supreme Council is that negotiations are continuing."

When he asked, "Have you started to train with Sharla and Cyborg yet?" Ananda answered no. Corgan knew that was the clue—he'd trained alone for fourteen years, until only three weeks remained before his own Virtual War was to take place. Only then had he been introduced to Sharla and Brig, and from then on, the three of them had trained together daily until the actual War began. So if Ananda hadn't yet met with her teammates, the new War must not be all that close. If there was going to be one at all. As Ananda said, negotiations were continuing.

Maybe he should ask Sharla if she'd heard anything. At least it would be an excuse to see her. But when he knocked on the door of her laboratory, she slipped into the hall, closing the door behind her. As he put his arms around her she seemed tense and distracted; when he tried to kiss her, she pulled away and said, "Someone might notice us."

"Can we go inside?" he asked.

"You can't come into the laboratory—I need to keep the place sterile," she answered, "and you might contaminate it with outside bacteria." But he could hear Cyborg in there. Or maybe it was Brigand, who was supposed to be in hiding—the clone-twins' voices sounded almost exactly alike.

"When can we get a chance to talk?" he asked her.

"Be patient, Corgan," she answered, brushing his cheek with the back of her hand. "I'm really stacked up with work. I don't have any spare time."

With Ananda it was different. Ananda always wanted to be with Corgan, even though their contact had to remain virtual. One day, after they'd done a particularly grueling race and both of them dropped onto the ground to catch their breath, she asked, "Corgan, did you know I've never been kissed by a boy?"

It came out of nowhere, startling Corgan, who wasn't sure what he should answer. He thought they were friends and nothing more; he believed he'd been acting protective toward her, like a big brother with a younger sister (at least he guessed that was the way brothers acted toward sisters; since he'd never had a sibling, he couldn't be sure). But hearing that question, he wondered if their dynamics were about to change. And whether he wanted them to.

"What am I supposed to say?" he asked. "Should I answer, 'No, I didn't know you've never been kissed,' or maybe, 'It's hard to believe some guy hasn't tried to kiss a girl as pretty as you—the guys in your domed city must be blind.'"

"You don't have to say anything," she told him. "Because it's me who's asking you. Would you give me my first kiss?" A breath later, she asked, "Now?"

Corgan looked beyond her, down the virtual track that stretched like an endless ribbon. The virtual paint that edged the running lanes gleamed white against blacktop, cutting clear and definite boundaries. The contrast made the course easy to follow. But what about his own boundaries? The lines that had kept him on course with Ananda seemed to be bending now, like marks seen through the bottom of a glass. What she was asking might be out of bounds. He was supposed to be helping her with her training and act as a friend—nothing more than that.

To buy time, he answered, "Ananda, we're in virtual reality. We can see and hear each other, but it's nothing like the real world. Kissing . . ." He swallowed, trying to put his thoughts into words. "It couldn't be the same as the real thing. I know, because I've lived it."

"You mean because you've been with Sharla. Did you kiss her? In the real world?"

"Yes," Corgan answered. He'd kissed her every chance he'd had. But that was then, not now.

Ananda sighed, then turned her dark eyes toward him to plead, "Couldn't we at least try? I mean, kissing each other? I want to do this, Corgan. Even if it isn't real for you, it will be real for me."

She was forcing him to make up his mind how he felt about her, and even more, how he felt about Sharla. What harm could there be in a kiss—mouth to virtual image, real to phantom?

So she wouldn't be disappointed, he tried to explain, "To me, here in my own domed city, I'm real but you're a digital creation. It's just the opposite in your city, where you're flesh and blood but I'm sitting beside you as an accumulation of tiny electronic signals. A virtual kiss won't be—"

Too late. He could feel the slight but sweet sensation of her lips on his, of her warm breath (temperature was one of the things virtual reality did well) against his mouth, the pressure of her arms around his neck (she must be holding tight to create that much virtual force). And it felt very nice. Not as good as kissing Sharla, but better than the quick, aloof touch that was all he'd had from Sharla the last time he saw her.

Color had risen into Anada's cheeks, russet beneath the bronze. Uncertain, hesitating, she asked him, "In the real world, did you and Sharla ever . . . do anything more than—"

"No," he answered quickly. That was the truth.

Sighing again, Ananda said, "Some day, Corgan, I hope you and I will be together. In reality." Then she stood up and raced down the length of the virtual track, her shiny black hair swaying, her powerful body moving as smoothly as ripples in a stream. Corgan didn't follow her.

The next day Corgan waited for Ananda to come to his virtual Box. They'd planned to work on Precision and Sensitivity training, the drill where they brought their hands to within mere microns of the digital images of soldiers, moving them without touching them. One mistake, one actual touch, and virtual soldiers died. But Ananda didn't come, and Corgan made no attempt to contact her. Maybe she was trying to figure out how they fit together now, just as he was.

The following day he happened to meet Cyborg near the hover cars. Now standing two and a half centimeters taller than Corgan, Cyborg had filled out and muscled up and—"What is that *thing* on your upper lip?" Corgan asked. "A hairy red caterpillar?"

"It's a mustache," Cyborg answered, grinning.

"You mean it's *going* to be a mustache one of these years," Corgan said, then remembered that Cyborg became a year older every couple of weeks.

"Yeah, well, look at you," Cyborg said. "You're all polished up like a silicon crystal. What's the occasion?"

It was true—Corgan had just spent a full hour in his Clean Room, grooming his thick, dark hair as carefully as he could, and shaving. Let Cyborg wear a mustache if he wanted. No facial hair for Corgan, by choice.

Mendor the Mother had made him a LiteSuit of material that shimmered with rich, dark colors. It closely fit the contours of his body, from his broad shoulders to the tops of his boots. As he turned to look at his reflection in the stainless-steel walls of the corridor, he thought he looked pretty good. "The occasion," he answered, "is that I'm on my way to see Sharla."

"You are? Good luck," Cyborg said.

"What's that supposed to mean?"

"Nothing. Forget it. Hurry up, here comes the hover car."

As they raced on foot along the tracks, Corgan easily outdistanced Cyborg. All that training was paying off.

SEVENTEEN

Once he and Corgan had climbed aboard the hover car, Cyborg flicked the switch that turned his artificial hand into a magnet, juicing up the current until it hummed. With a *thud* and a *click* the steel-rimmed dome of the car closed itself and locked into place.

"Good trick," Corgan told him.

"The magnet comes in handy sometimes. Listen, Corgan, Sharla's been pretty busy. She might not have time to see you."

Clamping his jaw to stem his irritation, Corgan waited a few seconds to answer, "She needs to see me. This is important. Two days from now is my sixteenth birthday, and Sharla's, too. We both were born in the genetics lab on the same day. I think we should be with each other for our birthday. I'm on my way to talk to her about it."

Cyborg touched his wispy mustache and stammered, "Uh . . . that's where you're going right now? To the lab?"

"Sure. That's where she is, isn't it? If she's doing all this extra work, she needs some time off. Turning sixteen is special—it's worth celebrating." Corgan leaned forward to examine Cyborg and said, "You look about sixteen now, too. So we're the same age."

And Brigand would be, too. Corgan remembered that afternoon at the waterfall, back on Nuku Hiva, when Sharla had teased him, "In a few more months they should be as old as you and I are right now. Then both you and Brigand will *really* have something to be jealous about." He pushed that memory out of his head. He did not want to think about Brigand. Not today.

Cyborg was right behind him when they got off the hover car to walk down the long corridor toward Sharla's lab. He seemed nervous, never staying exactly beside Corgan, but darting ahead a little and then falling behind.

"What's with you?" Corgan asked. "You're buzzing around like a mosquito."

"Yeah, mosquito," Cyborg agreed. "Certain things about Nuku Hiva I don't miss. Mosquitoes are one of them. Do you think you'll go back to the island, Corgan? Maybe that would be a good idea—for you to go back. You love it there."

Corgan didn't reply, because they'd reached the laboratory. When he knocked on the door, there was no answer. After waiting for thirty-seven and sixteen one-hundredths seconds, he grasped the latch. He'd managed to open the door only fifty-two centimeters when Cyborg's metal hand covered his.

"Don't, Corgan."

"Why not?"

"Just don't." Cyborg didn't explain.

The latch was made of some kind of metal, and Cyborg had apparently turned on the magnetism in his prosthetic hand, because Corgan felt a magnetic pulse that flowed through his own hand and bonded it to the latch.

"Turn that thing off!" Corgan yelled. When he still couldn't jerk his hand free, he hooked his foot behind Cyborg's legs so that both of them lost their balance and crashed through the doorway, landing on the floor. "What the crud were you doing?" Corgan demanded, scrambling up to glare at Cyborg.

Cyborg sprawled on the floor, not meeting Corgan's accusing eyes. Instead his gaze swept around the empty laboratory.

"Sorry," he apologized, getting up. "I must have pushed the magnetic switch on my hand by mistake. Okay, Sharla isn't here, so let's go."

"In a minute," Corgan answered. "I want to see what the place is like. I've never been inside Sharla's laboratory. She didn't start to work in here until after the Virtual War."

It was an altogether different type of laboratory from the one on Nuku Hiva, where Delphine labored to create transgenic calves. Cyborg pointed to what looked like a box with a vertical row of thin trays and said, "That's the DNA-sequencing machine over there. And the thermal cycler's in the corner. And this thing—she uses this metrix spotted array system to analyze custom microarrays."

"You know what?" Corgan said. "I don't have a clue what you're talking about. I'm impressed that you know so much about it." He circled the room, noticing petri dishes, test tubes, and other glass tubes whose functions were a mystery to him, boxes stacked on other boxes, papers with notes scribbled on them. Since the place wasn't exactly neat, he wondered why Sharla'd said he might contaminate it.

At the far end of the room was another door and he headed toward that.

"Don't go in there," Cyborg warned. "Anyway, it's locked."

"No, it isn't." When Corgan leaned his shoulder against the door, it swung open.

"Corgan! Oh, God—Corgan!" Inside the small, dim room Sharla stood with her back against the wall, staring at him like a startled doe.

As his eyes adjusted to the dimness Corgan got a look at the center of the room where two cots had been shoved side by side. On one of them lay Brigand, his naked chest decorated from shoulders to waist with tattoos of the same designs they'd seen on the chief in the tomb—lizards and tiki faces, crosses and squares, coils and ferns, and lines that had no discernible meaning. The boars'-tusk necklace still hung around his neck. Wearing blue jeans exactly like the ones Sharla had sent to Corgan, Brigand swung his legs over the side of the cot and sat up to switch on a lamp.

In the brighter light the image of those side-by-side cots seared itself into Corgan's brain. His voice gutteral, he said, "Looks like he still has to hold your hand every night before he'll go to sleep!"

Smiling, Brigand answered, "Something like that."

"Corgan, I know what you must be thinking," Sharla began. "I'll try to explain—"

"It's pretty obvious, isn't it?" Corgan interrupted. "No wonder you never have any time for me."

Anger mounted in Sharla's face as she shouted, "I don't have time for you because I've been working night and day in the lab trying to find an antidote for the clone-twins' aging!"

Her words didn't register with Corgan—all he could take in was Brigand, who wore that insolent grin as he lounged on the cot shoved right up against Sharla's. Next to it, the human skull from Nuku Hiva grinned just as insolently.

"How long has this been going on?" Corgan growled. "Ever since I got back? Stupid me! I thought you cared about me, Sharla."

"I do!" She reached out as though to touch him but then pulled back. "I happen to love Brigand, too. Don't forget—he's my creation."

"So is Cyborg—your creation," Corgan lashed out. "Does that mean you're taking care of both of them?"

Sharla drew back her arm, then swung it with such force that when it smashed against Corgan's cheek, he staggered. "You bastard!" she cried.

"Bastard!" he yelled back. "Yeah, you're right. All of us are bastards, aren't we? Created in a laboratory with no fathers. You and I, Sharla . . . and Brig . . . and Cyborg and

Brigand . . . . We're worse than bastards because we didn't have any mothers, either. No wonder we're all so screwed up. No wonder you think you can love two of us at the same time. Well—*you can't!*"

She was screaming at him now: "I *have* loved you! You don't even know what I did for you. I cheated in the Virtual War, but I did it for you, Corgan, because you were desperate to get to the Isles of Hiva. Do you think it was easy for me to manipulate the scores so expertly that the Supreme Council still can't figure out how I did it? Or *if* I did it."

Corgan couldn't answer. Any words he might have spoken died in his throat. For more than a year now he'd suspected her of cheating but never confronted her with it because he didn't really want to know. Now he knew. She'd cheated, but she said she'd done it for him. How could he deal with that?

"And the clone-twins—don't you understand? They're aging by two years every month. A year from now they'll be middle-aged. A year after that they'll be old. And soon after that they'll be *dead*. I'm trying to find a way to stop the process, Corgan. But what if I can't?" She grasped Brigand's hand and said, "That's why each day the two of us spend together is precious—because *it won't last!*"

"Do you know what he did with Cyborg's hand?" Corgan cried. "He's a cannibal!"

"Yes, I know about it."

"And you still love him?"

"Totally."

It was that word that sent Corgan's anger over the edge,

made the venom spew out of him. "Hey, do you know how easy it would be for me to put a stop to this? To break it up and keep the two of you apart? All I need to do is go to the Supreme Council and tell Them you cheated, Sharla. They'll throw you into Reprimand so fast your head will pop, and They'll keep you there for the next couple of years." He laughed bitterly. "By then Brigand will be too old to hold your hand in bed."

Sharla's eyes widened in fear. Brigand shoved her aside, then came toward Corgan with his fist clenched. "You think I'd let that happen?" he asked. "Not a chance. The time isn't ripe."

"Ripe for what?"

"For the revolt I'm going to lead against the Supreme Council. Grab him, Cyborg."

Corgan had almost forgotten Cyborg, until he felt the powerful mechanical hand circle his wrist. "The day you and Brigand got here," Cyborg explained into Corgan's ear, "Brigand started plotting to take over the domed city. Actually, he started long before that, back on Nuku Hiva. Pilot's in this with him, and Pilot recruited a lot of people who don't like the way the Supreme Council runs things."

"It's true," Sharla said. "Brigand has a rebel force of about fifty troops—more than enough to capture the Supreme Council, because the Council has been in power for so long They've grown careless. They never worry about security."

Incredulous, Corgan asked, "Sharla! Does that mean you support this craziness?"

"Sharla and I are still discussing it," Brigand answered

for her. "Sometimes she sees things my way, sometimes she doesn't." Standing with his face thrust right into Corgan's, he said, "I've been using you as an example to my troops. Isn't that right, Cyborg?" He laughed then, and added, "As an example of everything that's wrong around here. You were pampered all your life, Corgan, and given everything you wanted, while the rest of the citizens worked like drones. Sure, you won the Isles of Hiva, but you got the reward of going there, while all the other workers got nothing. Not very fair, do you think?"

"What about Sharla?" Corgan asked. "She went to the Isles of Hiva with me—at least at first."

"Then she came back here and dedicated herself to the DNA lab, where her brilliant work created Cyborg and me. The rebels all love Sharla for that. Especially for creating *me*."

Corgan would have hit him then with his one free hand if Cyborg hadn't gripped him from behind. Corgan might be fast, but Cyborg was strong!

"You're wrong if you think I'm going to keep quiet about this revolt business," Corgan threatened.

Tossing his head, Brigand told Cyborg, "Take him into the tunnels."

As Cyborg bent Corgan's arm behind his back he murmured, "Don't fight me, Corgan. I wouldn't want to hurt you. Just come along."

EIGHTEEN

Outside the laboratory Cyborg dragged Corgan along the corridor. "Hey, that metal hand of yours hurts," Corgan complained.

"Move your body!" Cyborg barked. "Or you'll get hurt a lot worse."

They stopped in front of a service door that was used only by maintenance people and was always kept locked. When Cyborg placed his metal hand on the door's surface, Corgan could hear a rattle, then the door swung open. "Through here," he ordered, giving Corgan a shove into a passageway filled with water pipes and electric cables. "Follow me, and stay close."

There was hardly enough room for the two of them,

and the passage was dark. "I thought you were my friend," Corgan said bitterly.

"I am. Move your butt."

Inside a narrow tunnel that snaked through darkness, Cyborg's hand began to glow with enough illumination to light the way. After they'd gone no more than eleven meters, they emerged into a small alcove, where Sharla waited. "You made it! I'm so glad," she breathed.

Amazed, Corgan asked, "How'd you get here?"

"By a different tunnel. Tell me quick—have you learned to fly the Harrier jet?"

"Just in the simulator—"

"Could you fly the real thing?"

"If I had to, I guess. Why?"

"You need to leave here," she told him, her voice trembling. "Brigand's getting ready to kill you. He's calling his troops—"

"Wait a minute! I'm not sure whose side everyone is on. You're telling me I'm going to get killed and I'm supposed to fly the Harrier—"

"Both of us are on your side, Corgan," Cyborg interrupted. He stood still, his eyes tightly shut.

Staring at him, Corgan asked, "Why are you standing there with your eyes closed?"

Sharla turned to Cyborg and asked, "Do we have time to explain? Can you get a psychic insight into what Brigand is doing now?"

Cyborg put the palms of both his hands, the real and the artificial, against his forehead. After four and thirty-two hundredths seconds he answered, "We have a little time. He's in a planning meeting with his troops."

"Sit," Sharla ordered, and the three of them dropped to the floor, their backs against the wall. Corgan's mind flashed back to the night when he and Sharla and Brig had met secretly in a darkened corridor to hear Brig's plan that they should ask for the Isles of Hiva as a reward for winning the Virtual War. But this wasn't Brig; it was a clone who looked strong and tall and the same age now as Corgan.

"Before he begins the revolt," Cyborg explained, "he plans to terminate you publicly, Corgan. Right now he's trying to block his strategy from me, so I can't get mental access, because he's not sure he can trust me—when it comes to you."

"Tell him I'll fight him one-on-one," Corgan said. "I'm not afraid of him."

"He won't do that. He wants to create a spectacle, with you as the scapegoat."

The coldness of the tunnel started to seep through Corgan's LiteSuit, and for the first time fear began to seep in, too. "So where am I supposed to go in the Harrier?" he asked.

"To Florida," Cyborg told him. "You'll be safe in the domed city there, but you won't be safe if you stay here."

Florida. Corgan mulled that over, then asked without much hope, "Sharla? Will you come with me?"

Crossing her arms on her knees, she lowered her head and answered softly, "I couldn't, even if I wanted to. I'm the only person who might be able to find an antidote for the clone-twins' rapid aging: I created them, and it's up to me to save them."

"Both of you, keep quiet for a minute," Cyborg said. Raising his metal hand, he announced, "I'm getting a mental image. Brigand and his troops are heading for the tunnel, Corgan, the one where I was supposed to take you but didn't. They haven't figured out that you're not there, because Brigand can't tune in to me when my eyes are closed. Get up now—we need to get you to the hangar fast."

"Sharla?" Corgan asked, trying once more, but she only answered, "I'll find Brigand and keep him . . . occupied . . . while Cyborg takes you to the hangar."

"Occupied! How do you plan to keep him *occupied*?"

"NNTK, Corgan."

Hearing that, those four letters that he hated so much, Corgan groaned in frustration, but Cyborg ordered, "Move it! We have to find our way through this maze of mainte-nance tunnels. And you'll have to lead me, Corgan, because my eyes need to stay shut. If I get a mental image of these tunnels or the hangar, Brigand will read it and know where we are." Without looking toward Sharla, he said, "Go ahead and keep Brigand busy, Sharla. Right now he's checking out your lab."

"Don't go near him, Sharla," Corgan begged.

"Corgan, will you please just leave?" she answered heatedly. "We're trying to save your life!"

Yeah, get a grip, he told himself. She wasn't going to come with him no matter what he said. "All right. I'm leaving. . . ." But for just three seconds he turned back to ask her, "When will I see you again?"

"Don't worry about that." She pointed down the tunnel. "Go! Be safe!"

Bent almost double, they crept through the tunnels, Cyborg's hand heavy on Corgan's shoulder for guidance, Corgan's chest heavy with pain and regret. To numb his mind so he would stop visualizing what Sharla would be doing after she found Brigand, he began to count the seconds. When he reached 847 and a fraction, he whispered, "We ought to be there by now."

"Good! As soon as I break through the door, you make a run for it, Corgan," Cyborg told him. "Here's the door—I'll have to open it with my eyes closed. Find the lock and put my hand on it, but be careful when I turn on the magnetic current, because it might spark. It does that sometimes."

The sparking was much hotter than Corgan expected, setting fire to the sleeve of his LiteSuit. Clamping his hand over the small flame to smother it, Corgan yelled, "Damn!" Which made Cyborg's eyes fly open in alarm.

"Damn for sure!" Cyborg yelled. "Brigand will connect to what I just saw, so he'll know where we are. Run for it, Corgan! Get to the jet!"

"How do I open the dome roof so I can fly the Harrier through it?"

"I'll take care of that. Just get into that cockpit as fast as you can."

Corgan sprinted. It was sixty-four meters from the door of the hangar to the Harrier jet, and he made it in six and twenty-two hundredths seconds. From hangar floor to cockpit, the Harrier's height was 3.55 meters, too high for Corgan to leap; instead he climbed onto the air intake, standing with his feet on the bottom of the curved metal while he wrestled to open the canopy. It was stuck.

"Corgan, hurry up!" Cyborg was shouting from behind him. "Brigand's on his way with troops." Just as he said that, Brigand burst through the door—not the one Cyborg had sparked open, but the main door to the large hangar. In his hand he held the spear from Nuku Hiva.

Brigand was the first one through the door, followed closely by Sharla and dozens of troops. Spreading her arms as though she could stop the small army from advancing, she kept talking to Brigand, who seemed to be only half listening. He shook his head, then grabbed her and pulled her against him. "She's mine!" he shouted across the distance to Corgan. "And you're dead."

"No!" Sharla cried, hanging on to Brigand to restrain him. Trying to loosen her grip, he knocked her to the floor, then started to run toward Corgan with the spear in his raised right hand, poised to throw.

At that instant Corgan managed to slide open the Harrier's canopy. Still standing on the air intake, he stretched his arms into the cockpit to feel around for some sort of handle to pull himself up. Finding none, he grabbed the back of the seat and slid in headfirst, but before he righted himself he looked up to see whether the panels in the dome had started to retract. They had.

When Corgan looked down again, Brigand was standing only four meters away. "You make a nice, easy target, Corgan," he shouted. At least Corgan thought that's what he said, but the last words were drowned out because Corgan had started the engines.

As he glanced at the instrument panel, the spear flew right past his nose. Corgan's reflexes worked fine: His arm shot out to catch the spear so it wouldn't fall back to the concrete pad, where Brigand could pick it up to hurl again. He dropped it behind him into the passenger seat.

But Brigand had only begun his assault on Corgan. "Finish him off," he ordered his troops—Corgan couldn't hear the words, but he could read them on his lips. Then he gasped in fear as one of Brigand's troops reached inside her shirt to pull out a gun!

Thirty years earlier, when the domed city had been built and populated by the lucky citizens who'd survived Earth's demise, the Supreme Council had confiscated, burned, and banned all firearms. Every citizen had been thoroughly searched to make sure that not a single weapon remained inside the city. Yet there, in the hand of one of Brigand's soldiers, was a gun, the first real one Corgan had ever seen. The female soldier who held it looked questioningly at Brigand, who told her, "Shoot!"

"Don't do it!" Sharla screamed at the same time Cyborg started to race toward the Harrier jet. As he ran he switched on the current in his metal hand, magnetizing it. While Sharla wrestled with the female soldier, Cyborg reached the aircraft and slammed his hand against its side, metal to metal, then began to pull himself up toward the cockpit. Corgan reached out to grab Cyborg's real hand— the flesh-and-blood one—and yanked him into the cockpit. Just as the gun went off, Cyborg's metal hand flashed in front of Corgan's face.

"Did Sharla get hit?" Corgan cried out.

"No. Here's the bullet. Some catch, huh?" Cyborg bragged, waving the metal slug that was stuck between two of his articulated, steel-coated titanium fingers. "I told you this magnetic hand was useful. But I don't know how many bullets it can catch, so you better lift this crate out of here."

"You're going with me?"

"What does it look like?"

With a roar of the vertical jets, the Harrier rose through the open dome. Wind blew wildly through the cockpit because Corgan couldn't close the canopy until Cyborg slid farther into the passenger seat, but just before the canopy slammed shut, Cyborg threw the spear down onto the concrete pad, not point first, but flat.

Over the headset Cyborg told Corgan, "Brigand knows now that I've betrayed him. But he's still my clone-twin, and he loves the spear. What does it matter if I give it back to him? He can't hit anything with it anyway."

Far beneath them Corgan could see Brigand and his troops waving their fists and yelling. And he saw Sharla, who'd risen to stand at Brigand's side. Her golden hair fluttered in the downdraft from the jets as she looked up at Corgan. She didn't wave, and from that distance he couldn't read her expression.

For thirteen and a half seconds the Harrier hovered over the domed city. Then Corgan retracted the nozzles and the landing gear, did a slow 180-degree turn that pointed the nose of the now sleek aircraft into the blue sky, and headed for Florida.

Where Ananda waited.

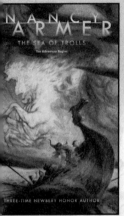

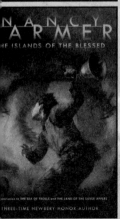

An unlikely romance.

A terrifying dream world.

One final chance for survival.

Nevermore

KELLY CREAGH

EBOOK EDITION ALSO AVAILABLE

From Atheneum Books for Young Readers

TEEN.SimonandSchuster.com

★ "A POWERFUL MIX OF POLITICAL INTRIGUE, ADVENTURE, AND MAGIC. . . . A STANDOUT."
—*SLJ*, STARRED REVIEW

Ancient secrets. Deadly danger.

Dark Reflections

THE WATER MIRROR ● THE STONE LIGHT ● THE GLASS WORD

KAI MEYER

FROM MARGARET K. McELDERRY BOOKS
TEEN.SimonandSchuster.com